ALSO BY LINDA CASTILLO

THE
HIDDEN ONE

A KATE BURKHOLDER NOVEL

Linda Castillo

St. Martin's Paperbacks

Published in the United States by St. Martin's Paperbacks, an imprint of St. Martin's Publishing Group.

THE HIDDEN ONE

Copyright © 2022 by Linda Castillo.
Excerpt from *An Evil Heart* copyright © 2023 by Linda Castillo.

All rights reserved.

For information, address St. Martin's Publishing Group, 120 Broadway, New York, NY 10271.

www.stmartins.com

Library of Congress Catalog Card Number: 2022004597

ISBN: 978-1-250-78107-9

Our books may be purchased in bulk for promotional, educational, or business use. Please contact your local bookseller or the Macmillan Corporate and Premium Sales Department at 1-800-221-7945, ext. 5442, or by email at MacmillanSpecialMarkets@macmillan.com.

Printed in the United States of America

Minotaur hardcover edition published 2022
St. Martin's Paperbacks edition / June 2023

10 9 8 7 6 5 4 3 2 1

This book is dedicated to my Ohio friends, Denise Campbell Johnson and Mark O. Thank you so much for that fun lunch in Amish country and the conversation that turned the spark of an idea into wildfire.

People look at the outward appearance,
But the Lord looks at the heart.

—I SAMUEL 16:7

PROLOGUE

He'd always known this moment would come. Judgment day. The great reckoning. The adjudication that had been lying in wait the entirety of his adult life. For years, he'd denied his guilt. He spent every waking hour proving he hadn't done what they said and making reparations because he had. He'd nearly convinced himself none of it had happened. That was his truth and he clung to that tenuous connection with the desperation of a man who knew his life depended on it.

But while he had duped the fools, and perhaps his own conscience, fate would not be hoodwinked. The wicked beast of his heart, the one he'd been running from for so long, had finally caught up with him.

He wasn't sure why he'd agreed to the meeting. Some dark compulsion. Curiosity at play. Or maybe it was some crazy notion that telling the truth would set him free. What did a master liar know about truth? Maybe his need to see this through, to finish it once and for all, was as simple as admitting he deserved what was to come.

Meet me at the windmill. Midnight. Come alone.

It was the third such note in two weeks. The kind an ordinary person would ignore or toss in the trash. The kind an innocent man might take to the police. As desperately as he wanted to believe otherwise, he was not an ordinary person. He sure as hell wasn't innocent. No, he thought darkly. He had no choice but to meet this problem head-on. Deal with it. Finish it. Make it right if he could. And then bury it once and for all.

But how could anyone know? How could anyone uncover a past he'd buried with such meticulous care? The most frightening question of all, the one that had kept him up every night since he received that first mysterious dispatch: How could anyone remember something that he himself had all but forgotten?

I know who you are. I know what you did. I know your secrets. All of them.

The words had tormented him for days now. He hadn't eaten or slept or had a moment's peace. He desperately wanted to believe he'd misinterpreted their meaning, their intent. That the cryptic words were the result of some petty incident or mundane proclamation he made that had provoked someone in the community. Is it possible he was reading something into it that had never been intended?

I know who you are.

No, he thought as he walked along the southern edge of the woods. There was no way he'd misinterpreted any of it. Right or wrong or somewhere in between, he needed to get to the bottom of this—put a stop to it before the situation spiraled out of control—and there was only one way to do it.

The wind rattled the leaves of the trees, the cold bite of it slicing through his coat and the layers beneath. It was a long walk to the old farm; he was glad he'd brought the walking stick. He'd brought the lantern, too, but he didn't need it. The three-quarter moon provided more than enough light for him to follow the old two-track.

At the turn in the road, he traversed the ditch and crossed to the barbed-wire fence. Hanging his cane on the top strand, he tested its strength, stepped onto the lowest wire, and swung his leg over the top. His knees protested when he came down on the other side. His feet followed suit. Such was the lot of a man who'd lived beyond his time.

He walked another two minutes before the silhouette of the ramshackle barn and windmill loomed in the distance. The steel blades spun, whining like a banshee, the vane shifting with a gust. Normally, he loved the sound. Tonight, the screech of steel against steel sent a shiver to his bones in a way that had nothing to do with the cold.

"Hello?" he called out. "Is anyone there?"

The only reply came from the squeak of the turbine. The rattle of wood siding come loose. The clang of the vane shifting in the wind.

Feet reminding him that he'd just traversed two miles, he waded through the grass to the base of the tower. Grunting, he propped the walking stick against the wood-rail fence and sat down on the crumbling concrete base of the windmill tower. Cold, his joints aching, he pulled his coat more tightly about his shoulders, shoved his hands into his pockets, and settled in for a wait. He'd give his midnight caller ten minutes to make his appearance. Another two to state his case and declare his intent. If no one showed, he'd walk home and throw away the notes. He'd forget about the silly messages, the way he'd forgotten so many other things over the years.

He was wishing for the gloves he'd left on the kitchen table back at the house, the tobacco pipe he kept tucked into his pocket, when the voice came at him from the dark.

"I didn't think you'd come."

He jolted, hefted himself to his feet, squinted into the dark recesses of the barn. He didn't need to see a face to know who it was. The thunderbolt of recognition slayed him as thoroughly as any sickle, and cut him to his soul—what was left of it.

"My bones are too old for a walk this far," he said, his voice calm despite the riot of emotions coursing through him. "Especially at a time when an old man should be home in his bed, sleeping."

"And how is it that you sleep?"

"'He grants sleep to those He loves,'" he replied, quoting a psalm from the Bible he knew so well. "God loves all of His children, after all."

A figure emerged from the shadows. The sense of betrayal punched him, hard enough to take his breath, with enough force to make his legs go weak. Never in a hundred years would he have imagined this. Not this.

"You know nothing of God," the figure said. "Only lies."

For the first time he noticed the rifle. His midnight caller held it muzzle down. Unthreatening. The way a hunter might carry his weapon when he's tired and on his way home after a long day of hunting. Even so, his heart rolled and began to pound.

"What is it you want?" he asked.

Bitterness suffused the laugh that followed. "I want you to be gone."

A dozen thoughts battered his brain at once. The realization that he was in danger. A rush of incredulity. Like ice water splashed on an exposed nerve. A tine against a broken bone.

The rifle came up and was leveled at him. Finger inside the guard, the quiver of the muzzle nearly imperceptible.

"I fear for your soul," he whispered.

"And I for yours. What's left of it. We both know you'll not make it to heaven."

The lantern slipped from his hand and clattered to the ground. The globe shattered, but he barely noticed. Breathing heavily, he raised his hands, stepped back. "Don't sacrifice your life for mine. I'm not worth it."

A whispered prayer floated on the breeze, as chilling as a scream in the night, and suddenly everything became crystal clear. Spinning, he launched himself into a lumbering run. Arms outstretched. Mouth open and gasping. The pain he'd felt earlier hijacked by terror. He looked around wildly as he ran, but there was no cover. No structure or tree. He shambled toward the fence a few yards away. The woods were his only hope. If he could scale the barbed wire, he might make it. He'd deal with the rest later.

He ran as fast as his joints allowed, his gait as teetering and clumsy as an old dog's. Twice he stumbled, arms thrashing, regained his footing just in time to avoid a fall. Behind him, the feet of his pursuer pounded the ground. He heard the racking of the rifle. The utterance of words he couldn't discern.

A tremendous blow slammed into him from behind. Like a baseball traveling at a hundred miles an hour striking between his shoulder blades. He pitched forward. A clap of thunder in his ears. A ping of confusion. And then he was falling. . . .

His face hit the ground. Nose breaking on impact. A spread of pain he couldn't quite feel. Grit in his mouth. The earth cold against his skin, winter-dead grass scratching his belly. He spit out a tooth, felt the gap with his tongue. He acknowledged the seriousness of his injury. A panic he couldn't react to. He lay still, his mind floating above him. Why couldn't he get up? Why couldn't he run?

Only then did it occur to him he'd been shot. That he was badly injured, bleeding, and unable to move. He watched his attacker approach and stop a few feet away. He wanted to look up. To know what those eyes would reveal . . .

"You cannot fool God," came the voice he knew so well. "He sees in your heart the things that others cannot."

He tried to reply, but his mouth was suddenly full. He opened it, tasted the salt of blood, felt the warmth of it as it flowed onto the ground. He saw the black steel of the rifle as it was lowered. He tried to focus, but his eyes rolled back. The muzzle nudged his temple. So cold against his skin. The smell of gun oil in his nostrils.

Closing his eyes, he listened to the screech of the windmill. The shifting of the vane. The whisper of wind through the grass.

An explosion of white light.

Another clap of thunder.

And the windmill ground to a halt.

CHAPTER 1

Eighteen years later

Doyle Schlabach was glad he'd purchased the mules. Datt had gone with him to the horse auction down to Belleville last winter and argued against the purchase. Get the Belgians, he'd said. They pull better; they're stronger. Doyle would never argue with his *datt* about anything, much less livestock, but while the two jennies weren't quite as strong as their equine cousins, they suited his needs just fine. They were smart and willing and easier to keep, too. According to the breeder, their donkey dam had been bred to a Dutch draft sire. As far as Doyle was concerned, there wasn't another team in the entire valley that could outpull these two. And they didn't eat him out of house and home.

He was cutting hay in the south field this morning. It was a new field he'd added to his farm when the old Duffy farm went up for auction. He'd gotten a good deal on the thirty-five acres. With Datt's help, he'd demolished the old barn, cleared the land, plowed it, and seeded for alfalfa. God had blessed the valley with an abundance of spring rain, and the hay was bountiful. It was going to be the best year he'd ever had.

The June sun beat down on the back of Doyle's neck as he steered the mules across the field. The smell of fresh-cut alfalfa filled his nostrils, and not for the first time today he thanked God for the bounty that had been bestowed upon him. He thought about the mock turtle soup he would be eating for lunch, and his mouth watered. He jiggled the lines to hurry the mules along.

"*Kumma druff!*" he called out. Come on there!

The clinking of the harnesses mingled with the rapid patter-patter of the sickle and lulled him into the state of peace he always felt when he worked the fields.

He'd just reached the far end and was in the process of side-passing the mules to turn around and cut the final swatch when the sickle bar clanked against a rock.

"Whoa." Doyle stopped the mules. "*Was der schinner is letz?*" he growled. What in the world is wrong?

This wasn't a particularly rocky area, but he'd run across a few in the course of plowing and seeding. Rocks in a hayfield spelled trouble, and the last thing he needed before lunch was a broken blade.

Leaning, he looked down at the spot where the sickle hovered above the ground and spotted the culprit. A big rock. Limestone, judging from the color. Muttering beneath his breath, he tied off the lines, set the brake, and climbed down. He went to the sickle bar and knelt. He reached for the rock, intent on chucking it over the fence and into the woods, but his hand froze mid-reach. The hairs at his nape prickled when his fingers made contact.

Doyle picked up the object and knew immediately it wasn't a rock. It was too light, hollow-feeling, and the surface was too smooth. He brushed away the dirt, turned it over in his hands. A creeping sensation skittered across his shoulders when he saw the jut of teeth. The eye sockets. The black hole of a nose. Doyle was an avid hunter; he butchered his own stock. He knew perfectly well what an animal skull looked like. This did not belong to an animal.

Lurching to his feet, Doyle dropped the skull and stepped back, nearly tripped over the sickle bar. He was suddenly aware of his proximity to the woods, the shadows within, the stories he'd heard as a kid about this place. Gooseflesh rose on his arms, despite the heat of the day. The sensation of eyes on his back was so strong he turned and looked to the place where the old barn had once stood. But there was no one there.

Schnell geiste, he thought. Ghosts.

His legs shook as he backed away. He couldn't take his eyes off the skull. He climbed onto the mower, settled onto the steel seat. His hands shook as he pulled the lever to lift the cutting blade.

He picked up the lines. "*Kumma druff!*" he called out to the jennies. "*Ya!*"

Hay forgotten, he urged the mules into a lope.

CHAPTER 2

There is a vibrancy in downtown Painters Mill on Saturday mornings. A pulse that beats a little faster. An energy that beckons motorists to roll down their windows as they idle down Main Street and drink in the sights of small-town USA. Or if they have time, plunk twenty-five cents into one of the vintage parking meters and spend the afternoon shopping.

My name is Kate Burkholder and I'm the chief of police of this charming little hamlet. I was born here and raised Amish, but left the fold when I was eighteen. I spent several years in nearby Columbus, Ohio, where I emerged from the mess I'd made of my life to earn my GED and a degree in criminal justice, and I eventually found my way into law enforcement. I spent years learning how to *not* be Amish. And though it was a time of profound personal and professional growth, it didn't take long for me to realize I missed home.

When the position of chief became available, I came back. Though I've remained Anabaptist, I've never returned to my Amish roots. For a lot of reasons, some of which I still haven't reconciled. I'm working on mending fences with my family. Some members of the Amish community still won't speak to me, but I don't let it get to me. Painters Mill is home, and like most relationships, it's a work in progress.

As chief of police, I'm off duty the majority of weekends, unless there's an emergency or I'm filling in for one of my officers. The only reason I'm in town this morning is to pick up a birdhouse for my significant other, John Tomasetti. He's an agent with the Ohio Bureau of Criminal Investigation, the best friend I've ever had, and the love of my life. His birthday is next week. I ordered the birdhouse from an Amish cabinetmaker who runs a workshop just off the main drag. He promised to have it ready this morning and I can't wait to get it home.

I'm in the Explorer, inching down Main Street, when a call on my police radio snags my attention.

"Ten-six-A," comes my weekend dispatcher's voice, using the ten code for "parking obstruction."

I reach for my mike. "What's the twenty on that, Margaret?"

"Main Street, Chief. I just took a call from Joe Neely. Some kind of disturbance outside his shop."

Joe Neely owns one of the newest businesses in town, a nice little upscale coffeehouse called Mocha Joe's, a place I've ventured too many times to count.

"A fight?" I ask.

"Not yet, but he says there are a bunch of people in the street, arguing. Parking slots are blocked and someone is refusing to move."

Painters Mill is a tourist town; gridlock on a Saturday morning is a serious offense. "I'm just down the street," I tell her. "I'll take it."

"Roger that."

Even as I rack the mike, I spot the disturbance ahead. Flipping on my overhead lights, I pass the vehicle directly in front of me, but traffic is at a standstill. I park where I am and start toward the crowd. The first vehicle I see is the Amish buggy. The harnessed Standardbred gelding looks uneasy being in the center of the throng. In the buggy, a woman wearing a gray dress and organdy *kapp* sits in the passenger seat, clutching a squirming toddler. I'm familiar with most of the buggies in the area and I recognize this one as belonging to Abner Nisley and his wife, Mary Jo. They're Swartzentruber and the parents of nine children. For years, Abner eschewed the use of a slow-moving-vehicle sign, which is illegal according to Ohio Revised Code. I've pulled him over half a dozen times. When my warnings didn't work, I issued a couple of tickets, the cost of which finally convinced him to add the signage to the back of his buggy, too ornate or not.

Parked at a cockeyed angle in front of the buggy is a silver Toyota RAV4. Ohio plates. A woman in blue jeans and a white blouse with rolled-up sleeves has her cell phone pressed to her ear. She's shouting into her cell, gesturing angrily, glaring at the Amish man standing next to her. Several passersby are taking videos with their phones, probably hoping to post the next viral hit on social media.

I tilt my head to speak into my shoulder mike, but of

course it's not there. I'm out of uniform because it's my day off. Sighing, I pull out my badge and make my way toward the kerfuffle.

"Chief Burkholder?"

I glance right to see Joe Neely trot toward me. I slow down, but I don't stop. "What's going on?" I ask him.

Wearing his usual coffee-spattered apron and Mocha Joe's cap, Neely keeps pace with me. He's usually an unshakable guy, keeps his cool even during the morning rush when caffeine-deprived customers are lined up at the door like zombies. This morning, he's breathing hard, his shirt wet beneath his armpits, and a bead of sweat on his upper lip.

"Buggy horse took a crap in the street," he tells me. "Lady in the RAV stepped in it."

"Bet that didn't go over very well," I mutter as I squeeze between two teenage boys who've stopped to see what all the excitement is about.

Joe's mouth twitches. "She's pissed, Chief. Went over to confront him. Just about tore my head off when I told her to move her car."

"Anyone get hit?" I ask.

"Not yet, but I sure wouldn't want to be that Amish dude."

"Let me see if I can calm things down." I leave Joe and make my way through the crowd.

I spot Abner Nisley first. The Amish man is standing in the street, leg cocked, his eyes fastened to the asphalt. He's wearing his usual straw hat and dark trousers, work shirt, and suspenders. His hands are shoved into the pockets of his trousers. The woman in the white blouse and blue jeans is standing a foot away from him, shouting something I can't yet hear. Judging from her frothing-at-the-mouth expression, it isn't very nice.

She's about thirty years old with blond hair, blue eyes, and cheeks infused with color.

I reach the edge of the crowd and approach her. "Ma'am?" I hold up my badge. "I'm with the Painters Mill PD. What's the problem this morning?"

The woman turns to me, motions toward the horse. "That horse shit all over the place! Right in my parking spot!" She jabs a finger down at her sandal-clad feet. "Look at that! All over my shoe! That's against the law."

I glance down at the shoe in question and try not to wince. She must have kicked the pile of manure, which ended up between her toes, and got beneath her artfully pedicured toenails.

"I just bought these shoes." Mouth taut, she shakes her head. "It's disgusting. Don't you people require them Amish to clean up after themselves? Why don't they use bags or whatever to catch the shit! I mean, think of the diseases!"

The Ohio Revised Code does not require manure bags for horse-drawn vehicles. Some townships and villages with an Amish population have enacted ordinances. Painters Mill is not one of them. Because this woman is visibly upset, I opt not to point any of that out to her and take a more diplomatic route.

"Look, I've got a couple bottles of water and paper towels in my trunk," I say calmly. "Let's walk over to my vehicle, and we'll rinse those shoes off for you." I look around, take in the blocked traffic. "If you'd pull your vehicle back into that parking spot." I offer her a smile. "Coffee's on me this morning."

She doesn't return the smile. "A bottle of water? Are you kidding me? I've got a luncheon to get to. I can't go smelling like crap." She stabs a shaking finger at Abner Nisley. "You. Hose it off! Right now!"

Abner catches my gaze and shrugs. "*See is weenich ad.*" She's a little off in the head.

The woman looks at him as if he's hurled a slur in her direction and she's thinking about slugging him. A motorist in the line of cars that have piled up behind the RAV4 lays on the horn. That's my cue to end this before it escalates.

I look at the woman. "Pull your car into that parking spot while we sort this out. Now. You're blocking traffic."

"Chief Burkholder! Katie!"

I turn at the sound of the familiar voice to see the owner of the flower shop next door striding toward us. Beatrice Graeff is a downtown Painters Mill fixture— all ninety-two pounds of her. White-haired and petite, she's dressed to the nines this morning in a Dior pantsuit and her trademark cloche hat. The crowd parts for her as she approaches and I notice the hand broom and dustpan in her hands.

"I've been picking up after those horses all summer," she says to no one in particular. "Let me tell you, it's pure gold. I got a composter out back and a boatload of tea roses just waiting for another dose of nitrogen."

The three of us fall silent when the tiny woman reaches us. She thrusts the dustpan and broom to Abner. "If you don't mind, young man, my knees aren't as flexible as they used to be."

Nodding, the Amish man kneels and sweeps the manure into the dustpan. Beatrice produces a plastic bag. "Dump it in. I'll take it all." She glances down at the woman's shoes and her brows furrow. "Honey, you might want to take those to the cobbler down the street. Mr. Shook'll get those cleaned up for you pronto."

It takes ten minutes for the buggy and car to disperse and the traffic to start moving along Main Street. I'm standing on the sidewalk outside Mocha Joe's, sipping a cup of dark roast when my cell erupts. I glance down to see DISPATCH on the display and pick up.

"Did you get that stinky situation taken care of, Chief?" Margaret asks, a snicker in her voice. "I heard that lady really stepped in it."

I smile. "Disaster averted."

"I'm sorry to bother you on your day off, but there are three gentlemen here to see you. Apparently, they've traveled all the way from Pennsylvania."

"Pennsylvania? Any idea what they want?"

"They wouldn't say, Chief. Just that it's important and they'd prefer not to wait until Monday." She lowers her voice. "They seem kind of serious about something."

I sigh, thinking about the birdhouse, and decide to pick it up later this afternoon. "I'll be there in two minutes."

I toss the empty to-go cup into the trash and head toward the Explorer.

The Painters Mill Police Department is housed in a one-hundred-year-old building dressed in red brick and sandstone. It lacks the character inherent in most of the town's historic structures. It's drafty in the winter, sweltering in the summer, and fraught with an array of inexplicable sounds and smells, most of which are not pleasant. Despite its shortcomings, it's my home away from home, and when I walk through the door, I don't see the cracks in the plaster, the battered dark molding, the outdated furniture, or the century of wear on the floor. Instead, I absorb a warmth that has nothing to do with temperature, but with the percept that I'm surrounded by people I admire and respect.

I enter reception to find my off-hours dispatcher, Margaret, sitting at her station, headset clamped over her head, fingers flying over a keyboard that's so well-used the letters are worn off. To my right, three Amish men—elders by the looks of them—sit on the sofa, looking out of place and uncomfortable.

"*Guder mariye,*" I say to them. Good morning.

The three men get to their feet, each of them showing some level of stiff knees and achy joints. Judging by the varying degrees of silver hair and stooped postures, I guess all of them to be in their seventies or older. They wear full salt-and-pepper beards and are clad mostly in black. Felt, flat-brimmed hats. White shirts. Black jackets and trousers. Nondescript dark shoes. Their expressions are as somber as their clothes.

The tallest of the group steps forward, his eyes meeting mine. "My name is Nelson Yoder. I'm the bishop over in Belleville, Pennsylvania."

I take his hand and we shake. "Lancaster County?" I ask, wondering why these men would travel so far to talk to me without so much as a call.

"The Kish Valley," he tells me.

My knowledge of the Kish Valley is limited to a vague perception that it's somewhere in central Pennsylvania and home to a small but diverse group of Amish. My expression must reflect as much, because the short man with bright blue eyes and fifty pounds of extra weight wrapped around his middle ducks his head and extends his hand. "That's the Kishacoquillas Valley," he says in a gravelly voice. "In the central part of the state. I'm Nathan Kempf, the deacon."

I shake his hand. His palm is cool to the touch, with the calluses of a man who still partakes in a fair amount of physical labor. "I've been to Lancaster," I tell him, "but never the valley."

He grins. "We won't hold it against you, Kate Burkholder."

I smile back, liking him.

The third man shuffles closer. He's thin, with the angular frame of a scarecrow, a beard the shape of a wet sock, and two missing eyeteeth. "I'm Mahlon Barkman," he says. "One of the ministers in the valley."

We shake hands.

"We are the *Diener* of *die alt gemee,*" Yoder tells me.

"*Diener*" is the *Deitsch* term for "servants," which means these men are, indeed, the elected officials of their church district. *"Die alt gemee"* translates to "the old church." While I'm able to translate the Pennsylvania Dutch, I'm not exactly sure what the words mean in terms of which sect they're part of.

"You gentlemen are a long way from home," I tell them.

The men nod in unison. Hands are shoved into pockets. Legs cocked. Eyes lowered to the floor, the occasional flick going to Margaret, who's covertly listening to every word, even as she burns up the computer keys.

"We have a problem," the bishop says solemnly. "We need your help."

He's the leader of the group. Their collective body language tells me they are in agreement about their mission, how they will accomplish it, and that I am somehow central to their goal.

"Let's go into my office." I motion toward the hall, and cast a glance at Margaret.

She raises her brows and gives me a what-the-hell-is-going-on shrug.

"Would you mind making coffee?" I ask.

"Are you sure you want to subject these nice gentlemen to that?" she whispers.

I can't tell if she's serious, but I'm smiling as I unlock the door to my cubbyhole office and usher the men inside. "Have a seat."

A few minutes later, having dragged in an extra chair, I'm sitting at my desk. The three men have settled in with their coffees.

I sip, try not to wince at the acrid bite that comes back at me. "What brings you to Painters Mill?"

Nelson Yoder grimaces. "Two months ago, human bones were discovered by one of our brethren while he was cutting hay. The police came. They took the bones and they did what they do with their machines and chemicals and such. A few weeks later, those bones were identified as belonging to Ananias Stoltzfus."

I'm not familiar with the name or the case, so I wait.

Deacon Kempf picks it up from there. "Ananias was bishop for many years. He was a good bishop and performed many communions, baptisms, marriages, and excommunications."

Mahlon, the minister, shakes his head. "Ananias disappeared eighteen years ago. Vanished without a trace." He grimaces. "It was a terrible time. For all of us. As you can imagine, his children and grandchildren were beside themselves with worry—and heartache—because no one knew what had happened to him. Of course, the Amish stepped in. We did what we could. We searched. We helped the family. Mostly we prayed, but . . ." The old man offers another shrug. "His safe return was not to be."

The men fall silent. I look from face to face, seeing the remnants of grief, not the kind that dulls with age, but a sharper, newer angst that comes with more recent news.

"Did the police determine what happened to him?" I ask.

The bishop raises rheumy eyes to mine and gives a single nod. "The sheriff told us Ananias had been shot."

"Twice," Mahlon adds.

"So it wasn't a hunting accident or suicide," I say

slowly, knowing there's more coming. That I'm not going to like it.

Nathan raises his hand and strokes his beard, thoughtful. "There was a rifle found with the bones. A muzzleloader. A rusty thing that was half buried."

"The muzzleloader belongs to one of our own." The bishop offers me a sympathetic look. "Jonas Bowman."

The name strikes me like a stick of dynamite igniting in my chest, unexpected and painful. For a moment, I'm so surprised, I think I misheard. "Jonas Bowman?" I repeat the name, even as I feel the rise of heat in my cheeks. "Are you sure?"

Glances are exchanged, the kind that make me wonder if they know more about me and Jonas and the past we share than I'm comfortable with.

Mahlon grimaces. "Brother Jonas was arrested two weeks ago. For murder."

The bishop stares down at his hands and sighs. "You didn't know?"

The Amish grapevine has a surprisingly long reach. For reasons I can't quite pinpoint, I don't want to tell him I'm not privy to Amish gossip. That some in the community prefer not to deal with me because I left the fold. So I simply shake my head.

I knew Jonas Bowman growing up. His father, Ezra, was minister of our church district here in Painters Mill. When I was a kid, Jonas was a minor character in the periphery of my life. I saw him during worship. He helped my *datt* a few times on the farm. As I grew older, we played the occasional game of baseball and hockey, went swimming in the creek. All of that changed when

I was fifteen and he drove me home after a singing. It was the first time I'd ridden in a boy's buggy without a chaperone. Or a sibling or parent or girlfriend. It was the first time I'd been alone with a boy. There were a lot of firsts for both of us that summer. Some good. Some . . . not so much. Jonas was nineteen and we were at an age in which four years might as well have been twenty. Of course, we were too young to care.

My composure snaps back into place. I stare at the men, aware that the cup has gone cold in my hands, that my pulse is thrumming a little too fast.

"Jonas has denied any involvement?" I ask.

"He says he did not do it," the bishop tells me.

"He is a man of his word," the deacon adds.

I think about the dynamics involved in the identification of a muzzleloader, especially one that's been exposed to the elements for eighteen years. Most blackpowder rifles have serial numbers, but some do not, especially if they're old, which may very well have been the case for an Amish hunting rifle.

"Did the police find the spent bullets?" I ask.

The three men seem to consider the question, but it is Mahlon Barkman who replies. "One of the round balls was found, I think."

"What about motive?" I ask.

The three men exchange looks, but it is Nathan Kempf who speaks. "There were hard feelings between Jonas and Ananias."

The minister takes it from there. "His father, Ezra, was a minister, you know. There was a disagreement about a tractor Ezra bought when his two horses died unexpectedly of the sleeping sickness. Ananias would not have it and put Ezra under the *bann*."

It's an all-too-common theme among the Amish. Ezra Bowman broke the rules and Ananias Stoltzfus punished him for it.

"Silenced him, too," the bishop adds.

"Two weeks later, Ezra passed unexpectedly." Mahlon heaves a heavy sigh. "Jonas blamed Ananias for his death. Said the stress killed him."

"Jonas held Ananias responsible," Nathan tells me. "He was angry. They argued. Publicly."

"Jonas behaved badly," Nathan adds. "He was young. Hotheaded. Just twenty-one. He did some things."

"Some things like what?" I ask.

"He damaged Ananias's buggy." Nathan shrugs. "He got caught. Had some trouble with the police."

"It was a minor thing," Mahlon puts in.

"Two months later, Ananias disappeared," Nelson finishes.

"Did the police positively link the muzzleloader to Jonas?" I ask.

"The sheriff took the gun to Jonas," the deacon tells me. "Jonas admitted it was his." Nathan shrugs. "They arrested him the next day. Put him in jail."

"Jonas would never commit such a sin," Mahlon says. "He would never take the life of another man."

"He asked for my help?" I ask.

The bishop shakes his head. "Jonas would not ask such a thing for himself," he tells me. "He would not impose."

"He understands that this hardship is part of God's

plan." Deacon Kempf looks at the other two men. "It is not Jonas who is asking for your help, Kate Burkholder. It is us."

I feel myself blinking, a jumble of denials and excuses tumbling through my brain in disarray.

"Jonas has a family to care for," Nathan tells me. "Children and a wife. A woodworking business to manage. And yet he sits in jail for a sin he did not commit."

"The English police do not understand our ways. They do not know Jonas the way we do." Mahlon tightens his mouth. "They will not listen to us."

"You are a police, Kate Burkholder," Nathan says. "You understand our ways. You understand the law of the land, too."

"More importantly, you know Jonas Bowman." The bishop's eyes burn into mine. In their depths I see discernment. An awareness that puts me on edge. And questions that, because of Amish decorum, will never be voiced.

I break eye contact first, look down at the notebook in front of me, and I scribble something meaningless. All the while I assure myself Jonas would never breach the tacit boundary of privacy that had been set.

"We read about the cases you've solved here in Painters Mill. You are a good police." Nathan gives a decisive nod. "We are asking for your help."

"We have money," Mahlon adds. "We will pay you for your time and travel."

The men fall silent, as if all of their persuasive energies are spent. For the span of a full minute no one speaks, the only sound coming from the occasional ring of the phone in reception and tap-tap of Margaret's fingers against the keyboard.

Everything that's been said churns in my brain. I can't stop thinking about Jonas. The boy I knew. The man he became. The time we spent together that last summer. The profound impression he made on my life. All at a time when I was vulnerable and confused and too young to realize some emotions cannot be contained. And some actions can't be taken back.

Jonas was charismatic, charming, and persuasive. When he wanted something, he was relentless. He gave his all whether it was baseball or woodworking—or something a hell of a lot more personal. He was a force to be reckoned with and touched my life in ways I could never have imagined at such a tender age. Was he flawed? Without a doubt—just like the rest of us. But those human imperfections were tempered by a keen sense of right and wrong—and zero tolerance for injustice. How is it that a man with such black-and-white views could be involved in or suspected of murder?

As these men stated their case, I wondered how much they know about me and Jonas. If they know we got into a lot of trouble the last summer he was here. That it cost his family their relationship with the Amish community here in Painters Mill. That I am the reason his family left for Pennsylvania.

"I'm sure you're aware that I have no jurisdiction in the state of Pennsylvania," I tell them.

"Even so, there are things you can do to help, no?" This from Bishop Yoder.

I look from man to man to man. "What I *can* do, is

make some calls and find out what's going on in terms of the case."

Another round of looks is exchanged, and this time there's an air of disappointment laced with an unmistakable I-told-you-so sentiment.

Deacon Kempf sits up straighter. "We're spending the night at the motel here in Painters Mill. Tomorrow, we will be returning to the valley."

"We'd appreciate it if you'd sleep on it, Kate Burkholder, before making your decision." The bishop gets to his feet and slowly straightens. "At this point, we've nowhere else to turn."

I watch the men shuffle out of my office, aware that I've broken a sweat beneath my shirt and there's a weight in my gut that wasn't there when they entered.

CHAPTER 3

My earliest memory of Jonas Bowman was an ice-skating outing on a cold and windy day on the farm where I lived with my family. I was eleven years old and I'd sneaked out of the house to join my brother and some other Amish boys for a game of hockey. They were older than me and when I arrived with my stick— borrowed from my brother, Jacob—and my ice skates, the other boys promptly excluded me from the game.

Undeterred, while two boys shoveled snow from the ice, I sat alone on the stump next to the bonfire and laced up, hoping they'd change their minds once they realized how good I was. When there was a good-size patch of ice cleared, I took my stick and skated out to warm up. I whizzed across bumpy ice, swatting at a make-believe puck, concentrating on my form, keeping an eye on the boys, hoping someone would notice me. At the far end of the pond, Marvin Beachy, whom I went to school with and was only a year older than me, was skating toward me, slapping his puck from side to side. I don't know what possessed me to do it, but I stole the puck right out from under him. I zipped across the ice fast, skates digging in and spraying ice, looking for an ally to pass it to. I was midway across the pond when someone whistled. I heard a cheer, and my heart surged. I heard Marvin yelling, too, but I was so busy stealing his puck I couldn't look.

"Hey! Look at her go!"

"She's faster than Marvin!"

My chest swelled with pride. I heard myself laugh. Twenty feet from shore, Eddie Weaver stuck out his foot and tripped me. No chance to break my fall. I tumbled headlong into a pile of crushed ice and snow, cutting my palms right through my mittens and my knees despite two pair of tights.

"That's what you get for stealing my puck!" Marvin yelled.

I extricated myself from the snow, rolled off the pile, and turned to see Marvin retake his puck. Next to him, Eddie Weaver leered, pleased he'd been the one to stop the female interloper. "Girls don't play hockey," he said.

"I do!" I shot back as I got to my feet.

Marvin pointed at me. "Yeah, look at those scrawny legs!"

Eddie snickered. "Bet her arms are just as scrawny."

"Probably got a flat top, too," muttered another boy, one I didn't recognize.

The boys cracked up as if it was the funniest joke they'd ever heard.

My knees hurt, almost as much as my pride, but I

wouldn't have cried even if my leg was hanging by a thread of skin. Not in front of them. No, I was just stubborn enough to wait for the walk home.

I looked past them for my brother, but he was standing on the other side of the pond, leaning on the shovel he'd been using, watching. I'd hoped he would come to my defense; he knew I could play as well as these boys, at least the ones my age. And yet he said nothing.

As I stood on the frozen bank and watched them warm up, my knees aching, my eleven-year-old heart burning with outrage, Jonas skated over, frowning, his eyes on my knees. "Not bad for a half-pint," he said.

Rolling my eyes, I brushed snow from my dress. "I'm not a half-pint."

We watched the boys play for a moment; then he motioned at my knees. "You're bleeding."

I wanted to see the carnage, but I didn't look. "Doesn't hurt."

"You're pretty tough, aren't you?"

"I'm a good hockey player is what I am."

He reached into his pocket and pulled out a kerchief. "Here. Tie it on."

"I don't need it."

"Yeah, you do." His face split into a grin. Bringing his fingers to his mouth, he whistled. "I want Half-Pint on my team!" he called out.

I became the girl who could play hockey that winter. The one who—despite my size and gender— was never last when it came time to choose teams.

Jonas made one hell of an impression on my nonconformist psyche that day. The part of me that was still a child was dazzled that an older boy would stand up for me. The part of me that was edging into my pre-teen years had her breath taken away. I had no way of knowing I'd been swept off my feet and the breathless-ness that made my chest swell was only a sampling of what lay ahead.

I'm thinking about that day on the ice when I pull into the lane of the farm Tomasetti and I share. After the three Amish elders left the station, I called the Mifflin County Sheriff's Department, which is the law enforcement agency for Belleville, Pennsylvania. The deputy I spoke to didn't know much about the case, but was able to confirm most of what the three men told me. Eighteen years ago, Bishop Ananias Stoltzfus and Jonas Bowman were involved in some type of dispute. Two months later, Stoltzfus disappeared. Jonas was questioned by the police, but there wasn't enough evidence to arrest him and the DA refused to pursue a case based on circumstantial evidence alone.

The skeletal remains were discovered two months ago in a farmer's field. The sheriff's department searched the area and unearthed an old muzzleloader and a .50 caliber ball at the scene. Because the gun was an antique, it didn't have a serial number. But when they took it to Jonas Bowman, he admitted the rifle was his and the arrest was made without incident.

Jonas was formally charged with second-degree murder and is being held at the Mifflin County Correctional Facility in Lewistown. Bail was set at five hundred thousand dollars. No trial date has been set. So far, he hasn't posted bail. A quick internet search revealed that in the commonwealth of Pennsylvania, second-degree murder carries with it the possibility of life in prison.

I also called the Mifflin County Correctional Facility, only to learn they don't allow incoming calls to inmates unless the call is from an attorney or an official involved in the case. I was able to locate Jonas's attorney, but today is Saturday and, evidently, he doesn't return calls on the weekend.

I park behind Tomasetti's Tahoe, snatch the birdhouse from the rear of the Explorer, and head toward the house. I'm nearly to the back door when I hear music coming from the barn. One of the front sliding doors stands open a few feet. Hefting the shopping bag, I head that way.

Our barn is an old German-style bank barn that shows every one of its hundred or so years. I take the earthen ramp to the door and walk inside. I find Tomasetti standing next to a beat-up solid wood door that's propped against the wall. He's built a wood frame against that wall. It's the height of a kitchen counter, and he's clipped a work light to a shelf he added at some point. I haven't seen any of the improvements he's spent the last week or so making, and I'm reminded that I work too much.

I set the bag on the ground and take a moment to simply watch. He's wearing faded jeans with scuffed work boots. There's a tape measure in his right hand. Worn leather gloves. A box cutter sticking out of his back pocket. His shirtsleeves are rolled halfway up his forearms. His elbow peeks through a small hole in the fabric.

"Looks like an interesting project," I say.

He glances at me over his shoulder. He doesn't quite smile, but I see pleasure in his eyes. I grin because he's happy to see me and he can't quite hide it.

"You're just in time," he says smoothly.

"For what?"

He tosses me a pair of gloves, which I catch; then he moves around to the top portion of the door. "Meet my new workbench."

"Looks solid." I go to the opposite end of the door.

"Found it at the junk shop out by the feed store."

"One man's junk is another man's treasure."

"Think we can lift it onto the frame?" He bends.

I do the same. "Never met a door I couldn't handle."

On the count of three we lift. The door is heavy, with a smooth top and a smattering of nicks. Grunting with effort, we shuffle right and lower it onto the frame.

I run my hand over the top. "Good find, Tomasetti."

"That's what I was thinking when I saw you walk in."

I can't help it; I laugh. "You're so full of it."

He crosses to me, puts his arms around my waist, and presses a kiss to my mouth. He smells of sawdust and man sweat and this morning's aftershave.

"What's in the bag, Chief?"

"And I thought I was going to get it inside before you noticed." I pluck the pencil from behind his ear and tuck it into his breast pocket.

"No such luck."

I lift the bag and hand it to him, knowing fully I'm

grinning like a fool. Feeling too serious because it's suddenly vastly important that I get this right, and that he like the gift.

"Happy birthday," I tell him, uncomfortable because my cheeks are hot. "A few days early."

Arching a brow, wondering about the premature giving of the gift, he reaches into the bag and pulls out the birdhouse. It's a rustic work of art made with repurposed barn wood, rusty tin shingles, and cedar perches, all of it constructed in the shape of an old German round barn.

"Nice workmanship." He carries it to the newly installed bench, sets it down, and steps back to admire it.

"Took me a week to make it," I tell him, deadpan.

His mouth twitches, but he's looking at me a little too closely. Tomasetti is an astute man; he knows I've got something on my mind. But he's also got a sense for timing and he knows this isn't the right moment to query.

"Going to look nice in the backyard," he says.

"Or out by the firepit," I tell him.

He nods. "I've got some steel pipe around here somewhere. I'll need to pick up a couple bags of concrete at the hardware store. If you dig the posthole, I'll mount it."

Suddenly unable to hold his gaze, I go to the birdhouse and run my hand over the roof. "It's a purple martin house," I tell him. "They like to nest in open areas, away from trees, with the birdhouse at least twenty feet off the ground." I'm not a habitual blatherer, but I can't seem to stop.

Noticing my discomfort, he approaches me, sets his hands on my shoulders, and tilts his head to snag my gaze. "Something on your mind, Chief?"

My eyes meet his and in that instant the floor beneath my feet seems to crumble so that I don't feel as if I'm standing on solid ground. I'm keenly aware of the warmth of his hands coming through the fabric of my shirt. My pulse throbbing at my throat. We've come a long way since we met. We've learned to trust. We've learned to love. To appreciate. Still, there are times when I feel as if I don't deserve this. To be this happy. To love this profoundly.

"I think I have to go to Pennsylvania," I say.

His brows go up in surprise. "A case?"

"Not an official case."

I tell him about the three Amish men I met with earlier and lay out everything they told me about the discovery of human remains and Jonas Bowman. "I called the sheriff's department in Mifflin County. They've charged him with second-degree homicide."

"Serious charge." He thinks about that a moment. "Bowman is from Painters Mill?"

I nod. "His family. I knew them when I was young."

I can tell by the way he's looking at me he knows there's more to the story. That there's something I'm not telling him. That it's important. He also knows I'm holding back and he's not quite sure how to get me to talk. Timing, I think, and I'm glad Tomasetti has it down pat.

"You were close?" he asks.

I stare at him, feeling like an idiot because my heart is beating too fast. My face feels hot. The weight of an uncomfortable emotion I can't pinpoint lies like a stone in my gut. It's all an overreaction. What happened between Jonas and me was a lifetime ago. We were kids. Reckless teenagers. I was still recovering from the ordeal I went through at the hands of Daniel Lapp, the Amish neighbor who raped me when I was fourteen. Despite all of it, the months I spent with Jonas were profound. They meant something. I can tell by the way Tomasetti is looking at me that he's taken note.

"Yes," I say.

It's as if he can't look away now, and his gaze is burning me from the inside out. Wondering why I didn't elaborate when I should have. In that moment, I know he's not going to take the conversation to the next level—or ask the question zinging between us.

How close?

"Do you think he did it?" he asks.

"The boy I knew growing up? No. He was a good kid. Amish. Still is." I shrug. "That said, you and I know people can change over time. So, I don't know."

"How long has it been since you saw him?"

"He left Painters Mill three years before I did. His family moved and he went with them." I don't mention that it was the bishop who asked them to leave. And that I was the reason.

Tomasetti is a complex man. He's a thinker, honest to a fault, and one of the smartest people I've ever met. Despite his many strengths, he's also human. He's still healing from the murder of his wife and children six years ago—losses that would have destroyed a lesser man. The one thing Tomasetti is not is insecure.

"Sounds like he could use your help," he says after a moment.

"I think so."

"How long will you be gone?"

"A few days." I shrug. "A week tops."

He looks at the birdhouse sitting on the workbench, then at me, and sighs. "I guess that means I'm going to have to put up this birdhouse all by myself."

I reach out, touch the side of his face with my hand. "I'm sorry I'm going to miss your birthday."

"I thought I might skip this year anyway. Give you a chance to catch up with me."

I laugh. "I'll see what I can do about that."

He sobers, gives me a long, thoughtful look. "You'll let me know if there's anything I can do?"

"You know it." I take his hand. "I'm not leaving until Monday, so we have the rest of the weekend. What do you say we find that pipe and get started on the birdhouse?"

"You're offering to dig the posthole?"

"Not a chance."

It's not often that I call for an unscheduled meeting with my team of officers. Painters Mill is a small, quiet town, after all. We operate on a skeleton crew, dealing with neighbor disputes or bar fights, domestic violence and speeders, and, of course, the rite of rounding up wayward livestock. Not exactly life on the edge for a cop, but my officers are professional and well trained. This morning, I'm compelled to let everyone know I'll be gone for a few days and ensure the department runs smoothly while I'm gone. My most experienced full-time officer, Rupert "Glock" Maddox, will be in charge while I'm away.

I spent most of last evening packing and digging around the internet and various law enforcement databases for information on the disappearance of Ananias Stoltzfus eighteen years ago. The case is ice-cold and there isn't much out there. The Mifflin County sheriff's deputy I spoke with wasn't much help. Neither the sheriff nor the district attorney returned my calls—it was the weekend, after all—but the lack of response reminded me that I'll be looking into the case not only as a civilian, but as an outsider. I have no law enforcement contacts in Pennsylvania, few resources, and zero in terms of backup. Not that I expect to need it. Belleville is smaller than Painters Mill, with an extremely low crime rate. In fact, there hasn't been a murder since Stoltzfus went missing.

Tomasetti and I got the birdhouse mounted and the pole sunk into the ground. We put it near the firepit, between the house and pond, and I have to admit it looks nice. We spent every minute together, but I was distracted. I spent too much time thinking about Jonas, the boy I'd once known, mulling the kind of man he's become, and wondering if he's the same person I remember.

It's just after seven on Monday morning now and I'm sitting at my desk in my cubbyhole office, putting together my notes for what will likely be a fifteen-minute meeting. My suitcase is in the back of the Explorer and I hope to hit the road inside the hour. Already, I miss Tomasetti.

"Chief?"

I glance up to see Mona Kurtz standing in the doorway. Though she worked the graveyard shift last night, she looks ready-to-take-on-the-day fresh. She was my dispatcher for several years. During that time, she earned a degree in criminal justice, devoured everything law enforcement, and garnered a good bit of training and experience from the rest of the team. She now graces the ranks of the department as Painters Mill's first female patrol officer.

"Team is wrangled and penned," she tells me.

"I'll grab the branding iron." Rising, I snag my coffee mug, round my desk, and walk with her to the closet-size meeting room.

I pause at the doorway, take in the sight of my team, and do my best not to acknowledge the quiver of pleasure. My relationship with the men and women who work for me is strictly professional. Aside from the occasional baby shower or celebratory meal, I don't socialize with them. As chief, I've always felt that it's important not to get too chummy. That philosophy in no way lessens my affection or respect for them. We're part of a brotherhood, and when you work together as closely as we do, that familiarity doesn't need to be shouted out, because we feel it where it counts and we know the officer standing next to us has our back.

Roland "Pickles" Shumaker is my oldest officer. He's

nearing eighty years of age now, but he'll be the last to admit it. If you ask, you're rewarded with a bald-faced lie or terse reply or maybe a robust cussing out. His law enforcement career spans fifty years. His glory days include an undercover narcotics gig that netted the biggest drug bust in the history of Holmes County and put a lot of bad guys behind bars. Pickles is my only part-time officer. He works fifteen hours a week, usually at the school crosswalk and the occasional football game. He's been known to nap in his cruiser and sneak a smoke when no one is looking. He took a fall last year and spent a month hiding a limp. While he may be getting older, only the unwise would underestimate Pickles. He is a sheepdog of the first order; he will guard his flock with his life, and fight any wolf that threatens them to his last breath.

Sitting next to Pickles, Chuck "Skid" Skidmore nurses a to-go cup of coffee from Mocha Joe's. He's the department's resident smartass. He upholds the honor with pride, but it's an unspoken reality that the rest of us appreciate his humor a little too much. He's a good cop with a laid-back personality and a unique ability to defuse even the most tumultuous of situations.

Glock sits at the head of the table, showing phone pics to Mona. Probably of his children judging by the smile on his face. He's a family man, a former Marine who spent several years in Afghanistan, and the first African American patrol officer to serve the citizens of Painters Mill. He's a good man and it gave me great personal satisfaction to hire him shortly after I became chief.

T.J. Banks is just twenty-eight years old. He's a single

guy with an active love life and high-drama relation-ships that garner him some razzing from his peers. He was the rookie until Mona came on board. He's come a long way since his early days and has accumulated some good experience in the years he's been on patrol. He's a dependable cop with a bright future ahead of him.

I tap my pen against my mug to call the meeting to order. "I appreciate everyone coming in early for a last-minute meeting," I say.

Skid raises his coffee cup. "No problem, Chief. T.J. was the only one complaining about not getting his beauty sleep."

"That's because he was out all night," Pickles mutters.

T.J. sits up straighter, paying attention now.

I glance at him. "We appreciate your sacrifice, T.J."

He hefts a sound of faux disgust and the room erupts with chuckles.

"I have to go out of town for a few days and wanted to touch base before I leave," I say. "Reports."

"Chief?"

I glance toward the door to see my newest dispatcher, Margaret, standing in the doorway, her hand raised, a student with an urgent question. Next to her, Lois, my first-shift dispatcher, has the headset clamped over her head, listening for incoming calls.

"I'd like to recommend our department invest in a new coffeemaker," Margaret tells me. "I can't tell you how many visitors come in and comment on how awful the coffee is."

A few chuckles ripple around the table.

Glock raises his brows and looks at me. "I say we

serve some of that coffee to Auggie," he says, referring to the mayor. "Might work to our advantage budgetwise."

"What are we going to complain about if not the coffee?" Skid puts in.

"I think the coffee's just fine the way it is," Pickles grumbles.

I give Margaret my full attention. "Put together a request. Get prices on three coffeemakers. I'll get it done."

"Yes, ma'am."

I glance at my notes. "The mayor says we've got vandals with paint out at the Tuscarawas Bridge. We need to step up patrols." I look at Pickles. "We could use you a few extra hours a week, if you can spare the time."

The old man takes his time answering, puffs out his chest a little. "There's nothing I'd like more than to bust those paint-huffing little shits."

"Clarice will be happy to hear it," Skid mutters, referring to Pickles's wife, who's been known to complain if he's home too much.

Another round of laughter ensues.

I turn my attention to Glock. "You're in charge while I'm gone."

He gives me a salute. "Roger that."

"Don't let it go to your head, dude," Skid mutters.

"Business or vacation, Chief?" This from Mona. She's not being nosy, just curious.

"A little bit of both." I outline the case in Belleville, mostly to quell further questions and deter any potential rumors. "If anyone asks, it's vacation." I scan the group, and for the first time I'm cognizant of the fact that I don't want to leave. That the trip is born of a sense of responsibility that doesn't fit quite right.

"My cell is on twenty-four seven," I tell my team. "Any problem, large or small, give me a call. Day or night."

At that, I adjourn the meeting.

CHAPTER 4

Twenty-three years before

When I was twelve years old, one of our English neighbors passed away, and his farm was left abandoned. That summer, my brother, Jacob, my sister, Sarah, and Jonas, and I transformed old man Delaney's pasture into a baseball field befitting a minor-league team. Jacob mowed a huge swatch of grass, leaving us with an acre or so of cleared land. Jonas set to work building a bench so people who came to watch us play would have a place to sit. Sarah and I sewed canvas bags that we filled with sand for the bases. We spread lime to demark the base lines. We piled a wheelbarrow of sand on the pitcher's mound, and partially buried a flat stone for home plate. Jonas even came up with a gnarled length of chain-link fence and transformed it into a batter's cage.

I spent my babysitting money on a leather glove. It was the first time I'd bought anything without my parents' consent; even at that early age, I'd known they wouldn't allow it. I was too competitive and too interested in partaking in activities better suited to my male counterparts. But I was crazy for baseball that summer. I loved hitting and I loved running. Most of all, I loved winning. Sometimes I was a sore loser. I remember vividly the mad rush to finish chores, so I could hit that diamond and make my mark.

On this particular day, I'd finished my chores early and was the first to arrive at the diamond only to find it had been commandeered by a group of English boys. There were six of them, a few years older than me, and they'd come in two ATVs wearing their strange baseball outfits with caps and cleats. I was wearing my traditional clothes—a mauve dress, an organdy *kapp,* and the fastest sneakers I owned—my glove and baseball in hand. I slowed as I approached, taking in the scene, keenly aware that all eyes were on me.

"Hey, look!" called out one of the boys. "We got us a new bat boy!"

A chubby red-haired kid with a catcher's mask cocked on his crown approached me. I guessed him to be one of the younger players, about my age, heavier but an inch or two shorter. He gave my clothes a thorough appraisal. "Does this field here belong to your mom and dad?" He enunciated the words slowly, as if he were speaking to a two-year-old—or someone who wasn't fluent in English.

"It belongs to Mr. Delaney," I told him, my mind rushing through how best to get rid of them. "You're not allowed to be here."

"Says who?"

I looked up to see a second boy approach, eyes

squinted against the sun. He was older, thirteen or four teen, brown hair sticking out of a Cincinnati Reds ball cap he wore backward. His eyes fastened to the ball and glove in my hands.

"Mr. Delaney," I blurted. "He gave us permission."

"She's lying!" The chubby boy laughed. "Old man Delaney croaked two months ago!"

My cheeks burned. I did my best to make up for my tactical error. "His family gave us permission," I told him.

"She's full of it," Chubby said to his teammate.

The kid in the ball cap frowned. "Hate to break it to you, kid, but we were here first. Get lost."

"Come on, dude! What's the holdup?"

I looked past him, saw two more boys approach. They were older, too, wearing baseball helmets and cleats, and they looked seriously put out that their game was being delayed by an Amish girl.

One of the boys jabbed a thumb at me. "Who the hell is that?"

I felt my big plans for an afternoon baseball game slipping away. "This is our diamond," I told them. "You can play until my friends arrive, but then you have to leave."

The boys cracked up.

The red-haired kid guffawed. "The only one leaving is you. Go on, beat it."

Another round of laughter ensued and the boys shuffled away, turning their attention back to the game.

"Let's play ball!" one of them shouted.

Dismissed, I stood in the hot July sun and watched the

boys prepare for their game. I thought about all the work that had gone into building the diamond—sewing the base bags, pilfering the lime from the barrel in the barn without my *datt*'s permission. All the money I spent on that glove. Mostly, I thought about the game I'd been pining for all morning. This was the day I was going to slam in that home run and show everyone how fast I could run. These English kids were going to ruin everything. In that moment, I was incapable of surrendering the diamond we'd worked so hard to build. How could I let them take it when they'd done nothing to earn it?

"This is my field and you can't play here!" I called out to them.

All six of the boys turned to face me. The chubby boy looked perplexed. One of the kids wearing a helmet laughed outright. The others exchanged looks ranging from uncertain to annoyed.

The boy wearing the backward cap stalked over to me. "What did you say?"

He had a mean look about him. The kind of kid who might kick a dog. Or pick a fight with someone smaller because he knew he could beat them up. I didn't like the way he was looking at me. His hands clenched into fists. I didn't want to talk to him. Worse, I was scared and wishing I hadn't opened my mouth. I looked over my shoulder, praying Jonas or Jacob or even Sarah would show, but there was no one there.

I was thinking about making a run for it when Backward Cap Kid snatched my glove from my hands and threw it as far as he could. "Beat it, you little shit!"

I watched my glove land in a muddy pond a few

yards away. In the silence that followed, the chubby boy giggled, but it was a nervous, unpleasant sound. My heart was beating so hard the blood seemed to sizzle in my veins. I knew I should walk away, do the right thing, be a good girl, and let these boys have the field. Instead, I smacked the glove from the boy's hand.

"Hey!" He reached for me.

I dodged left, scooped up the glove, and hurled it into the water.

One of the boys howled with laughter. "She's got an arm on her!"

The punch came out of nowhere. One moment, I was standing there, breathing fire. The next my nose was crushed. My head snapped back. Pain zinged up my sinuses. I reeled backward, landed on my rear hard enough to jar my teeth.

"Whoa!"

"Dude!"

"She's a frickin' little kid!" This, from Chubby.

Somewhere in the periphery of my consciousness, I heard the jingle of a harness, but the significance of the sound didn't register. I wiped my nose, saw blood on my sleeve. I was too furious to cry, but the tears came anyway. Part from pain, part from humiliation, but mostly because of the injustice of losing the diamond.

"You had enough, punk?" shouted Backward Cap Boy.

I didn't look at him as I got to my feet, but I was vaguely aware of Chubby placing himself between us. "Aw, come on, Jeffie," he said, darting a you-okay? look in my direction. "She's Amish. Leave her alone."

Shaking his head in disgust, the boy who'd hit me

stuffed his fingers into his mouth and emitted an ear-splitting whistle. "Let's play ball!"

I'd just gotten to my feet when someone shouted, "Skunk! What the—Frickin' *skunks*!"

"Shit!"

"Run!"

Out of the corner of my eye, I saw two of the animals in question waddle onto the diamond. Jonas, I thought, and I swung around to see him standing next to his buggy, eating an apple, watching the boys scatter. Despite the pain in my nose, the blood dribbling down my chin, I laughed.

A few weeks ago, he'd rescued half a dozen skunk babies when their mama was hit by a car. He bottle-fed them. Tamed them. Carried them around everywhere. He'd been planning to bring them here and turn them loose in the woods. Today must have been the day.

The boy who slugged me stabbed a finger at me, but his attention was riveted to the skunks doddering in his direction. "You ain't seen the last of us, you little shit!"

The boys clambered into their ATVs. Baseball bats and gloves tossed in the rear. The engines roared to life. A water bottle flew in my direction.

"This ain't over!" one of them shouted.

Dirt and dust spewed into the air as the two ATVs sped away.

I needed a minute to hide the evidence that I'd been crying, so I walked to the bank of the muddy pond, toed off my sneakers and socks, hiked up my dress, and waded into the mossy water to retrieve my glove.

"Looks like someone got slugged."

I turned to see Jonas walking toward me, his head cocked, his eyes taking in the blood on the front of my dress. He was sixteen now. Taller than me by a foot.

"I guess someone did," I muttered as I pulled my socks and shoes on over my muddy feet.

"You're still bleeding," he said. "Tilt your head back. Pinch your nose. I got a kerchief in the buggy. Come on."

Taking my hand, he led me to the buggy and sat me down on the step-up. I sat there, watching droplets of blood hit the dirt, praying I didn't start crying again.

"Here you go." Jonas handed me a crinkled kerchief.

I took it, trying not to wince when I pressed it against my nose and squeezed my nostrils together.

For a couple of minutes, we watched the skunks as they sniffed around, eventually moseying over to us. Jonas handed me a piece of his apple and I offered it to the runt of the litter, who took it and began to chew.

"Nose still hurt?" he asked.

I looked down at my muddy shoes and socks. "Mamm's going to be mad."

"I got some water in the buggy. We'll get that dirt off you and no one will ever know." He took the last bite of apple and offered the core to the other skunks.

I watched the animals eat, enjoying the way they held the apple core with their tiny clawed hands and wrinkled their noses when they bit into it.

After a moment, Jonas spoke. "You know that's not going to be the last time someone gives you a bloody nose."

"They were mean," I said. "I didn't do anything wrong."

"You should have let them have the diamond," he pointed out.

I sat up straighter, my hand falling away from my face, my sense of justice chafed. "We built it," I said. "Why should we give it up to those boys who did nothing but try to steal it? It's *ours*."

Frowning, he guided my hand back to my nose. "You're right. We built it. But this land belongs to the Delaney family, not us." He shrugged. "Besides, we're Amish, Katie. We don't fight. Over ball diamonds or anything else."

"Maybe that's why I don't fit in."

"You fit in just fine. You just have to try a little harder."

But while neither of us was quite able to put our doubts into words, we both knew my ability to conform wasn't an attribute that could be counted on.

I was well versed in all the Amish tenets. I knew their importance. I felt their goodness, the comfort of them. I wasn't mature enough to put my misgivings about the rules into words. But I was aware of the battle raging inside me and I wanted Jonas to know it wasn't because I didn't understand.

"You think I'm too rebellious," I murmured.

"I think your nature is rebellious."

I looked down at the kerchief, smeared with blood. I looked at the front of my dress and sighed, wondering how I was going to explain it to Mamm. Maybe if I told her I got hit in the face by the ball . . .

"If those boys were right to do what they did, why did you sic the skunks on them?" I asked.

"I didn't say they were right. But neither were you." I start to protest, but he raised his hand. "Besides, I didn't want to see you get punched again."

"Maybe I would have hit him back," I snapped.

Jonas laughed despite the fact that I was serious and he knew it. "That's the thing about you, Katie. You're muleheaded enough to walk the hard road."

"I don't know what you mean."

"You stayed true to yourself even though you knew it might earn you a punch in the nose." He shrugged. "In a way, that's a blessing. In another way, because you're Amish and a girl, it's a curse."

We got to play our baseball game that afternoon. We told Jacob and Sarah and my *mumm* I was hit in the nose by a fly ball. I never forgot what Jonas told me about staying true to myself. I recalled those words a hundred times growing up. Times when it would have been easier to compromise what I believed in and take the lesser road.

I felt closer to Jonas than my own brother. He listened to me. Treated me as an equal, as if what I had to say was important. He told me things he didn't share with others. Nothing inappropriate—we were innocents that summer—just observations and opinions that didn't necessarily jibe with all those Amish expectations. Later, when I began to get into trouble and the sum of my mistakes began to mount, Jonas was one of the few Amish who stood by me. He believed in me, even when I didn't believe in myself.

CHAPTER 5

Lewistown is a midsize borough with a pretty downtown peppered with historic buildings and architecture styles ranging from Greek Revival to Art Deco. Like most towns in this part of the country, it bears scars from the economic downturns of decades past. I see evidence of that as I make the turn onto Market Street and idle toward the square.

The Mifflin County Correctional Facility is located in a nondescript brick building at the corner of Market and Wayne. It took half a dozen calls and a bit of cajoling to get approved for a visit. That I'm a member of law enforcement was my saving grace. I've still not been able to speak to Jonas. As I take the steps to the glass doors and head for the central desk, I'm hoping everything is in order and I'll be able to meet with him.

The detention officer inside the glassed-in office gives me a quick once-over as I approach. I identify myself and drop my driver's license and badge into the pass-through drawer.

"You here to see an inmate?" She taps a few keys on the keyboard in front of her.

I nod. "Jonas Bowman."

"You're not on the visitation list," she informs me.

"I called ahead," I tell her. "The deputy sheriff added me to the list over the weekend."

She frowns. "Gotta check."

It takes twenty minutes for me to get through security. I'm questioned about my service firearms, both of which are unloaded and locked in my vehicle. A male detention officer leads me to the visitation hall, where I'm taken to a row of plexiglass-encased booths, each containing a stool, a slab Formica desk, and a phone that doesn't look quite clean.

"He'll be out in a few," he tells me. "Hang tight."

I wait fifteen minutes. I'm thinking about flagging down a detention officer when the door to the visitation room opens. Jonas starts toward me, craning his neck to see who has come calling. Some prisons and county jails accommodate the religious needs of inmates. Not so with this one. He's clad in a wrinkled orange jumpsuit. No hat. Rubber flip-flops on his feet. His hair is long and cut in the "Dutch boy" style that's typical for Amish males. Some prisons won't even allow their inmates to retain their facial hair, because it makes it more difficult for the officers to identify them. To my relief, they allowed him to keep his beard, which is of great significance for a married Amish man.

He recognizes me instantly and stops cold. A quiver moves through his body. He blinks, as if his eyes are playing tricks on him. I feel a similar quiver move through my own psyche. The urge to rise and go to him for a handshake or embrace is powerful. Of course, I can't do either.

He looks much the same as he did last time I saw him, some twenty years ago. A few pounds heavier. Leaner face. Troubled eyes the color of dark roast coffee. When I was a kid, he'd seemed as big as a giant, but he's only a few inches taller than me. His face has seen too much sun over the years, evidenced in the crow's-feet at his eyes, the tanned-leather appearance of his neck. He didn't wear glasses last time I saw him, but he does now. The frames are black and unadorned.

He holds my gaze as he slides onto the bench seat and picks up the phone. "You always did know how to surprise a guy," he says matter-of-factly.

His voice is the same, too. Deep and melodic with a hint of the Amish-English accent I myself have been accused of having. Despite the reason for our meeting, I smile. "Not all of those surprises were pleasant."

"This one is."

"I guess we both wish it was under different circumstances." I hear the words as if they were spoken by someone else. A person whose pulse isn't pounding, whose emotions aren't swelling and a little too close to the surface, and a gut that isn't knotted into a ball of emotions I'm not sure I could unravel even if I tried.

"You look the same." He leans back in his chair and studies me intently. "After all these years, you're exactly as I remember."

"Less the *kapp*."

"I always knew you wouldn't remain Amish. The signs were there. Even when you were twelve years old."

I don't know what to say to that. Inexplicably, I can't meet his gaze. An awkward combination of self-consciousness and discomfort, neither of which I can reconcile, stirs uncomfortably in my chest. I pretend to look past him at the door from which he emerged, and I use that moment to shore up.

"English suits me," I say.

"I can tell. You look happy."

"I am."

"You didn't have to come."

"Yes, I did." Settled now, I take his measure. He looks tired. Embarrassed. Ashamed. Humiliated. But like so many Amish I know, he has a serenity about him that transcends the negativity of the situation. "How are you holding up?"

"I'm fine." He raises a hand to encompass the room, as if to dismiss any worry about his well-being. "The officers have been decent. You know, professional. Polite. Food isn't too bad. They give me three meals a day."

"You're still not a very good liar." They're harsh words, but I soften them with a smile because it's true.

He makes a sound of dismissal, but before he can look away, something darker peeks out at me from behind the mask of composure. It's the first sign of a crack I've seen and I suspect it will grow the longer he's incarcerated and as the reality of the situation hits home.

"I worry for my wife," he tells me. "The children. They're probably confused."

"I'm happy to check on them for you," I say.

He scrubs his hand over his face, but it's not enough to wipe away the pain etched into his features. "Thank you."

I recall the day my sister told me Jonas had married. I was sixteen, and though he'd been gone for a year, I still pined for him. I couldn't believe he'd fallen in love with someone else and moved on so quickly. It wasn't my first heartbreak, but it was the first time in my life I felt the fangs of that green-eyed beast Jealousy.

He hefts his gaze back in my direction. "The *Diener* came to you?" he asks. "In Painters Mill?"

"They thought I might be able to help."

Frowning, he shakes his head, as if the three elders are misguided teenagers. "They're good men and they meant well, but I asked them not to involve you."

"They did the right thing, Jonas. I might be able to help."

His mouth curves. "You never would take no for an answer."

"Especially when I'm right."

"Which is all the time, no?"

We share a smile.

Jonas sobers first. "The thing is, Katie. I know God has a plan. Sometimes we don't know what that plan is. But it is divine and this is part of it. I'm in His hands, as are all of us. The one thing that I know for certain is that everything will work out the way it's supposed to."

It is the quintessential Amish mindset—one of many

reasons I didn't fit in and left the fold. The impulse to point out that he's been charged with murder and faces spending the rest of his life in prison is powerful, but I don't succumb.

"I read a newspaper story about your being a police," he tells me. "It said you're good at what you do."

"I'm good at digging."

"You always were one for asking questions." The hint of a smile touches his mouth. "Too many, according to some, eh?"

I smile back, but a hundred of those questions swirl in the forefront of my brain. The need for hard information is tempered by the knowledge that all visitor conversations, attorney-client exchanges aside, are recorded and may be used any way a prosecutor sees fit.

"Jonas." Without consciously thinking about it, I switch to *Deitsch*. "Everything we say is being recorded."

He takes the information in stride, as if it's the last thing on his mind and he doesn't care one way or another. "You think I'm going to admit to something that will put the nail in my coffin, Katie?"

"Just so you're aware." I don't smile this time. "I need to know what happened."

He leans back in the chair and shakes his head. "I didn't kill Ananias Stoltzfus, if that's what you're asking."

"They arrested you," I say.

He heaves a sigh, as if the thought of wading into the explanation of how he ended up here exhausts him. "It's a long story that goes back a few years."

I motion to our surroundings. "I think we have time."

He ducks his head, sheepish. The exhale that follows is a disconsolate sound that goes through me as wrenchingly as a sob.

"I was nineteen when we left Painters Mill and moved here to Big Valley," he tells me.

I stare at him, wait, surprised because even after all these years I have to steel myself against the punch of remembrance. The pain of the fifteen-year-old girl I'd been and the dark days that followed his departure was excruciating and real. I'd never felt so lost. So betrayed. I was broken in so many ways I didn't think I'd ever be able to put all the pieces of me back together.

"Ananias Stoltzfus was our bishop," he tells me. "A year or so after we arrived, Datt was struck by the lot."

Being "struck by the lot" is an Amish term for the process of electing a new member of the *Diener*—a bishop, deacon, or minister—by the congregation.

"Ezra was a minister?" I ask.

"A good one," he tells me.

I remember Jonas's father well. Ezra Bowman was a respected member of the Amish community in Painters Mill. He had a booming voice, a big laugh, and a demeanor that made no bones about what he believed or where he stood. He was charismatic and unfailingly adherent to his Anabaptist beliefs. I was too young at the time to fully comprehend the complexities of the adult relationships around me. But even as a kid, I sensed some of his views weren't popular among some of the Amish. My own *datt* used to call him *druvvel-machah*. Troublemaker.

"Everyone in the church district agreed to the ordination," he explains, "though we'd only lived in Belleville for a year. Datt was born in Belleville, you know. Grew up here." Jonas pauses as if to get his words in order. "My father served well for months. He was a good preacher. In full fellowship. Preached in other church districts on the off Sundays."

Jonas grimaces. "He'd been minister for about year when the mess with the tractor happened. It was diesel powered, you know. Datt had been pushing for more relaxed rules. But Ananias wasn't happy with him, even though he allowed those who own dairy farms to use diesel machinery to milk. After a lot of discussion and arguments, Ananias put Datt under the *bann*. When Datt still refused to get rid of the tractor, the bishop silenced him."

To be placed under the *bann* is emotionally traumatic for any Amish person. None of your fellow Amish will do business with you. Friends, and even family, will not share a meal with you. Some Amish won't speak to you. Contrary to popular belief, it is not done to punish, but to bring the fallen back into the parish. For a minister to be "silenced" is worse. The minister's voice is taken away; he is no longer allowed to preach. It's a harsh punishment for a man who has been charged with preaching to his congregation.

Seemingly lost in the memory, Jonas shakes his head. "Datt was distraught. He was a good minister. Some of the families in our church district rallied and supported him. People took sides and, in the end, several families rebelled. They chose Datt over the bishop. It was a painful time."

Church disagreements aren't unheard of among the

Amish. Over the last hundred years, several factions of Amish and Mennonite groups have broken off to begin new settlements with different rules. The reasons for the splits range from clothing types to the rules surrounding excommunication to the types of buggies allowed.

"There were a lot of hard feelings. On both sides." He runs his fingers over his beard, his expression troubled. "Two weeks later, Datt passed. They said it was a heart attack." Jonas's expression hardens. "Maybe it was the stress. But he was gone."

I nod, wincing against the stab of guilt that follows. I'd heard about Ezra's passing and yet I didn't write a note or send condolences to Jonas or his family.

"I'm sorry about your *datt*," I tell him.

"He's with God now." He waves off the condolence and for the first time I catch a glimpse of anger. I'm surprised because his *datt* has been gone eighteen years. Too long for him to still hold a grudge.

"A couple weeks later, church Sunday, I got into an argument with Ananias," he tells me. "I lost my temper. I shouted. Said some things I shouldn't have."

"Did you threaten him?"

"No."

"What about the vandalism incident?"

"Ah." He gives a wry smile. "The old men didn't leave anything out, did they?"

I say nothing, wait.

"I was young and stupid. Not to mention angry. I went out with a sledgehammer and wrecked his buggy."

He looks down, shakes his head as if in self-disgust. "I'm not proud of it."

"You got caught?"

"Paid a fine."

A documented indictment of character that likely played a role in his being arrested. . . .

He sighs. "Two months later, Ananias disappeared. No one knew where he'd gone or what happened. But there was talk. Too much talk."

"About you?"

He nods. "The police questioned me, but I wasn't too worried. I had the truth on my side. Even so, the suspicion was there."

"Do you have any idea what happened?" I purposefully leave the question open ended.

"You mean who killed him?"

I nod.

"All I know is that he was a hard man, Katie. If someone took offense to being treated harshly . . ." He lets the words trail.

"Tell me about the muzzleloader."

"The police found it in the field where the bones were discovered. It was mine. An old thing I hadn't seen for years."

"How did it get there?"

"I don't know."

"Jonas, how can you not know? The gun must have been missing from your house, right? Did you give it to someone? Or let someone borrow it? Was it stolen?"

He scoffs. "No. I just . . . lost track of it, I guess.

The muzzleloader belonged to my *dawdi*." Grandfather. "He passed it down to my *datt*. My *datt* to me. I'd had it for years. Kept it in the mudroom." He gives another shrug. "I didn't hunt much, you know. I don't know when it went missing."

"So the muzzleloader disappeared from your home and you didn't notice?"

"I know that sounds odd, but it's true."

"Did you file a police report?"

He gives me an are-you-kidding look. "I did not want to speak to the police, especially about a gun. I knew they suspected me of wrongdoing. I forgot about it."

The muzzleloader found at the scene is damning, particularly since, according to the newspaper stories I read online, the victim sustained two gunshot wounds. Only one large-caliber round ball—the kind of ammo used in a black-powder rifle—was found at the scene.

"Do you have any idea who might've taken the gun?" I ask.

"No."

"Who knew it was there?"

"It was in plain sight, I think." He shrugs. "We kept it in the corner, out in the mudroom. Anyone who visited would walk right by it."

I think about that a moment. "Jonas, do you have any idea who might've killed Stoltzfus? Did he have any disagreements with anyone else? Amish or English?"

"All I can tell you about the bishop is that he was strict. Some Amish were okay with that. Others . . ." He ends the statement with a shrug.

Another pause ensues while I mentally file away everything that's been said. "Is there anyone who might want to see you get into trouble?"

"There is no one who would do such a thing."

The statement is naïve. But I've been around the Amish enough to realize he likely believes it. The problem is that while the Amish are nonviolent and generally make good neighbors, they're subject to all the same frailties as the rest of us.

"Do you have an attorney?" I ask.

"I'm innocent, Katie. I don't need one. Lawyers charge a lot of money and I'm capable of speaking for myself."

"The legal system is complicated," I tell him.

"The truth is simple."

"They're going to assign you a public defender," I tell him. "Will you at least work with him? Let him help you?"

"If you think it's important, I'll do it." He studies me a moment. "I would like to go home. With my family. I've got a woodworking business to run. Customers who'll be expecting their cabinets or whatnot."

I don't point out that his woodworking business is the least of his worries. "What about bail?" I ask. "Are you trying to raise bail?"

"I don't know anything about bail."

I think about the teenager I knew a lifetime ago. I think about everything I know regarding the case and I'm a hell of a lot more troubled now than when I walked into this room.

"I'll look into it," I tell him.

"All right."

"Jonas, is there anything else you can tell me that might help me find out what happened to Ananias Stoltzfus?"

He considers the question, then shakes his head. "Most of the Amish thought he was a good bishop, Katie. But like I said, he was heavy-handed and set in his Old Order ways. He wasn't open to change. Sometimes he took things too far. Like with Datt. Ananias wasn't always fair, but no one wished him ill."

Someone did, a little voice whispers.

I think about my own experiences growing up Amish. "What about excommunications?" I ask.

"You know as well as I do that most Amish straighten up when the bishop gets involved." His thoughts seem to turn inward. "There were two I can think of that didn't end well. Roman Miller and Duane Mullet. Neither man could change their ways and left."

"Do you know what happened?" I ask.

"Roman is Mennonite now. Mullet . . . he's English. Lives up in the hills doing God only knows what."

"Did things get ugly?" I ask. "When Ananias put them under the *bann*?"

"They didn't like it much. I don't know the details. Dorothy probably knows more than I do."

The sound of a door opening behind Jonas draws my attention. I look beyond him to see a corrections officer peek out at us, give me five fingers to let me know my time is almost up.

I nod at him and turn my attention back to Jonas. "Do you need anything?"

"No, I am fine." His eyes skate away from mine, but he quickly forces them back. "If you could let Dorothy know I'm all right. She worries, you know."

"I will." I rise, anxious to get started, but there's another part of me that's hesitant to leave.

I want to say more. To reminisce about the past. To reassure him, bolster him, but there are no words. Instead, I set my hand against the plexiglass divider. He does the same and we stare at each other for the span of several seconds.

"I'll let you know about bail," I tell him.

His hand is still pressed against the glass when I walk away.

CHAPTER 6

The Mifflin County Sheriff's Department is housed in the same building as the jail. Due to security, I have to exit the prison and reenter as a visitor. Before leaving Painters Mill, I tried to schedule an appointment with the sheriff or second-in-command, but neither man was available, so I'm relegated to meeting with whoever is on duty this afternoon.

Sergeant Rick Gainer keeps me waiting nearly twenty minutes. According to their webpage, he's the fourth man down from the top of the organizational chart. Judging by his demeanor he's well aware it's nearly four P.M., official business hours are about to end, and he's in a hurry to get this end-of-the-day meeting over with quickly.

He shakes my hand with a too-firm grip as I introduce myself. I guess him to be about forty years of age. He's in full uniform. Still in good shape, but starting to go soft around the middle. His hair is cut military style. His biceps are the size of cantaloupes.

"And you're a police officer where?" he asks, giving me only part of his attention.

"Chief of police," I tell him. "In Painters Mill, Ohio."

He utters a noncommittal "Huh," and motions toward the door that will take us into the main part of the building. "How is it that you grew up with an Amish guy?"

"I used to be Amish," I say as I go through.

He looks at me over his shoulder, curious now, as he leads me down the hall. "Never met a formerly Amish police chief before."

"I guess there's a first time for everything."

He takes me down a hall, then motions to a small, windowless office. "Sheriff got the view." He gestures to one of two visitor chairs. "Have a seat."

I take the chair and pull my notebook from my pocket.

"What exactly do you want to know about the Stoltzfus case?" he begins.

"I'm looking into it for the Bowman family," I tell him. "Any information you can share would be helpful. Anything you're comfortable sharing about the case."

He studies me a moment. I can tell by his expression he's not an information-sharing kind of guy. "If you don't mind my asking, Chief Burkholder, what exactly is your reason for being here?"

It's a simple question with a complex answer that likely won't help my cause. I've been around enough law enforcement types to read between the lines. "I just want to get to the bottom of what happened," I say simply. "Help if I can."

He looks at me over the tops of his reading glasses. "Help who?"

In that instant, I see in his eyes that he considers me an outsider despite my badge. "I'm not here to second-guess or get in the way," I tell him.

Nodding, he opens a drawer and pulls out a file. "You close to Bowman?" He asks the question in an offhanded manner, but there's nothing offhand about it. He's gathering information. Not only on Jonas, but me. Been there, done that, so I give him what he wants.

"Like I said, we grew up together," I tell him.

"You must have been pretty tight for you to take time off and drive all the way over here to help him out."

I tell him about the three elders who came to see me in Painters Mill. "Until this afternoon, I haven't talked to Jonas in almost twenty years."

"Ample time for someone to change," he says.

I don't respond.

He opens the case file and begins to page through. "Most of this information has been made public," he tells me, letting me know in advance he's not going to give me anything that's not. "I'm sure you know there are some details I can't share."

"Of course."

He outlines the timeline first, giving me the framework of events in the order they occurred. I put my pen to use and write down all of it.

"Stoltzfus went missing in October 2004. Widower. Eighty-six years old. Lived on a farm out on Indian Ripple Road. Son, thirty-five-year-old Henry Stoltzfus, went out to see his dad, couldn't find him, and reported him missing the next day. We searched the area most of the day and into the night. Ananias Stoltzfus was elderly, so as you can imagine the family was concerned. There were dozens of volunteers, both Amish and English. We brought in dogs. The whole nine yards."

"You were there?" I ask.

"I was a rookie back then. Spent a cold night tromping through the woods out there by his house. We didn't find so much as a single footprint."

He licks his finger and turns the page. "We didn't know if he'd left or collapsed or if there was foul play involved. Next morning, deputies began interviewing people. Family. Friends. Neighbors. Most were Amish. We learned pretty quick the old man was on the outs with an Amish dude by the name of Ezra Bowman, who was deceased. He'd been shunned or whatever it is they do. Evidently, that caused bad blood between the son, Jonas Bowman, and Stoltzfus. We looked into that and learned there had been an altercation between the victim and Bowman a couple of months before Stoltzfus disappeared. Multiple witness statements say Bowman threatened Stoltzfus."

"What was the nature of the threat?"

He frowns as if I'm questioning his assessment, so I quickly add, "I'm curious. The Amish are pacifists. A physical threat would have been unusual."

Even as I make the statement, Jonas's words come back to me.

I lost my temper. I shouted.

I'm not proud of it.

Gainer squints down at the file in front of him.

"According to one witness, Bowman told the victim something like: *Your time is coming, old man. Sooner than you think. When it does, you won't be going to heaven.*

"Witnesses paraphrased, but that's how the threat was framed."

"Got it."

"We also have the vandalism charge. It was enough to pick up Bowman for questioning. We conducted an interview, and he was released without charges. He paid a fine." He flips the page, looks at the back side. "By then, we were pretty sure Stoltzfus was dead. Whether his demise was from natural causes or foul play, we had no way of knowing. All we had was a missing elderly man and a handful of circumstantial evidence. We had no body. No witnesses. We didn't have enough to make an arrest, so the case went cold."

He leans back in his chair and crosses his leg over his knee. "Of course, the case remained open. Every year or so, we'd look at the file. Send a cadaver dog out to the woods around the Stoltzfus farm. We kept an eye on Bowman. He never gave us cause to take any kind of action." He slips off the eyeglasses, puts an endpiece in his mouth. "Until that muzzleloader was found, anyway."

I let my eyes flick to the file. "It would be tremendously helpful if I could read the file."

"Some elements of the case weren't made public, Chief Burkholder. I'll check with the sheriff and get back to you."

A polite way of saying no without having to say no. "Are the state police assisting?"

"Yes, ma'am."

"You've brought in a forensic anthropologist?"

He sits up a little straighter, tilts his head in a way that tells me he's surprised that I can pronounce the term let alone that I'm familiar with it. I hold on to my neutral expression.

"We worked with a guy out of the university up in Buffalo," he tells me.

"Was he able to determine official cause and manner of death?"

"Ananias Stoltzfus sustained two gunshot wounds. One to the torso. One to the head. Manner of death is homicide."

"Can you tell me anything about the muzzleloader found at the scene?"

"Evidently, both the body and the gun were buried in a shallow hole. Back then, the area had been wooded, but it was cleared a few years back. Anyway, we took a metal detector out there and found the gun straightaway."

"Spent bullets? Casings?"

"A single ball. Fifty-cal. Buried a few inches in the ground."

I think about that a moment. "But there were two wounds?"

He lifts one shoulder, lets it drop. "Investigators figured one hit him while he was standing and the ball got away. The other—the one we found—when he was on the ground."

I nod. "How did you identify the muzzleloader?"

"It was a damnedest thing." Smirking, he scrubs his

hand over his shorn head. "A couple of deputies took it out to Bowman and the guy admitted the gun was his. He's like: 'Oh, that's mine. Thank you for returning it.'" The sergeant punctuates the statement with a laugh. "At that point, we had motive, means, and opportunity. We had a body and a suspect. So we secured a warrant and made the arrest."

It doesn't seem to have occurred to him that while they do, indeed, have a case, it's not rock solid. For example, why would Jonas leave his muzzleloader at the scene and so readily admit it was his?

"We searched the Bowman house, too," the sergeant adds. "We found a half-empty box of fifty-caliber balls. Same brand as the one found at the scene."

"Is there any other information you can share that hasn't been released to the public?"

"Not at this time."

I can tell by the way he's looking at me that he's not telling the truth. And that he doesn't mind that I know.

The sergeant glances at his watch, which is my cue to wrap it up. "Is the DA going to stick with second-degree murder?" I ask. "Is there any chance the charge will be reduced?"

"Last I heard, the DA's of the mind that Bowman threatened the victim and then made good on it. He's gotten off scot-free for eighteen years. Rumor has it, he's going to go with first-degree murder."

CHAPTER 7

Jonas and his wife live in a modest midcentury frame house just outside Belleville. The property isn't in town per se, but the place is a far cry from rural. There are no barns or pastures, no livestock or pens—just the low-slung house and a large metal building at the rear. An ancient hackberry tree shades the entire front yard. A sign next to the driveway tells me this is also home to Bowman Cabinet and Wood Design.

As I make the turn, I'm thinking about my meeting with Jonas earlier, the number of years that have passed since I knew him, and how little I really know about him and his family. I've no idea what to expect. The driveway takes me to a parking area behind the house and the red metal building. The door stands open and when I get out I'm met with the whine of a saw and what sounds like the rumble of a generator. I'm about to head that way when the slam of a door from the house draws my attention. I glance toward the house to see a boy of about ten bound down the steps of a small porch. He's wearing dark trousers with a blue work shirt and single-strap suspenders. A banded straw hat is clamped down over a headful of curly red hair.

He freezes upon spotting me, his eyes going wide. I see a freckled face, a turned-up nose, and lips that are smeared with something purple. He's cute in a puppy-dog kind of way. Hazel eyes dart from me to the Explorer and back to me.

"*Wie geht's?*" I smile and start toward him. How's it going?

His mouth opens. I can't tell if he's surprised because an *Englischer* spoke to him in *Deitsch* or if he thinks I'm about to grab him and cart him off in my spaceship.

"I'm Katie from Painters Mill," I say. "Is your *mamm* home?"

The boy lets out a squeal akin to the screeching of tires, then turns on his heel and runs as fast as he can back into the house.

Laughing, I ascend the steps and knock.

An Amish woman answers with the caution of a woman who's been forewarned about a potentially dangerous foreign invader. She's pretty and in her mid to late thirties, with the same features as the boy: hazel eyes, freckles, and a mane of curly red hair pulled back and tucked into a *kapp*. She's wearing a green dress with a white apron that's stained with what looks like tomato juice, and off-brand sneakers. Judging from her expression, she has no idea who I am, so I quickly introduce myself.

"I'm the chief of police in Painters Mill," I tell her.

"Chief Burkholder." She softens, presses a hand against her chest, and lets out a laugh that speaks more of nerves than humor. "Jonas might've mentioned you a time or two."

I try not to show my surprise. "Call me Katie." I pause. "The *Diener* thought I might be able to help."

"Oh." Her smile fades and for an instant, I think she's going to burst into tears—or collapse. Instead, she motions to the doorway. "*Kumma inseid.*" Come inside.

She steps back and swings open the door. An awkward moment ensues and she sticks out her hand for a shake. "Where are my manners? Scattered all over the place, just like the rest of me. I'm Dorothy, Jonas's wife."

Her laugh is more polite than genuine, and as we shake hands, I discern the signs of stress on her face. Circles beneath her eyes. A too-quick smile that trembles. A demeanor that's outwardly energetic, but under scrutiny fails to cover the exhaustion beneath.

"He's fond of his childhood in Painters Mill." She looks at me from beneath her lashes. "Fond of you, too."

I have no idea how much Jonas told her about me. About us. *Ancient history,* a little voice whispers. Even so, better to stick to the topic at hand.

"It's a good place to grow up," I tell her.

"You were Amish." Tilting her head, she looks at me, wondering, curious.

"I wasn't very good at it," I tell her.

She hefts a genuine laugh. "*Kumma. Ich habb kaffi.*" Come. I have coffee.

She leads me into the kitchen. "*Sitz dich anne un bleiva weil.*" Set yourself there and stay awhile.

The kitchen is modern for an Amish home. Eggshell-white walls with gleaming oak cabinets. A big walnut table with six ladder-back chairs. High-end gas stove. A big stainless-steel refrigerator hums from its place against the wall, state-of-the-art and powered by gas.

"You and Jonas have a nice home," I say as I take a seat at the table.

"Jonas built most of what you see, including that table and the cabinets." At the counter, she pours coffee from an old-fashioned percolator into mugs. She's in her comfort zone now. The kitchen is her domain and she's in charge. It's a precarious grip, but she's got her hands on it and she's going to maintain her grasp until she figures out exactly who I am and why I've come here.

I run my hand over the tabletop. "He's good."

"The English sure like him." She sets a steaming cup of coffee in front of me. "Maybe a little more than the Amish."

I'm not sure what to make of that or how to respond, so I pick up the cup and sip, file the comment and its implications away for later.

"How are you holding up?" I ask.

She waves off the question. "Oh, I'm fine. Work around here is piling up a little, but what else is new? Jonas'll have plenty to keep him busy when he gets home." She's making small talk. Nervous. Hesitant to bring up the business at hand with a stranger, especially an *Englischer*.

It's a typical Amish response. Even when faced with a devastating situation, they don't complain. They make do. They accept their problems and deal with them in silence, changing what they can, and leaving the rest to God.

"The kids?" I ask.

She closes her eyes briefly, but not before I see the flash of pain. "I haven't told them. I mean, they know something's wrong. Their *datt* has been gone for two weeks. They're confused. I just don't know what to say to them. How do I tell them their father is in jail, accused of murdering his own bishop?"

It's a devastating question. One I couldn't begin to answer myself. All children are innocent. But there's an added ingenuousness in Amish children that makes the situation even more heartbreaking.

"Hopefully, we'll be able to get him home soon." I tell her about my visit.

She sits up straighter, the need for news lighting her eyes. "How is he?"

"Okay, I think. More worried about you and the kids than himself. He asked me to check on you, see if you needed anything."

She looks down at her coffee, but not before I see the quick jump of guilt in her eyes. "He told me not to come, so I've not been to visit him yet. I know that's bad, but I can't imagine. Seeing him in a cage . . ." She lets the words trail as if unable to finish.

"Dorothy, bail has been set at five hundred thousand dollars," I tell her. "Do you have a bondsman?"

"Katie, we don't have that kind of money."

"With a bondsman, you only pay ten percent, and Jonas will be released."

"That's fifty thousand. . . . I don't know. . . . Maybe."

"Think about it," I tell her. "I'll help if I can."

I don't know the dynamics of her and Jonas's standing in the Amish community, but I do know the Amish will help. Even if there's some kind of rift, the Amish will set it aside and do what needs to be done.

She blinks back tears. "It's such a foreign thing. Murder and jail and legal problems. I don't know what to do." The tears spill, but she swipes them away. "I can tell you one thing, Kate Burkholder. Jonas Bowman is a lot of things and he's sure not perfect, but he is not a killer."

"I'm a civilian here in Big Valley," I begin. "I don't have any authority or resources, but I'll help any way I can."

"We're not ones to ask for help, but if there was ever a time when we needed it, this is it." She sets her hand over mine. "Thank you."

I pull out my notebook and set it on the table in front of me. For twenty minutes we cover the situation from beginning to end. Jonas's father being put under the *bann* and silenced. Ezra Bowman's death. The ensuing feud. What I'm looking for now is new information and insights from someone close to Jonas rather than the perspective of a stranger.

"What was Jonas's state of mind after the death of his father?" I ask.

"We'd been married a little over a year at the time."

The smile that follows is fraught with angst. "Losing Ezra was a shock. He was such a strong man. Sometimes he didn't even seem mortal. It was as if nothing could ever stop him or take him down, not even the nature of life itself."

Hearing her speak of the larger-than-life Ezra Bowman is like watching a silent, black-and-white film. I remember him as an outspoken man with a piercing gaze that could send even the toughest of the tough running home to Mamm. When he spoke, it was with great passion—and you listened. More than once I recall him arguing with my own *datt* over some topic to which I wasn't privy. Ezra Bowman was never unkind, but I was afraid of him.

Dorothy heaves a sigh. "Heart attack finally got him. He was plowing the field and collapsed. He fell and . . . the plowshares tore him up something awful. Jonas found him." She shakes her head, takes another sip of coffee as if in an attempt to wash away the terrible image. "Jonas was crushed. We'd lost two babies that year and not once did I see him cry. He's stoic, you know. Keeps it all tucked away the way men do." She looks away, blinking, remembering. "Jonas cried that day. And in the days that followed, he grew angry."

I'm familiar with grief and all of its gnarly repercussions. I've been handed my share by a Fate who's rarely fair about how she doles it out. I've watched Tomasetti suffer with losses that hollowed him to the core. I'm no stranger to the anger stage.

"Jonas blamed the bishop," I say.

"Right or wrong, he did." She shrugs. "Ezra and Ananias had been at each other's throats for a year. Ezra, the stubborn fool, had been put under the *bann*. But it was the silencing that did him in, Katie. He couldn't preach and that destroyed him."

"Tell me about the argument between Jonas and Bishop Stoltzfus," I say.

"I'll never forget it." Her eyes meet mine. "Church Sunday after the funeral. Jonas was just . . . raw. He wasn't himself. Wasn't eating or sleeping. I figured worship would be good for him, you know. It always is. But when he saw the bishop that day. And his own *datt* wasn't there to preach." She shudders. "I've never seen him like that. Jonas went for the bishop and he didn't stop. They had words. Terrible things were said. They nearly came to blows. Can you imagine? Right in front of everyone."

"What was the argument about exactly?"

"Jonas blamed Ananias for his *datt*'s death. Called him cruel. Said the stress of the *bann* and the silencing killed him."

"How did Ananias respond?"

"The bishop didn't help. He said Ezra had fallen to error and sin. He said that God took him because of that tractor." Dorothy puts her hand over her mouth as if to smother a sob. "I couldn't believe he would say such a thing. To blame a dead man and point out the error of his ways."

"Did Jonas threaten him?" I ask.

Her brow creases as if there's more to be pulled from her memory. "I was so shaken up, Katie. I've likely misremembered some of it. One thing I do recall is Jonas telling the bishop that there were a dozen families who supported Ezra's use of the tractor. Jonas said he was going to rally those families, and that they were going to form a new church district. You can imagine how that went over."

Dorothy lowers her head, sets her fingers against her forehead, sucks in a deep breath as if to compose herself. "There were so many ugly things said. I could barely take it all in. I don't want to say it, Katie, but Jonas lost some friends that day. He was too angry. Some of the Amish thought he was just wrong."

"How long after that argument did the bishop disappear?" I ask.

"Two months to the day."

"The police spoke to Jonas?" I ask.

"The sheriff's department picked him up. Talked to him for hours. When they brought him back, Jonas was shook up something awful."

I think about the case against Jonas in terms of motive and realize that, as a cop, I would have done the same. Pick him up. Question him hard. Apply pressure. Shake him up.

"What about the muzzleloader?" I ask.

She huffs. "That old thing sat in the mudroom gathering dust for years. Jonas likes his meat just fine and that includes venison, but a hunter he isn't. You know how he is. Got a soft spot for animals."

I think about that long-ago day when Jonas unleashed the family of skunks on those bullies at the baseball diamond, and something warm flutters in my chest.

"Do you know what happened to the gun?" I ask.

"I must have walked by the thing a hundred times. It sat in the corner for so long I didn't even notice it anymore. Then it was just . . . gone." She shakes her head. "I've been racking my brain, trying to figure out when it disappeared and who might've taken it, but I just don't know."

"Could it have been a neighbor or friend who borrowed it?"

"We asked. No one did."

"Can you show me where you kept it?"

"Sure. We walked right by it on the way in." She gets to her feet. "Mudroom. Come on."

I follow her to the narrow porchlike room I passed through upon entering. A row of windows on the outside wall lets in a generous amount of sunlight. A big chest freezer rattles against the opposite wall. There's a shelf unit littered with canning jars and a few gardening tools. Next to it, hooks set into the wall for hats and jackets.

"Kept that old gun right there in the corner." Dorothy points. "Propped against the wall."

"Loaded?"

"I don't think so. To tell you the truth, I don't even know."

"Do you keep your door locked?" I ask. "I mean, at night?"

She smiles tiredly. "No one in Belleville locks their doors."

I stand there a moment, taking in the proximity of the place where the gun was stored in relation to the door. It wouldn't take much for someone to slip inside unnoticed and snatch it up.

"Was Bishop Stoltzfus having problems with anyone else in the community?" I ask.

"Well, Ananias *was* strict. He was tough on anyone who broke the rules." She purses her lips. "Now that you mention it, there might've been a time or two when someone got their back up."

"Anyone in particular?"

"Duane Mullet. That one was trouble from the day he was born. His poor *mamm*. He talked like a demon with all the cursing and taking the Lord's name in vain. Drank like a fish. The bishop wouldn't have it and put him under the *bann* straightaway. Duane was just twenty years old and he sure didn't take it sitting down. Cussed out the bishop right in front of everyone."

"Did the police question Mullet?"

"He was a truck driver at the time, and he was up in Alaska when Ananias disappeared."

I write down the name anyway. "Is he still around?"

"Lives up in the hills last I heard. Still a roughneck from what I hear."

"Anyone else?"

"Roman Miller comes to mind. That boy was as cute as a speckled pup. He'd been courting a nice Amish girl. Going to the singings and whatnot. Rumor had it, he was messing around with a Mennonite girl up to Lewistown at the same time. I don't know how the bishop got involved; someone probably saw Roman with the girl and told him. Ananias came down hard."

"Did Roman come around?"

The Amish woman scoffs. "Got mad is what he did. Roman's a firebrand. He denied all of it. Refused to confess. Kept on seeing both them girls. Strutting around like a rooster. Believe me, he was no catch. Ananias finally put him under the *bann*."

"How did that go over?"

"Didn't like it one bit. Roman's a farrier, you see. Lost all his Amish business. From what I hear, it put him into financial ruin."

"So he was more worried about the financial impact than being ousted from his friends and family," I say.

"Tells you something about the man, doesn't it?" she replies.

"How long ago did this happen?" I ask.

"A few months before Ananias went missing."

The timing makes the back of my neck itch. "Does he still live in the area?"

"Last I heard, he joined a Mennonite church. Married that floozy and had a herd of little ones. Still a farrier, though. Does mostly English horses now. Cowboys and such. Lives on the other side of Belleville." She rattles off directions.

I write all of it down. "Did the police talk to Roman?"

"I wouldn't know." She looks down at her hands and shakes her head. "They seem to have their sights set on Jonas."

I think about other sources of information. Family or friends of the bishop who might be able to shed some light on his life. "I understand the bishop was a widower."

"Mrs. Stoltzfus passed away when I was barely a teenager," she tells me. "I think it was in 1999 or so."

"Do they have children?"

"Mary Elizabeth lives right here in Belleville. Last name is Hershberger. Henry lives a ways out of town. Only had the two far as I know."

I jot down the names. "Do you think they'd talk to me?"

"Probably. They're Amish. Decent folks. Not too fond of Jonas and me, as you can imagine." Her brows furrow and she drops her gaze to the floor. "Mary Elizabeth had some trouble a while back."

"What kind of trouble?"

"Vandals. She and her husband own an old paper mill at the back of their property, you know. Place has been abandoned for years. They were renovating it with plans to turn it into a bed-and-breakfast for all the English tourists that never seem to come. Anyway, someone set fire to the place. Did a lot of damage."

"Were the police called?"

She gives me a what-do-you-think look. "The Amish like to handle things on their own when they can."

"Any idea who did it?"

"Mary Elizabeth blamed Jonas. Accused him of holding a grudge." She makes a sound of distress. "I suspect it was teenagers. English youngsters out drinking and driving around the way they do."

I glance at my notes. I don't have much, but it's a start. I slide the notebook into my pocket and finish my coffee.

"The little boy I met in the driveway," I begin. "He looks like you."

"That would be Junior, our youngest." Her grin

reaches all the way to her eyes. "He's a shy one. Smart. Good little worker, too. Short on words, though."

"Jonas tells me you have three."

Her expression lights up at the mention of her children. "They've been in the shop all day, like little worker bees. Wouldn't come in for lunch, so I took soup to them. Poor things. They've been working on some cabinets Jonas promised a client." She glances at the clock on the wall and gets to her feet. "It's past time for them to come in and eat. Come on, Katie, and I'll introduce you."

CHAPTER 8

I follow Dorothy across the parking area toward the
metal building. A generator is still rumbling from somewhere on the other side. I catch sight of a large air tank
and realize the equipment inside is run on pneumatic
power. A cinder block props open the door. I hear the
scream of a saw, the hiss and chirp of compressed air.
It's after hours; I wonder if the Amish community has
stepped in to keep the business running while Jonas is
in jail.

If you're Amish and get into a jam, the community
will rally. They will come even if they are not asked,
and they will do what needs to be done to keep the
home or farm or business up and running until you're
on your feet. It's one of the things I admire most about
the Amish.

The interior is a well-lit, state-of-the-art woodworking shop—Amish style, of course. The smell of fresh-
cut wood mingles with the oily pong of wood stain. I

see a long bench with air hookups above. A drill press. An impressive-looking lathe. Air lines snake along the ceiling, smaller lines hanging down. To my left, an Amish girl of about fifteen is on her knees, vigorously rubbing stain into a two-tone ladder-back chair. She's so immersed in her work, she doesn't notice us.

Junior, the little boy I met earlier, stands at a small bench, drill in hand, screwing brushed-nickel hardware into cabinet doors. He's putting a good bit of muscle into the task, tongue poked out with the effort. An older boy, who looks astoundingly like a teenage Jonas, runs a sander over a tabletop, sawdust flying.

I ponder Dorothy's comment about the children working on some cabinets and I realize there are no other workers. The Amish did not come to help this family. Has the community turned against them because they believe Jonas is guilty of murder?

My heart quivers uncomfortably in my chest as I watch the kids work. There's no music. There are no masks or safety glasses. No gloves or hearing protection or steel-toed shoes. There's little in the way of ventilation despite the heat, dust, and vapors from the stain. Still, I see intent concentration and adept hands that are likely callused because this kind of manual labor is a regular part of their day.

Dorothy brings her hands together. "We've got a visitor!" she calls out to be heard above the noise. "And then supper."

Three heads swivel in our direction. The sander goes silent. The girl sets her staining rag on a bench and gets to her feet. Uncertainty overtakes her features as her eyes move from me to her *mamm*.

"This is Kate Burkholder," Dorothy says in *Deitsch*. "She's here in town to . . . visit for a few days."

The girl is red-haired with a smattering of freckles on cheeks blushed pink from the heat. Not quite pretty, but she'll grow into it. She's wearing a light blue dress. White *kapp*. A smear of stain on her chin. Knees chafed from kneeling and covered with sawdust.

"This is Effie," Dorothy tells me. "Fifteen years old already."

"Almost sixteen." She's got a chipped front tooth, but it suits her. Hazel eyes. I amend my earlier assessment that she's yet to grow into her prettiness.

I offer my hand. "Stain looks good."

Grinning, she gives my hand a hearty shake. "Junior said you spoke *Deitsch*. Are you Amish?"

"Now you just mind your manners," Dorothy says.

"I was," I tell the girl. "I think maybe I broke too many rules."

"Oh." Her laugh is a musical sound that reminds me of simpler times, when such things didn't need to be stifled.

Dorothy turns to the little boy. "I think you met Junior."

The boy in question holds his ground a few feet away. He's got a sweaty face. Sawdust on his cheeks. Lingering purple stains around his mouth. Hat cocked back. Red hair sticking to his forehead. He looks as if he's thinking about bolting again.

I approach the boy and extend my hand. "It's nice to meet you, Junior."

The boy backs up a step, eyes darting left and right.

"Junior don't talk much," Effie proclaims. "He's only eleven but he's good with the drill. Knows how to measure, too. Got an eye for color."

I back off, motion toward the cabinet he'd been working on. "Is that hardware stainless steel?" I ask, knowing fully it's not.

He looks at the cabinet and the flight response seems to wane. Still, he doesn't like being the center of attention. "B-b-brushed nickel," he says.

"He stutters when he's nervous," Effie announces.

"Or when you pay him too much attention."

At the sound of the deep male voice, I look over my shoulder to see the older boy approach. He is, indeed, the spitting image of Jonas when he was a teen. Dark hair and eyes. A surly demeanor that's as charming as it is off-putting. And a direct stare that speaks of attitude and self-assurance.

He comes up behind his younger brother, sets his hands on the boy's shoulders, and eases him toward me. "She's not going to bite you," he says in *Deitsch*.

"And this is Reuben," Dorothy tells me. "Our oldest."

We shake hands and for an instant, I can't look away. It's as if I've been swept back in time and I'm seeing the Jonas I knew twenty years ago.

"Just turned seventeen," Dorothy says with a shake of her head. "Already works like a man."

"Seventeen going on ten," Effie whispers.

Grinning, Reuben tosses his shop rag at her. "Who asked you?"

The girl bats the rag aside, then smiles at her *mamm*. "Acted like he was twenty at the singing Sunday. Especially when Miriam Miller came around."

Reuben falls back into surly mode, bends to pick the shop rag off the floor, but not before I catch the rise of color in his cheeks.

The girl turns her attention back to me, tilts her head. "What brings you to Belleville?"

Since Dorothy hasn't explained to them the situation with their father, I keep it vague. "I'm here to help your parents with a couple of things."

Reuben's eyes flick from me to his *mamm*. "Does it have something to do with Datt being in jail?"

Dorothy puts her hand over her mouth, her eyes darting to her other children. "Reuben."

"Mr. Gleason told us," he tells her. "He came to check on his cabinets when you were in town. He figured there wasn't any work getting done since Datt was sitting in a jail cell."

Effie steps closer and takes her *mamm*'s hand. "He told us everything. Everyone in town knows, too. Mr. Gleason said."

"Oh, dear Lord." Dorothy looks helplessly at me, at her children, and grapples for composure.

"He w-wanted his m-money back," Junior puts in.

"He tried to cancel the contract," Effie adds. "Reuben talked him out of it."

Reuben slings the shop rag over his shoulder. "We're

going to show the old big-bug we know a thing or two about cabinets." "Big-bug" is an Amish term for a rich person.

"Reuben told him they'd be finished on time," Effie says.

"Which is tomorrow," Reuben finishes.

"W-we know D-D-Datt didn't do anything b-bad." This from Junior, and somehow it is the most profound of statements.

Dorothy winces, blinking back tears, but regains her equanimity quickly. "Katie is a police from Ohio. She's going to help if she can."

The kids eye me with a combination of wonderment and awe.

"Are you going to get our *datt* out of jail?" Effie asks.

"I'm going to do my best," I tell her.

Dorothy cuts in before any more questions can be voiced. "There's fried chicken inside. I want your hands washed. Effie, grab a jar of beets out of the cellar on your way."

"But we have to finish the cabinets tonight!" the girl exclaims.

"Mr. Gleason is going to pick them up first thing in the morning," Reuben puts in.

The Amish woman doesn't miss a beat. "Well, you can't work on empty stomachs, can you? Go wash up. I don't want to see any dirty fingernails." She turns to me. "Katie, you'll be staying for supper. I've got enough for an army."

Had the circumstances been different, I would have happily joined them. But with the clock ticking and an innocent man charged with murder, I decline. "I need to talk to the bishop's family," I tell her.

Dorothy doesn't respond until the children file past and are out of earshot. "I hope they cooperate. Mary Elizabeth is decent enough, but that Henry is as prickly as his *datt* and twice as mean."

CHAPTER 9

Dorothy didn't have an address for Ananias Stoltzfus's daughter, but Amish directions are usually spot-on. Just west of town, she'd told me, take a right on Blue Run Road. Past the chicken farm. Over the bridge at Little Kishacoquillas Creek. Second place on the right. There's a big "Brown Eggs for Sale" sign out front. Can't miss it.

I pass the sign for eggs, which spells out NO SUNDAY SALE in bold caps, and pull into the gravel driveway. The house is nestled in a pretty spot with half a dozen shade trees and a white picket fence. As I get out of the Explorer, I notice the square of cardboard crisscrossed with duct tape covering a front window. A plump Amish woman stands at the clothesline, laundry basket at her feet, watching me through the space between two pairs of trousers. I guess her to be in her mid-fifties. She wears a gray dress with dark stockings and shoes. Blond hair streaked with silver is tucked into a gauzy white *kapp*.

"Mrs. Hershberger?" I say as I pass through the picket gate.

She cocks her head, wondering who I am and how I know her name. "That's me."

I extend my hand for a shake and introduce myself. "I hope I'm not catching you at a bad time."

She unpins a shirt, folds it, and places it in the basket. "Always nice to take a break, especially on such a pretty evening."

I've debated how to best approach Ananias Stoltzfus's family. Asking questions about the death of a loved one, even after so many years, requires tact. That's particularly true in this case because the remains were just recently discovered—and I'm friendly with the accused.

I lay out the reason for my visit, my background, and my connection to Jonas. "The *Diener* came to me in Painters Mill and asked me to look into the case."

"The *Diener,* huh?" Her expression remains impassive as she takes in the information, with no indication of wariness or hostility. "I reckon it took some nerve for you to show up here."

"I know this is a difficult time for you and your family," I tell her.

"As long as you're not here to get that no-good friend of yours off the hook."

"I'm just looking for information," I say simply.

She snaps a shirt from the line, shakes out the wrinkles. "The police seem pretty sure Jonas Bowman shot my father with that old muzzleloader of his."

"Sometimes things aren't always as they appear," I tell her.

Frowning, she tosses the shirt into the basket without

folding it. "Jonas Bowman." She huffs the name like a curse. "Shot his own bishop like an animal. Left him for the vultures and critters to pick at. Not a shred of decency or a thought for the family. Eighteen summers and winters and not a word. The awfulness of that tears me apart to this day."

I look past her at the house where the shadows of the trees play against the siding, give her a moment before continuing. "What do you think happened?"

"What do I think?" She chucks a clothespin into a small wicker caddy. "I think the devil lured my *datt* down to that abandoned farm. Nearly two miles and the man was eighty-six years old, for goodness' sake. Spry for his age, but not a spring chicken." She sighs. "Once we realized he was gone . . . we figured he'd fallen somewhere or had a heart attack. The kind of thing that happens to an old person." She's not telling me anything I don't already know, but she's talking, so I don't interrupt.

"We looked for him for days," she says. "Even the *Englischers* pitched in with their ATVs and horses and whatnot. All the while, we worried and we prayed."

"Was there anything unusual going on in your father's life at the time he disappeared?" I ask. "Anything out of the ordinary?"

"Nothing of the sort. Like I said, he was old. Liked to take walks and tend his garden. Feed the birds. He was a godly man. A loving man who lived simply and plainly."

"Had there been any disputes or arguments with anyone?" I ask.

"Everyone loved Datt." Even as she snaps the words, I see a flash of hesitation in her eyes, and I wonder if she truly believes it—or if she's convinced herself of it because she loved her father. "He was a good bishop. Must have done a hundred communions and baptisms. Dozens of marriages." She clucks, a sound of irritation, as if I'm trying to sully his good deeds.

"What about excommunications?" I ask.

"Datt brought them backsliders right back into the fold."

"Not all of them came back, though, did they?" I ask. "Roman Miller?"

"Now there's a backslider for you. Two-timing a nice Amish girl with some *Mennischt* floozy." *Mennischt* is the Deitsch word for Mennonite.

"Was Miller upset with your father?"

"You'll have to ask him." She straightens and gives me a level look. "My *datt* helped a lot of people here in Big Valley, Chief Burkholder. He did a lot of good. Don't let anyone tell you otherwise."

I nod my acceptance of that and press forward. "Was he a strict bishop, Mary Elizabeth? With the rules, the following of the *Ordnung*?"

"Someone's been handing you a lot of talk." She chucks a handful of clothespins into the wicker basket, but misses and they scatter in the grass. "You'd be wise not to listen to the gossipmongers."

She's getting herself worked up, so I kneel and pick up the pins, place them in the container. "I'm just gathering information," I tell her. "Trying to figure out what happened."

When the clothesline is bare, she steps back and looks at me as if trying to decide if I'm friend or foe. "Look, my *datt* kept people in line. A bishop has to keep things in order. Things are just better that way."

"Fair enough." I motion toward the house. "I couldn't help but notice the broken window when I pulled up."

She turns and looks, shrugs dismissively. "Someone threw a rock. English kids probably. You know how they are."

"Did you report it to the police?" I know the answer before she answers.

"I don't know how it is where you come from, but around here we like to handle things on our own."

"I understand there was a fire, too," I say.

Her eyes narrow. "You know a lot for having been here only a day."

"Any idea who did it? Or why?"

"Wasn't much of a fire, really. We lost some lumber is all. Adrian is renovating that old mill at the back of the property. Thinks he's going to turn it into a bed-and-breakfast." She shakes her head. "I reckon someone would rather we not do that."

"How long ago did it happen?" I ask.

"Been about a month now."

"Interesting timing, don't you think?"

Her eyes probe mine. "Jonas Bowman was still on the loose."

"Are you saying you believe he started the fire?"

"You're the one mentioned timing."

I nod. "Did you report the fire to the sheriff's department?"

"Like I said, we prefer to handle things our own way. Nothing much they could do, anyway." Bending, she picks up the laundry basket. "I know you don't mean any harm with all these questions, but I think I've had enough."

I pass her a card with my cell phone number scribbled on the back. "Let me know if you think of something that might be important, or if you just want to talk."

After a brief hesitation she takes the card. "I don't think I will, but thank you."

I'm midway to the Explorer when a final question occurs to me and I turn back to her. "Mrs. Hershberger, can you tell me where your *datt* was living when he disappeared?"

Holding the basket at her hip, she motions toward the road. "He'd been living out to the *dawdi haus* since Mamm passed." It's *Deitsch* for "grandfather house" and is generally a small abode where Amish grandparents live with — or close to—their grown children when they become too elderly to manage on their own. "Little cottage on Indian Ripple Road. It's been vacant since we lost him."

"Would it be all right if I took a quick look around?" I ask.

"I don't know what you expect to find. A mouse or two maybe." She shrugs. "I don't think my brother keeps it locked, so go ahead."

"Thank you." I turn and start toward the Explorer, but she calls out to me.

"You want to know what the worst part of this was, Kate Burkholder?"

I reach my vehicle and turn to her.

"The not knowing," she tells me. "Eighteen years of wondering. Is he alive or dead? Is he hungry and cold and hurting? Did he suffer? Cry out for us? Think about that while you stand there and ask questions so you can get that *hohchmeedich* friend of yours out of jail." It's the *Deitsch* word for prideful. "All the talk of justice. Tell me, where's the justice in that?"

According to my GPS, Indian Ripple Road runs east and west on the north side of Belleville. There's a good bit of daylight left, so I head that way and quickly realize it's a barely-there asphalt two-track shrouded with trees and marred with potholes. I've just spotted the dead-end sign when I notice the narrow opening in the trees to my right. I slow, discern the patches of gravel, and pull in.

The canopies of seventy-foot-tall trees fill the cab with shadows. Spindly fingers of bramble scrape at the doors. I'm wondering if I made a wrong turn and thinking about turning around when the forest opens and I find myself looking at a small cottage. The siding had once been fresh and white, but time and the elements have worn it to gray. A porch encompasses the front, but the character is lost due to a dozen or so missing rails and a warped floor that gives the place a lopsided appearance. A stone chimney juts from a steeply pitched steel roof that's gone to rust. There are no shutters or landscaping. A tiny one-horse barn is the only other building. The attached pen is filled with weeds as tall as a man's shoulders. In the side yard, I see the scar of what had once been a garden, the picket fence grinning a hit-or-miss smile.

I park in front of the cottage and get out. A breeze eases past me from the west, carrying with it the scent of the forest and fresh-cut hay. Taking in the sight of the house, the place where the garden had once been, and the old horse pen, I get a sense of what the place might've looked like in its heyday. Peaceful. Quiet. Pretty. The perfect dwelling for an elderly widower to live out his twilight years.

A blue jay scolds me from the branch of an elm as I start toward the house, my feet swishing through weeds. The sidewalk is uneven and cracked. The wood steps creak beneath my feet as I take them to the porch. I know there's nobody inside, but I knock anyway.

"Hello?" I call out. "Is anyone home?"

No answer.

I try the knob, but it's locked. "Crap," I mutter.

I didn't come here expecting some earth-shattering piece of evidence to fall into my hands, but I've got enough experience under my belt to know it can be helpful to see the residence of the victim. Not giving myself time to debate, I leave the front porch and head around to the back.

I wade through hip-high weeds and a profusion of thistle to reach the rear. An antique-looking hand pump stands guard over a galvanized trough that's eaten through with rust. Between the house and barn, a chicken coop not much bigger than an outhouse is nearly swallowed up by saplings and weeds. A hitching post slants up from the ground at a forty-five-degree angle.

The porch is a small slab of concrete that's surprisingly intact. Half a dozen wasps buzz around a nest beneath the eave. A clay pot lies on its side next to the step. A screen door hangs by a single hinge. I take the steps to the door and find it unlocked.

"Hello?"

I step into a small kitchen. The stink of mildew and rotting wood hangs in the air. The linoleum floor is covered with dirt and indistinguishable debris. Yellow Formica counters are littered with rodent droppings. Plain wood cabinets line walls painted robin's-egg blue. A battered porcelain sink has collapsed into the cabinet below. Through the opening, I see water damage and a tangle of insulation that's become a nest for some lucky mouse.

Dirt and grime crunch beneath my boots as I cross to the doorway. The living room is small, with three narrow windows and the front door. The only furniture is an old sofa that's been shredded by some animal, stuffing scattered all around. A rusty oil lantern lies on its side in the corner. The floors look like oak and are still in pretty good shape. There's nothing of interest. Just a nice little cottage that's seen better days.

There are no stairs or second level, so I make my way to the hall. There's a bathroom ahead. A bedroom to my left. In the ceiling, a small square door likely leads up to an attic. I walk into the bedroom. There's a night table. An old-timey blue-and-white-striped mattress. No closet. A rocking chair with a broken armrest sits forlornly in the corner.

Nothing to see here. Move along.

I traverse the hall, go back through the living room. In the kitchen, I pause and look around. Ananias Stoltzfus was eighty-six years old. He lived alone. A widower for five years. Did someone come into his home, murder him, and dump his body in the woods? According to reports, there were no signs of forced entry. Did Ananias know his killer? Mary Elizabeth had said her father enjoyed walking. Did he go for a walk and encounter his killer? Or did Ananias leave his house to meet someone?

I go through the door and walk outside. The house and yard are surrounded by trees, which makes it difficult to figure out exactly where I am in relation to where the bones were found, but I have a general idea, so I head in that general direction.

There's no visible trail. No fence line to follow. I've only gone about fifty yards, and I'm thinking about going back, when my foot catches on something in the weeds. I glance down to see the remains of an old barbed-wire fence. Most of the wood posts have been broken off at ground level, the barbed wire rusted through and snapped. Blackberry and bramble have pulled all of it to the ground.

I stand there a moment, look around, and I realize the trees are smaller here; I'm standing in a corridor of sorts and wonder if this was once a two-track that ran parallel with the fence. Did Ananias take this route the night he disappeared?

Weaving through saplings, doing my best to avoid

blackberry stickers, I walk along the broken-down fence, keeping an eye out for fallen posts and tangles of wire. The trees thicken; shadows ebb and flow all around. A chipmunk scampers across a fallen log. The tempo of the birdsong rises. Not for the first time, the beauty of the place strikes me, and I wonder what these trees would tell me if they could talk.

I walk for several minutes and reach a shallow ditch and a cross fence. The original fallen fence veers right, little more than a hump in the land that's covered with knotted foliage. The newer woven-wire fence, topped with a single strand of barbed wire, runs straight as an arrow right to a neighboring field. How far away from where I'm standing were the remains found?

The question gnaws at my brain as I make my way back to the cottage. I'm so embroiled in my thoughts, I don't notice the sheriff's cruiser parked behind my Explorer until I've stepped into the clearing and I see the flashing red and blue lights.

A deputy in full uniform is walking around my vehicle and looking in the windows.

"Hello!" I call out to him as I approach.

He looks in my direction, and tilts his head to speak into his radio. "Ten-twelve," he says, which is the ten code used to check the registration and to see if a vehicle is stolen.

He's a tall guy with a runner's build and sandy hair shorn into a crew cut. I guess him to be in his late twenties. Probably a rookie.

"We received a trespass call." His voice is amicable, but he's got those cop's eyes and they're sizing me up as I get closer. "What are you doing out here?"

"Mary Elizabeth gave me permission to look around." I reach him and stop about ten feet away. "I was—"

"I don't know who Mary Elizabeth is," he tells me. "Henry Stoltzfus owns this place. He called us and said someone was breaking into the house."

"I didn't break in. The back door was—"

He cuts me off again. "I need for you to walk over to my vehicle." He points. "I want you to lean against it. Nice and easy. Keep your hands where I can see them. Do you understand?"

"No problem." I nod, raise my hands in submission. "I'm a police officer from Ohio."

"Uh-huh." He responds with a dismissive motion toward his cruiser. "Go lean against the vehicle and be quiet."

"You got it."

He's being an asshole, but I do as I'm told. He doesn't know me from Adam, after all. As far as he knows, I was kicking in walls and stealing copper plumbing or maybe burying a body somewhere on the premises. In the back of my mind, I wonder if Mary Elizabeth decided she didn't want me out here after all, and ran down to the pay phone to make the call.

I reach the vehicle and lean.

"Anyone else out here with you?" the deputy asks.

His badge tells me his name is K. Vance. "Just me," I tell him.

He crosses to me. "You got your driver's license on you?"

"Sure." I reach into my rear pocket, pull out my driver's license and shield, and hand both to him.

He takes both, looks carefully at them. "Chief of police, huh?"

"Last time I checked." It's a flip response; I don't want to get on his bad side, so I add a smile.

"You got a weapon on you?"

"Both of them."

One side of his mouth curves as he hands my license and shield back to me. "I'm Kris Vance." Now that he knows I'm not a mass murderer, he relaxes. "What are you doing out at this old place, Chief Burkholder?"

"I'm a friend of Jonas Bowman," I tell him. "I just wanted to take a look around."

He speaks into his radio. "Ten-twenty-four," he says, letting the dispatcher know his assignment is complete.

"You know him?" I ask.

"I bought my kitchen cabinets from Bowman last year. He and his kids helped me install them." He shakes his head. "Nice family. Never had him figured for something crazy."

"Me, too." I wipe sweat from my temple with my sleeve. "You guys probably don't have much crime in this area."

"Not at all. I mean, it's pretty rural. Quiet. A lot of Amish and they keep to themselves. Those human remains were big news."

"Same in Painters Mill," I tell him. "Do you know much about the case?"

"Just that it was cold for a long time," he tells me. "To tell you the truth, the brass is being kind of tight-lipped about it. Probably because there's going to be a trial."

He's warming to me. Probably bored. Likable.

"Do you think Bowman did it?" I ask.

He takes the question in stride. "From what I understand, there was some kind of feud between Stoltzfus and Bowman. Sheriff's department questioned him when the old man disappeared, but without a body . . ." He shrugs. "Nothing ever came of it. Then Doyle Schlabach found the bones and the case heated up quick."

"So, investigators went back to Bowman."

"Well, we found Bowman's muzzleloader with the bones. That kind of sealed the deal. And, of course, Bowman doesn't have an alibi."

"That doesn't help." I look out across the field. "You guys look at anyone else?"

"Well, I'm not really involved in the case," he tells me. "I mean, directly."

He's getting nervous about my asking too many questions. Once again, I'm reminded that I'm an outsider here, so I slow down, stop pushing. "I'm not trying to pressure you into telling me anything you're not comfortable with."

He smiles. "I appreciate that, but most of what I've told you is already out there for public consumption."

"I'm just trying to sort through all of it." I smile back. "Help the family negotiate the legal system."

He shrugs. "Basically, everyone we talked to pointed a finger at Bowman." He laughs. "Gotta hand it to him for being honest, though. A couple of deputies took that old muzzleloader that was found at the scene out to Bowman's place, and he tells us right off the bat that it's his. He didn't try to lie or explain it away." He shakes his head. "No offense, but if he's trying to avoid prison, that didn't exactly help his cause. The muzzle-loader doesn't have a serial number. Had Bowman kept his mouth shut, we probably wouldn't have been able to prove it was his. Go figure."

"Doesn't seem like the kind of thing a guilty man would do," I say.

"Maybe." He looks at me a little more closely, sizing me up again. "You think we got the wrong guy, or what?"

I shrug, noncommittal. "I knew Jonas when he was young and I can tell you he was a good person. So when the Amish elders asked for my help, I told them I'd look into it."

He looks past me, nodding, saying nothing.

I keep going. "Were you around when the old man went missing?"

"Naw. I was just a kid." He laughs. "Went out with my dad and searched though. We had an ATV and looked high and low for that old dude. Everyone figured he'd fallen down and hurt himself."

"Do you guys have a theory on what happened?" I ask. "I mean, do you think Stoltzfus left his house to meet someone? Did he run into someone he wasn't expecting? Or was he killed in the house, his body moved?"

"No one knows for sure."

I think of the short walk I just took. "How far is the field where the remains were found from here?"

He motions in the general direction of where I just walked. "A couple of miles."

"Was the field wooded back when Stoltzfus went missing?"

"This whole area was wooded. Farmers are clearing as they need more land. I think Schlabach and his daddy cleared that field a couple of years ago. The general consensus is that the body was buried in a shallow grave. Between the plowing and natural erosion, the bones worked their way to the surface."

I think about that a moment. "Back when Stoltzfus went missing, do you recall if anyone happened to notice tire marks? From a car or buggy? Anything like that?"

He smiles. "I guess you *are* a cop."

I smile back. "Character flaw."

"I hear you." He cocks his head. "To tell you the truth, I don't know. I'm not part of the investigation. Did you talk to anyone at the sheriff's department?"

"Sergeant Gainer wasn't too inclined to share information."

"Ah." He clears his throat. "He's not known for his congeniality."

"There's one in every department."

"Ain't that the truth." He lets the silence ride a moment and then adds, "I'll see what I can find out for you."

I give him my card. "I appreciate it."

We stand there in companionable silence for a minute

or two, enjoying the breeze, the cacophony of birds all around.

"I reckon I ought to get back to work." He pushes away from the vehicle.

I extend my hand. "Thanks for not writing me a ticket."

"Glad I didn't have to write up the report."

We shake and go our separate ways.

CHAPTER 10

As is always the case at the start of a homicide investigation, there are a hundred things to do and they all needed to be done yesterday. While experience has taught me the art of prioritization, I don't fare as well when it comes to keeping my impatience in check. Not only do I have little in the way of hard facts, but I'm out of my jurisdiction and operating without my usual resources. Worse, I'm personally involved in a way that will likely work against me—at least in terms of my contemporaries. Sergeant Gainer made it clear that my law enforcement credentials will not garner me preferential treatment. In fact, I'm under the impression that he'll go out of his way to keep me at arm's length—and in the dark.

I'm in the Explorer, heading toward Belleville, where I have reservations for a room at the Kish Valley Motel and RV Park. I'm anxious to get checked in and unpacked, but there's one more thing I want to do before I run out of light.

The land where the remains were found is owned

by an Amish man by the name of Doyle Schlabach. According to newspaper accounts, he was cutting hay when he discovered the skull. I have no idea if visiting the scene will be helpful, but it's a starting point. I'm not sure if he'll grant me access to the property, but it's worth a shot.

The Schlabach farm is on the north side of Belleville at the foot of a verdant green ridge. I make the turn into a long gravel lane, and I'm rewarded with a view so spectacular, I roll to a stop just to admire it. Lush with forest and surrounded by the gray veil of evening humidity, the mountain is a majestic sight. A four-rail wood fence lines both sides of the lane. Farther in, an ancient German bank barn is built into the hillside, with the livestock pens facing the front and the upper, bank side of the barn looking out at the ridge. These kinds of barns are common in Ohio. What differentiates this barn is a forebay where the upper-level wall over-shoots the foundation.

The lane curves left and a frame house looms into view. It's a typical Amish farmhouse with the appearance of having been added on to several times over the decades and not all of those additions executed with forethought.

I do a double take upon spotting the buggy parked beneath a giant oak tree, its shafts resting on the ground. I've heard of the Pennsylvania yellow-topped buggies, but I've never seen one and it's a shocking sight to behold. The lemon-yellow top is anything but plain. I park next to it and get out of the Explorer. The brightly colored top isn't the only difference from the buggies I'm used to seeing in Painters Mill. There are rearview mirrors on both the driver's and passenger sides. At the rear, someone has installed brake lights, taillights, half a dozen reflectors, and two slow-moving-vehicle signs. Nearly as astounding as the yellow top is an interior decked out with green velvet and a gleaming burled-walnut dash more befitting a Rolls-Royce.

"She's a nice one, ain't she?"

I turn to see an Amish man approach. I guess him to be in his mid-thirties. A longish beard that tells me he's married. He's wearing typical Amish garb—trousers, work shirt, and a flat-brimmed straw hat. A single suspender crosses at his chest.

"It's the most amazing workmanship on a buggy I've ever seen," I tell him.

He grins. "I'm no craftsman—just ask my wife—but I do appreciate all that walnut. Too pretty for a buggy, if you ask me. Definitely got all the bells and whistles. Watch this." He leans into the buggy and punches a button. He tugs a cigarette pack from his pocket, taps one out. By the time he's got the cigarette in his mouth, the lighter has popped out of its place in the dash, and he lights up.

"Comes in handy if there's a smoker in the family," he says.

I'm not sure which surprises me most, the lighter set into the dash or the fact that he's smoking. At a loss for words, I extend my hand and introduce myself. "I'm the chief of police over in Painters Mill, Ohio."

"Burkholder, huh?" He squints at me. "There's a good name for you."

"I'm an old friend of Jonas Bowman's," I tell him. "The *Diener* asked me to look into what happened."

"Ah. Holy cow." The mention of Jonas seems to deflate his mood. "Awful thing. About the bishop. Jonas, too."

I glance toward the fields spread out to my left. "I understand you discovered the remains."

He puffs the cigarette and motions toward the rear of the property. "I was out cutting alfalfa that day. Thought the blade hit a rock. I stopped to toss it and . . . there it was." He feigns a shiver. "You don't expect to see something like that. At first, I thought it might be some historical thing. You know, an old grave. A pioneer or forefather. Then I remembered the bishop disappearing and a shiver went right through me." He exhales smoke. "I called the police. They came out with all their tools and such. Spent two days digging around in that field. Had those bones identified in a couple of weeks."

The laugh that follows sounds forced. "I'm no believer in ghosts, but I ain't been in the field since."

"Would you mind if I took a look at the scene?"

He hesitates, his smile faltering. "I reckon I could walk back there with you."

"I know you're busy," I say, giving him an out if he wants it. "If you point me in the right direction, I'm happy to walk on my own. I shouldn't be but a few minutes."

"Well, my wife *is* wanting me to finish that raised

flower bed by the garden." He flicks the cigarette to the gravel and crushes it beneath his boot. "I'll walk you part of the way."

It's a half-mile hike to the field. As we walk, I learn that Doyle and his wife are Byler Amish. I don't know much about them. My *datt* used to refer to them as "bean soupers," ostensibly because they regularly served bean soup for lunch after the preaching service. The men wear their hair shorter than some of the other sects. The women sometimes wear brown bonnets. And, of course, the yellow-topped buggies.

"Do you know Jonas?" I ask.

We're on a dirt two-track. A cornfield to our right. Thick woods to our left and, beyond, the steep ascent of the ridge.

"Sure. I've talked to him a hundred times over the years. Church Sunday, you know. Helped him on that workshop he built a few years ago. My wife spent some time with Dorothy down to the auction last summer, selling bread and cakes and whatnot." He shakes his head, his brows knitting. "Good family. I always liked Jonas. Some people say he has a temper, but I never saw it. To tell you the truth, I didn't know what to think when I heard they arrested him. Didn't seem right."

"Ananias was your bishop?"

"Bishop Stoltzfus baptized me. Got me married off." He slides his hand under his hat and scratches his head. "In fact, that was the last time I saw him. I was about twenty, I guess."

"What kind of bishop was he?"

"Some people thought he was strict. You know, kind of set in his ways." He laughs. "Ananias was tough on backsliders."

"The sergeant at the sheriff's department told me there were problems between Jonas and the bishop."

"Well . . ." The Amish man ducks his head, looks out across the field, away from me. Hesitant to engage in gossip or say anything negative about one of his brethren. For the span of a full minute, the only sound comes from our shoes against the ground.

"I'm not here to make judgments," I say. "I'm just trying to get a handle on the relationship between the two men, so I can figure out what happened."

Doyle nods, shoves his hands into his pockets. "Fair enough, I guess."

A rustle in the grass, the breaking of brush to my right startles both of us. I glance over to see a deer and fawn bound across the road and disappear into the trees.

Doyle sets his hand against his chest and bursts out laughing. "That'll get your heart started."

"Or maybe stop it."

We start walking again. Not for the first time, I'm drawn to the beauty of our surroundings. The razor-straight rows of corn in the field we just passed. The lush greenery of the woods and the cacophony of bird-song. Farther, the hulking form of the ridge. I've almost given up on getting any useful information out of Doyle when he speaks.

"Jonas's *datt* was a minister, you know. Ezra was a good man, too. A good *Amisch*. More lenient than Ananias, I guess." He whistles between his teeth. "From what I hear, the two men butted heads a time or two. Ananias could be a hard man. He enforced the rules with an iron hand and was always looking to add more. Bowman was more moderate, willing to ease the rules, especially when it came to technology."

"Phone?" I ask. "Computer? Electricity?"

"All of it." He laughs. "And that's not to mention the tractor!"

We reach a gate. He unlatches the chain, opens it, and we go through. "Boy, did it cause a stir."

"I bet." To a non-Amish person, the purchase of a tractor doesn't sound like a big deal. If you're Amish, it's huge. I think back to my own upbringing and I know that not only would such a bold act have been eschewed by the community, but Bishop Troyer never would have allowed it.

"Ezra argued that the tractor was fine because it was a diesel. He even modified the wheels so they were without rubber. Wasn't good enough for the bishop. Ananias saw the purchase as worldly and claimed the tractor would do violence to the land. He told Bowman to get rid of it."

Doyle casts a smile in my direction. "Those Bowmans are a stubborn bunch. Ezra used that tractor all spring. Plowed and planted every field. He bought implements, too. Worse, a couple of his Amish neighbors borrowed the thing. That's when the bishop put him under the *bann*."

Doyle shrugs. "What made all of this really bad is that people started taking sides. Some thought we should be able to use tractors—if the engines are diesel—to make life easier, you know. Others were put out by the idea. The situation got so bad Ananias stepped in and silenced Bowman.

"Two weeks later, Bowman died. Just keeled over when he was working in the field. English doctor said it was a heart attack. From what I hear it hit Jonas hard." Doyle shakes his head. "It was a bad time. Everyone figured things would get back to normal. They didn't."

"How so?" I ask.

"Well, all those Amish who supported Bowman still wanted to leave and form their own church group." Grimacing, he looks down at the ground, then at me. "You'd have a better understanding if you were Amish, I guess."

"I was," I say simply.

He gives me a lopsided smile, not sure if I'm pulling his leg.

"I left when I was a teenager," I say in *Deitsch*.

"I guess you do know how it is then," he says. "It's not the *bobblemoul* you have to worry about." The blabbermouth. "But the silent dissenters who leave." He taps his chest. "They keep all of their discontent inside."

I nod, understanding.

"I saw Jonas and Ananias go at it that Sunday after the preaching service. It was ugly. No one knew what to think. The one thing we *did* know, is that we didn't like it." He shoves both hands into his pockets and shakes his head, as if he still can't believe the incident even happened. "In his defense, Jonas was young. Hurting, you know. Just lost his *datt* and all. He basically accused Ananias of killing his father." He heaves a sigh. "A couple weeks later, Ananias Stoltzfus disappeared."

We reach another gate. This one is steel pipe and held in place with a wire loop. Doyle lifts the loop and pushes open the gate, but he doesn't go through.

"This is as far as I go, Chief Burkholder."

It's another pretty spot. The alfalfa is bright green. The fence is newish. Trees growing along the fence line. To my right, a rusty windmill tower lies on its side, the fan blades bent and entangled in hip-high weeds. Beyond, I can just make out the jut of a brick chimney where a house had once stood.

"This was once a farm back here?" I ask.

Doyle nods. "It's been abandoned for as long as I can remember." He points to the old chimney. "House burned down a few years ago. My *datt* and I tore down the barn. Windmill collapsed in a storm last spring."

I nod. "Was anyone living here when Ananias disappeared?"

"No, ma'am. No one has lived here since before I was born. Land went up for sale a few years ago." He motions toward the alfalfa field. "I bought that field there. Thirty-five acres. Abuts my own property. My *datt* and I cleared the trees and strung that wire fence. I planted alfalfa first spring I owned it. It's given me a good crop every year since."

"Where did you find the bones?"

He touches my shoulder and points. "About twenty feet from that end post there. I was cutting with my two jennies and I'd just made the turn for the final cut." He makes a sound to indicate fright. "Never forget the way those teeth grinned at me when I turned it over in my hands." He gives himself a shake. "I'd best get back to work."

"I appreciate your bringing me back here and letting me look around. I won't be long."

"Take your time, Chief Burkholder." Grinning, he mimics another shiver. "You might want to keep an eye out for *kshpukka* though." Ghosts. "I hear there's one haunts those woods when the sun goes down."

CHAPTER 11

I'm not exactly sure what I hope to accomplish by coming here. Law enforcement agencies have thoroughly searched for—and extracted—every shred of meaningful evidence. According to reports, cadaver dogs and metal detectors and a small army of forensic anthropologists were brought in to sniff out, detect, and dig up anything that might have been part of, or related to, the human remains.

But while I won't uncover anything earth-shattering or new, it can be beneficial to see the crime scene. It helps to visualize what might've happened and get a feel for the scale and proximity of the scene and surrounding area. Is this location private enough to murder someone and not be seen? Is it far enough away from neighbors so that no one would hear two shots? Is this location isolated enough to dump or hide a body? Ananias Stoltzfus was eighty-six years old. Did he walk from his farm to this location? Did someone drive him? Or was he killed elsewhere, his body dumped?

Jonas and his wife own a home on the other side of Belleville. Is the distance between the two locations relevant?

The alfalfa is still stubby from being cut, and the sweet, green smell of it conjures a rise of nostalgia as I start toward the place where Doyle found the skull. The area has been thoroughly trampled, the alfalfa pounded to dirt in places by dozens of feet and the tires of official vehicles. A strip of yellow caution tape flutters atop an end post where someone had taped it off. A few feet away, a red stake flag is the only other sign this was a crime scene.

I stop next to the flag and look around. I'm in the corner of the field. The end post is about twenty feet away. To my right, the land sweeps upward toward the ridge. To my left is the wire fence that demarks the edge of the field. Beyond is a dirt two-track and a wooded area. According to Doyle, the hayfield had once been wooded, too. He and his father cleared the land to grow hay. If that's the case, the place I'm standing was once wooded. Is the theory Deputy Vance laid out correct? Did the killer bury the body here in a shallow grave thinking it would never be found? Were the bones uncovered by the simple mechanics of natural erosion and plowing?

I walk to the fence and climb over. There's a dirt road about ten feet wide and then a virtual wall of trees. I traverse a drainage ditch. Shadows descend as I enter the forest. Leaves from last fall crunch beneath my feet. Within just a few yards, I'm completely hidden from view. Is this what the field looked like eighteen years ago? If so, it would have been an ideal place to bury a body with a reasonable belief it would never be found.

As I scale the fence and walk back to the hayfield, I think about Jonas Bowman, locked in a cell, accused of murder. He'd been twenty-one years old when Ananias disappeared. He'd just lost his father. He'd been grieving. According to everyone I've spoken with, he blamed Ananias for his father's death. Was he angry enough to lure the bishop to this remote location and shoot him? Why would an elderly bishop agree to meet him? The questions circle my brain in an endless loop. I try to get my head around the notion of Jonas marching an old man—a bishop—into a wooded area and committing premeditated murder, and I simply can't do it. Not the boy I'd once known.

I reach the stake flag, kneel, and set my hand against the ground. "What did you do?" I whisper.

The only reply comes with the caw of a crow as it takes flight, and the sinking sensation that none of the answers I need are going to come easily.

The Kish Valley Motel and RV Park is located just west of Belleville proper. It's a midcentury modern motel with a neon sign above the office and two wings of rooms, each with a clattering window-unit air conditioner and turquoise door. A smattering of cottages and RVs are nestled in the trees at the back. Two cars are parked in the lot. Half a dozen kids play in a courtyard pool that's more green than blue, but no one seems to mind.

It's fully dark by the time I check in. Hoping for quiet away from the pool kids, I choose one of the "honeymoon" cottages at the rear and lug my overnight bag into a room that smells of air freshener and old carpet. But the place is clean and cool, the bed covered with fresh linens, and according to the online reviews, the Wi-Fi fast.

I call Tomasetti while I unpack.

"How's the trip so far?" he asks.

"Interesting. Strange. Seems like I've been here longer than a day."

"If I'm not mistaken, that's a Grateful Dead song."

I laugh, missing him, and take a few minutes to update him on everything I learned today.

"Weapon found at the scene is damning," he says.

"Most of the evidence is circumstantial."

"Pretty strong set of circumstances, though."

I sigh. "I was hoping the sheriff's department would be more open to sharing information."

"I've no doubt they'll warm up to you," he says. "Any hostility from the victim's family?"

I tell him about my visit with Mary Elizabeth Hershberger. "She wasn't hostile, but shut me down pretty quickly. The Amish are generally pretty well behaved. I'm hoping to speak with the son tomorrow."

A buzz of silence and then he asks, "So what's your take on Bowman?"

"I met his wife and kids," I tell him. "Nice family."

He pauses. "And Bowman?"

A quiver of tension creeps up the back of my neck,

but I swish it away. "I only saw him for a few minutes at the jail. He's . . . the same. Seems like a typical Amish guy. Husband. Father. Cabinetmaker. His wife is working on bail."

"Do you think he did it?"

I let the question sink in, force my mind into all those corners I initially didn't want to explore because I was afraid of what I'd see. "I don't think so. I mean, I knew him a year or so before the murder happened. Before his family left Painters Mill. I can't see him murdering his own bishop."

"Sounds like you have your work cut out for you."

"I think that pretty much sums it up."

"Will you do me a favor?"

"You know I will."

"Keep in mind that this is a homicide investigation, Kate. The stakes are high. We're talking life in prison without parole—or the death penalty. People get squirrelly when their life is on the line. The case may be cold and the players Amish, but it's still murder no matter how you cut it. That old man didn't get shot twice and buried all by himself."

"Is that your way of telling me not to trust Jonas simply because I grew up with him?" Despite the teasing note I add to my voice, I hear the underlying seriousness buried in the question.

"I'm telling you a person can change a lot in twenty years," he says. "Don't forget that."

"I don't have to remind you that I'm not a rookie, do I, Tomasetti?"

"I wouldn't be doing my due diligence as a domineering lover and know-it-all ex-cop if I didn't remind you that sometimes you care a little too much."

"I'll be careful," I tell him. "And you're not a domineering lover."

He laughs because I didn't mention know-it-all ex-cop.

We spend a few minutes engaging in small talk. About the farm. He tells me about the just-hatched chicks. The purple martins checking out the new birdhouse. All the while I sense something unsaid between us. A hovering presence I don't want to acknowledge. A subject he doesn't want to broach.

This time, we let it go.

I'm wakened from a dead sleep by the rattle of my cell phone against the night table. For an instant, I think I'm home, but Tomasetti isn't there. I roll, grapple for my cell, squint at the incoming number. I don't recognize it and answer with a coarse, "Yeah."

"Chief Burkholder?"

It takes me a moment to place the voice. "Effie?" I sit up, look over at the clock on the table next to the bed. 5:15 A.M. "Is everything okay?"

"The police came to our house. They're yelling and being mean. Mamm told me to run to the pay phone and call you."

"Do you know what they want?"

"All I know is they knocked on the door really hard and woke everyone up. They were mean to Mamm. She asked them what they wanted and they told her to just read the papers. She doesn't know what to do."

"Where are the police now?"

"Um . . . outside, I think."

I can only assume the papers she's referring to are a warrant. But that doesn't make sense because the sheriff's department has already searched the house. Jonas is in custody. Why would they return to the house for a second search?

"All right," I tell the girl. "Go back to the house. Tell your *mamm* I'm on my way. Tell everyone to stay calm."

"They're not going to take my *mamm,* too, are they?"

I try not to wince. "No one's going to take your *mamm,* honey," I assure her. "Everything's going to be okay."

"That's what Datt said right before they put him in jail," the girl whispers.

As I end the call, it occurs to me that there's probably more I don't know about the case than I do.

CHAPTER 12

I call the sheriff's department twice on my way to the Bowman house. Once, I'm put on hold and never gotten back to. The second time I'm transferred to the public relations officer's voicemail. I don't bother leaving a message.

The Bowman property is alight with the flashing blue lights of law enforcement vehicles when I arrive. I count three cruisers as I pull in to the driveway. A state police crime scene unit truck. A fifth vehicle—a white van—belongs to an NBC affiliate from nearby State College. A lone deputy stands in the driveway, pacing and talking on his phone. I catch sight of Dorothy on the front porch, huddled in a big cardigan sweater, lantern in hand, and I pull over and get out.

"What happened?" I ask as I start toward her.

The Amish woman is disheveled, hair sticking out from beneath her *kapp*. Sockless feet jammed into plain white sneakers. All of it telling me she was roused from sleep with no time to dress properly.

"They just came pounding on the door." She brandishes the warrant, the papers rattling because her hand is shaking. "Gave me this. Said they were going to search that old well out back."

"A water well?" Even as I say the words, I take the warrant and skim. *Executed in the Commonwealth of Pennsylvania.* The warrant application was approved by the district attorney. In the description of the premises to be searched is the address of the home, but neither the house nor the workshop is listed. Instead, the area to be searched is listed as a *nonoperational water well*.

Farther down, I come to the place on the page where the specific evidence to be obtained is listed.

Firearms, ammunitions, biological evidence, multimedia devices, and any other physical evidence related to the crime in question.

Puzzled, I look at Dorothy. "Do you have any idea what they're looking for?"

"I can't imagine." She shakes her head. "That well's an old thing that was here when we bought the property. I've asked Jonas a dozen times to fill it in to make sure no one fell in."

"*Mamm!*"

The three of us spin to see Junior burst through the front door. "They're beating up Reuben!"

"Oh, Lord."

"Stay put," I tell them. Then I'm through the door, the living room, and kitchen. I hit the back door with both hands. I spot lights through the trees as I take the steps two at a time to the walkway. I hear raised voices, but I'm too far away to make out what's being said. The one thing that's clear is that there's some kind of scuffle taking place, and if I don't get there quickly to deescalate the situation, Reuben might end up in jail with his father.

I yank my mini Maglite from my pocket as I jog across the grass. I enter the trees, see a deputy sheriff.

Flashlight in hand, he strides toward me. "Ma'am!"

"I'm a cop," I tell him. "What happened?"

"You can't be out here," he says.

"I know, but there's a minor child over there." I slow down, keep moving toward the lights and the sounds of a heated confrontation. "Can you give me a hand?"

I'm aware of the deputy following me, keeping pace though I'm moving fast.

Another ten yards and I catch a glimpse of two deputies kneeling over someone on the ground. Reuben. Facedown. Arms behind his back. Shit. *Shit.*

"Reuben." I slow, take a moment to crank it down a notch, calm myself. "He's a minor child," I say to the cops. "I can help."

"Get her out of here!" a deputy shouts.

A second starts toward me. Face grim. Mouth taut. "Ma'am."

"I'm a cop." I point at Reuben. "A family friend. Let me get him out of your hair."

The deputy stops a few feet away. In his eyes, I see a reluctant acknowledgment of the connection I'd been hoping for. The blue brotherhood. Right or wrong or somewhere in between, he's recognized that I'm one of them. However tenuous the connection, I seize it, hold it tight.

"I'm the chief of police in Painters Mill, Ohio," I tell them. "I need someone to tell me what the hell is going on."

One of the deputies that had been kneeling next to Reuben gets to his feet. He's sweating and disheveled. Pissed off. Leaves and dirt stuck to sweat-slicked arms. "If you want to keep this little shit out of jail, I suggest you take him to the house. Right now."

"No problem." I reach them as both men haul Reuben to his feet. The Amish boy's shirt isn't buttoned. His skinny, white chest is heaving and covered with dirt and dried grass. Hands cuffed behind his back. Single suspender dangles at his hip. He's not wearing a hat. Head hanging down. Eyes not meeting mine.

"*Bleiva roowich,*" I say to Reuben. Stay calm.

The boy raises his eyes to mine, but he quickly looks back down at the ground.

"I can take it from here, guys," I say to both deputies. "Thank you." I turn my attention to the pissed-off deputy. "You okay?"

"I'm fine," he says nastily.

I jab a thumb at Reuben. "He won't cause any more problems."

The boy looks at me as if I've betrayed him and chokes out a sound of anger and frustration, his eyes sweeping to the deputy. "*Eah sheeva mei mamm!*" He pushed my *mamm*!

I point my finger at his face. "Don't say another

word." I address him in English, my harsh tone leveled as much at the cops as at the boy.

Reuben hangs his head.

"Chief Burkholder."

My heart sinks when I spot Rick Gainer approaching, the sergeant I spoke with at the sheriff's department yesterday.

"Temper must run in the family." He smiles, but his expression isn't friendly.

"Teenagers aren't exactly known for restraint," I tell him.

He looks from the boy to me and frowns. "I'm an inch away from taking him down to juvie."

I hold his gaze. "I'd appreciate it if you didn't. This family has been through a lot."

In the too-long pause that follows, sweat breaks out on my back, at my nape. I feel my own temper rise, but I force it back. Finally, Gainer nods at the deputy holding Reuben. "Cut him loose."

While the deputy unlocks the cuffs, I look past him at the well. "What are you guys looking for?" I ask Gainer.

"It's all in the warrant." It's the standard-issue response when you don't want to answer. I've uttered those very same words myself dozens of times.

"Timing is interesting," I say. "You get some new information?"

He offers up a wouldn't-you-like-to-know smirk.

I smile. "I guess you're not going to cut me any slack, are you?"

"Not a chance."

Keeping my expression neutral, I focus on the well. The stone wall surrounding the pit is about two feet high, some of which has collapsed. There's no cover or bucket. The crime scene unit investigator has set up a work light on a scaffolding. A second investigator is in the process of lowering something into the well. A light? A camera? Both?

When the cuffs are off, Reuben looks at the deputy, awkward and sheepish, then at me.

"Let's go," I say firmly.

Reuben gapes at me, incredulity flaring in his eyes. "But they can't—"

"Yes, they can." I set my hand on his shoulder and squeeze. "They have a warrant."

A sound of resignation and disappointment hisses between his lips. "I thought you knew how to stand up to people."

I stop and face him. "There's a difference between standing up for what's right and getting yourself thrown into some juvenile detention center for no good reason. You should take a few minutes and think about that."

He looks at me, nostrils flaring, mouth taut. At that moment, he looks so much like Jacob when he was that age that my chest aches.

"Go inside," I tell him. "Ask your *mamm* to make coffee. I'll be there in a few minutes."

Without a word, he turns and starts for the house.

I linger on the periphery of the scene. Twice, I'm told to back away and keep my distance. Twice, I slowly work my way back, but I can't get close enough to see what they're doing. Someone brought in a generator. The roar of the engine makes it difficult to hear. Despite the work lights, there's not enough light to see. I talk to a couple of deputies, one of whom tells me they sent someone into the hole and that he's encountered water. They're being tight-lipped about what they're looking for. Whatever it is, it's got them wound up. It chafes to be left in the dark.

Dawn spreads pink and gray across the eastern horizon when I spot the deputy I met yesterday at the old Stoltzfus place. I search my memory for his name. Kris Vance. He's brought coffee for his peers, and both arms are laden with cardboard trays containing to-go cups. An underling relegated to providing the creature comforts of his higher-ups.

"Need a hand with that?" I ask.

"Ah . . . better not since you're . . ."

"The opposition."

He laughs. "Right."

I give him a few minutes to distribute the coffee, then approach him, not getting too close. "You been on duty all night?" I ask.

He nods, sips from his cup. "Pulled a double."

"Coffee helps." For the span of several minutes, we watch the deputies mill about.

"I think they sent someone down the well," I tell him.

"Huh." Noncommittal, then, "Interesting."

"Any idea what they're looking for?" I ask.

He looks around to see if anyone has noticed him talking to me. "Not sure," he says, without looking at me. "I was on patrol when Sarge called and asked me to bring coffee."

The tempo of the men's voices rises. Deputy Vance makes eye contact with me then saunters over to the well for a look. I stick with him in time to see a man in a Tyvek suit being raised from the depths. He's wearing a headlamp. Gloves. A face mask. Shoe covers. As if he's expecting to encounter some kind of biological contaminant or evidence. Even more interesting is the fact that he's carrying two small cardboard boxes.

What the hell is in the boxes and what does it have to do with Jonas? Does it have anything to do with the murder of Ananias Stoltzfus? More importantly, how did the sheriff's department know to find it in the well?

I try to get closer, but I'm stopped by a deputy. I've lost track of Vance. I hang around a few more minutes, but the deputies and crime scene investigators are starting to break down the lights and generator. Whatever they were looking for, they found.

A few minutes later, I'm sitting at the big table in the kitchen, working on my second cup of coffee. Junior and Effie sit across from me, eating scrambled eggs and toast without enjoyment or enthusiasm, staring into their plates, unspeaking. Dorothy pours herself a cup of coffee from the old-fashioned percolator and joins me.

"Do you have any idea what the police were looking for?" I ask the question of no one in particular, knowing any one of them might have an answer.

Dorothy shakes her head. "No one would say."

Reuben enters the kitchen. He's fully dressed in

trousers and a blue work shirt, single suspender looped over his shoulder. He doesn't look at anyone as he goes to the counter and pulls a plate from the cupboard.

Dorothy starts to rise, but he raises his hand. "I'll get it, Mamm."

The Amish woman settles back into her chair, worried eyes moving from Reuben to me and back to her son. "*Es is dunk-oiyah,*" she tells him. There are eggs.

Without responding, he goes to the stove and shovels two eggs onto his plate. I can tell by his body language he's still angry. That he'd prefer not to deal with any of us this morning. Likely, that he's not proud of getting himself handcuffed and nearly arrested.

"I was just asking your *mamm* if she had any idea what the police were looking for," I say to him.

He glances at me over his shoulder, sets down the spatula, and joins us at the table. "I shouldn't have lost my temper," he mumbles. Still not making eye contact with anyone.

For the first time I notice the abrasion on his cheekbone. The burgeoning bruise beneath his eye. And I wonder how much those deputies roughed him up. If they had cause.

Dorothy scoots a small bowl toward her son. "*Es is gebacht brot un abbel budder zu.*" There's toast and apple butter, too. "Now eat."

Reuben raises his gaze to his mother. "That deputy pushed you," he said.

Dorothy waves off the statement. "I got in the way is all."

Mouth tight, he snags toast and slathers it with apple butter. "They're not supposed to do that."

Junior sets down his fork. "I-I threw r-rocks into the well," he blurts.

All eyes turn to Junior. The boy has stopped chewing. He sits stone-still, his eyes moving from me to his *mamm* to Reuben. "Melvin M-Mast said you can c-c-count the seconds between when you let go and it hits the water and f-figure out how deep it is. We w-wanted to know."

Dorothy gives him a sympathetic look and pats his hand. "I don't think the police are looking for rocks."

"They were looking for bones," Reuben says.

That gets my attention. "What bones?" I ask.

He shrugs. "I don't know, but I heard the deputy say something about bones. When they lowered that light and camera. He was talking on the radio. To the guy down in the well."

"Are you sure they weren't talking about the bones in the field?" I'm keenly aware that Junior and Effie have stopped eating and that this isn't the kind of conversation to have in the company of young children, especially when they know their father is in jail.

Reuben raises his gaze to mine. "He said the bones in the well."

"Any idea who they belong to?" I ask. "Or who put them there?"

He shakes his head. "That's what I was trying to find out when the deputy jumped me."

Effie sets down her fork, blinks at her *mamm*. "Do

the police think Datt did something bad to someone else?"

"Those police don't know what they think." Dorothy gets to her feet. "Pounding on the door at five o'clock in the morning like they did." She brings her hands together. "If you kids are going to get those cabinets finished today, I suspect you ought to get started."

I'm barely aware of the youngsters taking their dishes to the sink and clattering out the back door. Is Reuben mistaken about what the sheriff's deputies were talking about? Human remains are the last thing I'd expect them to be looking for. Even so, it would explain the predawn raid, the crime scene unit, and the Tyvek-clad investigator.

Such a discovery would raise a lot more questions than it solved. Who do the remains belong to? Is there a second murder victim I'm not aware of? How did the bones get in the well? And how did the sheriff's department know they were there? Most importantly, what do the bones have to do with Jonas and the murder of Ananias Stoltzfus?

CHAPTER 13

Information is a priceless commodity during an investigation. The more you know, the closer you are to the big solve. Unfortunately for me, information is the one thing the sheriff's department won't share. I'm no stranger to being stonewalled. When you're a cop, there's always someone with an agenda who's willing to lie, cheat, and steal to keep you in the dark.

Being shut out of an investigation by fellow cops is different. I'm involved in this case as a civilian; no one is obliged to work with me. They don't have to share information or answer my questions or even return my calls. I'm an outsider with a personal connection to the suspect which places me squarely on the opposing team.

Frustration sizzles like acid on skin as I toss my cell onto the passenger seat and pull onto the highway. All I can do at this point is push forward, keep digging, and add as much information to my arsenal as I can. As hopeless as it seems at the moment, things will eventually come together. That's what I keep telling myself, anyway.

The key to working a cold case is to treat every piece of information as if it's fresh. Start at the beginning and retrace every step. Go through the motions and don't make the rookie mistake of taking shortcuts because you know it's already been done. If the murder of Ananias Stoltzfus had just happened, I'd start by looking at anyone who'd had a disagreement with him. While Jonas would be at the top of that list, Roman Miller wouldn't be far behind.

He lives west of Menno, several miles outside of Belleville proper. It's a nice-looking spread with a red-brick ranch house surrounded by a split-rail fence, and a pretty horse barn at the rear. I pull into the gravel drive and park next to a rusty two-horse trailer hitched to an old pickup truck. Two blue heelers rush from the barn, hackles up, barking.

I'm trying to decide whether to get back into the Explorer or try to make it to the house without getting bitten when a voice calls out.

"Girls! That's enough!"

I look over the hood of the Explorer to see a woman on a big paint horse trotting toward me. Leather saddle squeaking. Buckles jangling. Shod hooves clanking against gravel.

The dogs back off, wagging their tails now, but keeping eyes on me nonetheless. The woman stops the horse a few feet away. "Can I help you?"

"I'm looking for Roman Miller," I tell her.

"You and me both," she says with a huff. "The man

disappears every time there's an inkling of work to be done around here." She makes the statement good-naturedly, but I can tell by her expression there's a thread of truth to it.

I cross to the horse and run my hand over its neck. The animal's nostrils are flared. Its coat is sleek and damp with sweat. A bit of lather where the saddle pad meets shoulder. "He's a beauty," I tell her.

"She," the woman corrects. "And she's the biggest bitch I've had since that Appaloosa gave me two broken ribs and a concussion last summer. If I didn't love 'em so much, I swear I'd ship them off to the glue factory."

I make a noncommittal sound as I run my fingertips over the animal's muzzle, liking the velvety feel of it, the smell of the horse.

The woman is a talker and just getting warmed up. "If I had a steady income, I'd do the same to that no-good husband of mine." Somehow, she makes the statement with affection. "He knows it, too."

She looks down at me, tilts her head. "What do you want with Roman?"

I introduce myself. "I'm a family friend of Jonas Bowman and I'm looking into the Stoltzfus case."

"Heard they found his bones." She blows out a breath. "That's some creepy stuff."

I nod, aware that the horse is nuzzling me, and I get the impression that despite this woman's tough talk, the animal gets its fair share of carrots.

"I suspect Roman's in the barn." Making a sound of supreme irritation, she motions. "He goes in there, makes all sorts of noise so I'll think he's working. Saw.

Hammer. Whatever. I go in to check and he's sitting on his ass with a beer in his hand. I swear I'm going to cut him loose one of these days."

I clear my throat, reach down to pat one of the dogs, pleased when the animal wags its tail.

She gathers the reins. "Go on in," she tells me. "I suspect he'll give you an earful about Stoltzfus. I'm going to finish my ride."

The dogs follow her. I start toward the barn. It's a newish structure with a wide center aisle and horse stalls on both sides. I see the silhouette of a horse cross-tied at the far end, a man in a Western hat bent over, working on the animal's hoof. A floor fan blows warm air on both of them.

"Mr. Miller?"

He lowers the horse's hoof and straightens, looks at me over his shoulder. "You found him."

The smells of horses and wood and fresh-cut hay play at my olfactory nerves as I approach him. "Nice place you have here."

"We like it." He tips his head, looks at me from beneath the brim of his cowboy hat. "I'm not taking on any new clients right now."

"I'd like to ask you some questions about Ananias Stoltzfus."

He pushes up the brim of his hat, gives me a once-over. "You some kind of cop?"

I introduce myself. "I'm the chief of police in Painters Mill, Ohio, but I'm here as a friend of the Bowman family."

"Burkholder, huh? You Amish or what?"

"I was."

"Huh." He sets down the rasp he'd been using and gives me his full attention. "Wouldn't want to be in Jonas Bowman's shoes. Dude's in a shitload of trouble."

I nod. "I hear you had some problems with Ananias Stoltzfus yourself."

"Word gets around, don't it?" He laughs, but there's an edge to it. "You'd think after all these years those Amish pricks would find something else to talk about besides me."

"I was probably asking pointed questions," I tell him.

"At least you're honest about it."

"I understand you were excommunicated." I make the statement in *Deitsch*. I'm not above using whatever connection I share with this man to gain his trust and get him to talk to me.

He blinks in surprise, but takes the question in stride. "Broke my parents' hearts, but there was no going back. No one to blame but Ananias Stoltzfus. Not to speak ill of the dead, but that sumbitch was mean as a damn snake."

"What happened?"

"He didn't like me dating a Mennonite girl." His eyes sweep to the doorway to indicate the woman on the horse. "Ananias found out and tried to warn me away from her. When I didn't give her up, he put me under the *bann*. When I didn't come around, he lowered the boom." He levels a knowing gaze on me. "If you were Amish, you know what that means."

"I do."

"Not only was it tough on my family, but it ruined

me financially. I'm a farrier, you know. My clients were Amish. They refused to let me shoe their horses. I'd just bought some equipment so I could hot-shoe, and then there goes my business. My equipment got repossessed. Credit got ruined." He spits out the last word as if it's gone rotten in his mouth. "So, yeah, I wasn't real happy with the bishop."

The level of animosity after so much time surprises me. "Did you argue with him?"

"He was trying to run my life and when I didn't let him, he ruined me. So, yeah, we had a go of it a few times. He was too strict and he wasn't very nice about it. I wasn't the only one who thought so."

"Anyone in particular?"

"It was kind of a general consensus kind of thing. The Amish don't go around complaining about their bishop, if you know what I mean."

"Did the police talk to you when Ananias disappeared?"

"Oh, yeah. They came pounding on my door first thing, pointing their fingers and asking questions. Had me on their radar for years. No offense, but I'm not a big fan of cops."

"None taken."

"Lucky for me, Bowman left that old muzzleloader at the scene." He lets out a nervous laugh. "Or else it might've been me stuck in jail instead of him."

"What do you think happened to Ananias Stoltzfus?" I ask.

"As far as I'm concerned, Bowman did all of us a big favor."

When I don't respond, he shakes his head. "Look, I have no clue who offed the old man. All I'm saying is people have their limits."

"You think someone reached their limit and decided to do something about it?"

"I think a lot of the Amish didn't care for his heavy-handed ways. Ananias Stoltzfus bullied people in the name of the *Ordnung*. If you were Amish, you know what that means and it ain't right."

I think about the thoughtful and careful process the Amish use for the selection of their *Diener*—the bishop, deacon, and ministers—which is by lot. They eschew any notion of power as being worldly.

"If Ananias Stoltzfus was a tyrant, how is it that he was elected bishop?" I ask.

His brows knit as if he's trying to recall. "I don't think he was overbearing from the start. From what I hear, it got worse after his wife passed away."

"How so?"

"I think that's when he started cracking down on people. Especially the backsliders. Like me." He offers a self-deprecating smile. "Guess you can't blame him for being a crotchety old bastard. The way his wife died and all."

"How did she die?"

He looks at me as if he's surprised I don't already know. "She walked into the Lutheran church in Belleville and slit her wrists right there by the altar. Pastor found her. She died before they could get her to the hospital."

"Any idea why she did it?" I ask.

"Everyone was pretty tight-lipped about it. Even the newspaper didn't go into much detail."

"How long ago did it happen?"

"A few years before Ananias disappeared." He uses a kerchief to blot sweat from his temple. "But, damn, cutting your wrists in a Lutheran church when you're Amish? Who does something like that?"

CHAPTER 14

I have no idea if the suicide of Mia Stoltzfus is related in any way to the death of her husband, but the story follows me as I pull onto the road and head east. The suicide rate among the Amish is slightly lower than the general population. But, of course, it happens. Depression and despair are human conditions and the Amish are not immune. What sets Mia Stoltzfus's suicide apart is that she chose to do it in a Lutheran church. Why would an Amish woman, an Anabaptist, choose to take her life in a Lutheran church?

The question nags me as I glance at my GPS and head toward the address for Henry Stoltzfus, Ananias's son. He lives on a postcard-perfect farm nestled between two hills with a small creek running through the dale between. A grain silo overlooks the field to my left. A massive red barn and three smaller structures are connected by a jigsaw of wood fences dressed in fresh white paint. On the right, a windmill nearly as tall as the two-story farmhouse dominates the side yard, green vines snaking toward the bladed topper.

I idle past the barns and stop in the gravel area at the side of the house. It's a frame structure with a green composite roof, a redbrick chimney, and a porch that stretches across the front elevation. I'm midway to the door when I notice the midsize barn behind the house. It's a workshop of sorts and the door is open. Seeing light and movement inside, I head that way.

There's a picnic table in front of the building. A giant stockpot simmers atop a homemade tripod set over an open fire. An Amish boy of about twelve emerges from the interior. He's wearing blue trousers and a work shirt. Straw, flat-brimmed hat. Single suspender crossed over his chest. He's carrying a headless chicken by its feet. Butchering day, I realize.

"Hello there," I say.

The boy nods a greeting, holding the dead chicken far enough away to keep blood off his shoes.

"I'm looking for Henry Stoltzfus," I say. "Is he around?"

The boy points toward the open door.

I enter the dimly lit interior to the sound of clucking chickens. Two headless creatures hang by their feet from the low-slung rafter overhead. Three roosters await their fate from wood crates stacked on the floor.

"What do you want?"

At the sound of the voice, I turn to see a stern-faced Amish man approach from a darkened corridor. He's blond-haired and blue-eyed with a coarse-looking beard the color of straw. He's dressed similarly to the boy.

His expression tells me he's not thrilled to see an *Englischer* standing in his barn.

I go to him, extend my hand for a shake, and introduce myself. "I'm looking into what happened to your father. The *Diener* asked me to help."

He doesn't accept the handshake. "Help who?"

"Anyone interested in the truth," I say.

"Why you?" He gives my clothes a pointed look. "You're *hohch*."

It's a slightly derogatory term for a non-Amish person. It's not the first time I've heard it; I don't take it personally. Sensing my time is limited, I make my point in *Deitsch*. "Any information you can share will be very much appreciated."

Unimpressed, he bends and pulls a chicken from one of the crates. The animal's wings flap as he lays it on the bench in front of him. With deft hands, he wraps baling twine around the bird's feet and draws it tight. "The police said he'd been shot. They found Bowman's muzzleloader next to him. That is the only truth I need."

He picks up the ax. I brace an instant before he brings it down on the chicken's neck.

I glance away, give him a moment to hang the bird to drain. "I know it was a terrible time," I say. "Mr. Stoltzfus, I just want to make sure the right person is found and brought to trial."

The boy I saw earlier enters, his eyes flicking from his *datt* to me and back to his *datt*. He knows something's afoot and wants no part of it. Stoltzfus and I fall silent and watch as the boy picks up the headless chicken and takes it outside to scald and pluck.

Stoltzfus sets down the ax. "Tell me this, Kate Burkholder. What kind of man hates an eighty-six-year-old bishop so much that he strikes him down with a gun? What kind of man buries the body so that the family will never know what happened? Perhaps you should consider those questions before you come to my home and ask for my help."

"Whoever did that to your father deserves to be punished," I tell him.

A knowing light enters his eyes. He gives a satisfied nod. "You've strayed far since leaving the church, no?"

"This has nothing to do with me."

"If you were Amish, you would know it is God who makes the final judgment. Not the police or judge or jury. Certainly not a backslider like you."

I take the insult in stride, keep going. "That may be true, Mr. Stoltzfus, but what if Jonas Bowman didn't do it? He's Amish. With a wife and children. The truth matters."

"I leave the truth to God."

"Even if the person who did it is still out there?" I say. "What if he kills again?"

He stops working and gives me his full attention. "You need proof that Jonas did this thing?"

"I'll take any information you have."

"Maybe you should ask my sister about the letter."

I blink, confused. "What letter?"

A smirk slinks across his mouth. "Jonas Bowman threatened to kill my *datt*. Judging from the look on your face, I'd venture to say he forgot to mention it."

It's the first I've heard of the existence of a letter. "I

talked to Mary Elizabeth yesterday. She didn't mention it."

"For having been Amish, you know little about our ways." He bends and removes the last chicken from its crate. "Now leave me and my family in peace. Do not come back. I do not wish to talk to you or expose my children to your kind."

"Well, that went swimmingly," I mutter as I climb into the Explorer and start the engine.

I expected a certain level of mistrust, especially from the family of the victim. Forgiveness may be one of the most fundamental Amish tenets, but there are times when emotion transcends ideology. Evidently, if there's any helpful information to be had, it's not going to come from Henry Stoltzfus.

I've gone just a mile or so down the road when my cell phone chirps. I glance over, see a local number I don't recognize.

"Chief Burkholder, this is Deputy Vance."

"The deputy who didn't write me a ticket for trespassing." In the back of my mind, I wonder if Sergeant Gainer has relegated an underling to deal with me and my questions.

"Look, I probably shouldn't be talking to you," he says. "Especially about the Stoltzfus investigation. But I've got something to say."

I pull over and park. "Something bothering you about the case?"

"When we talked before, I told you I bought my kitchen cabinets from Jonas Bowman."

"I remember."

"Well, I spent some time with him and his kids the week they installed those cabinets and worked on my kitchen."

"They're a nice family," I say.

"Yes, they are." When he speaks again, his voice is so low I have to turn up the volume of my phone. "I shouldn't be telling you what I'm about to tell you."

"If you're asking me if I'll keep my mouth shut, the answer is yes."

Another pregnant pause and then, "The investigator found human remains in that well. Bones."

"They found another body?"

"Not a whole body. Just . . . hand bones."

"Hand bones?" I mull the possibilities, come up short. "Who do they belong to?"

"We sent them to the lab up in Erie for DNA testing. It's going to take a while, depending on how backed up the lab is."

My cop's antennae are cranked up and on high alert, my heart beginning to thrum. I know that even though the bones were sent to a police lab for identification, chances are the cops know more than they're letting on or making public.

"You're sure this is related to the Stoltzfus case?" I ask.

"You know it is." The pause that follows is so long that for a second I think he hung up on me. Then he continues. "The detective in charge thinks those remains belong to Ananias Stoltzfus."

"I thought his remains were found in the hayfield."

"They were. Investigators never made it public, but the hands were missing."

"Someone . . . ostensibly the killer . . . cut off his hands?"

"Both hands were severed at the wrists."

I'm so gobsmacked that I can't find my voice. I break the silence by posing the obvious question. "Why would someone do that?"

"No one has a clue," he tells me. "I mean, usually when that sort of thing is done, it's to hide the victim's identity. You know, fingerprints or whatnot. But Stoltzfus was local and missing. With or without hands, he'd be identified the moment he was found. The whole thing's a mystery."

"What's the theory on how the hands ended up in the well?" I ask.

"The general consensus is that Bowman panicked. He removed the hands thinking it would make the identification process more difficult."

"But why would he hide the evidence on his own property?"

"I know," he says. "Doesn't make sense. Hence my call to you."

"How did you guys know the bones were in the well?" I ask.

"I'm not privy to the details, but from what I understand an anonymous tip came in."

"Kind of convenient, don't you think?"

"I'm not calling you because I'm buying in to all of this, right?"

"Any idea who the tipster was?"

"No clue and no one's talking." He sighs. "The thing is, Chief Burkholder, the sheriff is up for reelection this year. Word has it, he wants a slam dunk on this case."

"Whether he has the right man or not."

"No comment. Look, I need my job. Word gets out that I called you and I'm done."

I think about my conversation with Henry Stoltzfus. My mind is trying to connect dots that simply don't connect. "I understand Ananias Stoltzfus received a threatening letter from Jonas Bowman. Do you know anything about that?"

"Don't know anything about a letter."

Which makes me wonder if Henry Stoltzfus was just blowing smoke.

Vance heaves an unhappy sigh. "Look, you didn't hear any of this from me."

"Kris who?"

His laugh is short-lived. "I don't like what's going on. I sure don't feel good about calling you. But I thought it was the right thing to do."

"I'll keep this between us," I tell him.

He ends the call without responding.

One of the most difficult aspects of investigating any crime is not knowing if you're on the right track. Early on, there's always a certain amount of wheel spinning, false leads, and incorrect assumptions, all of which leads to hours and days and sometimes weeks of wasted time and energy. It's part of the process. When I arrived in Belleville, I had my doubts about Jonas's innocence. There is, after all, a fair amount of physical evidence against him, namely the muzzleloader. He had motive, means, and opportunity. Add the circumstantial evidence—bad blood between Jonas and the victim—and the police had just cause to make the arrest.

One of the most telling things I look for is motivation. The presence of bones in the well doesn't make sense on any level. For one thing, Jonas had no reason to remove the hands; he would have known that any body discovered would be assumed to be that of Ananias Stoltzfus. Even if, in a state of panic, he did remove the hands, why would he dispose of them on his own property? And who called in the anonymous tip? The discovery raises a hell of a lot more questions than it answers.

It's ten P.M. now. I'm sitting at the table in my motel room, my laptop humming, a yellow legal pad open and scribbled upon. I'm tired, but too wired to sleep. The only thing I've managed to accomplish so far is a stiff neck.

One of the most troubling questions raised is the source of the anonymous tip. Who called the sheriff's department? How did the caller know the bones were in the well? And why now? After eighteen years?

I pick up the pen and write: *Who knew the bones were there?*

The killer.

An accomplice?

"Why cut off the hands?" I whisper.

The killer would have known that removing the hands would do nothing to slow the identification process. Any human remains would be assumed to be that of a missing person. Furthermore, if Jonas had murdered Ananias Stoltzfus, why would he bury the body in a shallow grave in one location and then transport the victim's hands to his own property and toss them in a well?

The short answer is, he wouldn't.

Knowing I'm not going to figure it out tonight, I swivel to my laptop and type "MIA STOLTZFUS SUICIDE" into the search engine. Her death doesn't produce many hits. I click on the first link—a newspaper out of Lewistown—and read.

WIFE OF AMISH BISHOP COMMITS SUICIDE
IN LOCAL CHURCH

A spokesman with the Mifflin County Sheriff's Department said the woman whose body was found at Big Valley Lutheran Church appears to be the victim of a suicide. Pastor Russell Zimmerman stumbled across the woman sprawled on the floor a few feet from the altar at 6 this morning.

The sheriff's department spokesman said the death appears to be suicide, but left the final determination up to the county coroner.

Repeated calls for comment were not returned from the coroner's office.

The woman, said to be Amish and in her 70s, was not named pending notification of family.

"Nothing like this has ever happened in Big Valley Lutheran Church before," the pastor said. "Whatever problems she suffered with, she is now in the loving arms of our Lord and Savior."

I go back to my search engine, but there's no mention of the official cause or manner of death or if there was an investigation. Normally, a seemingly unrelated story wouldn't be important in terms of the case I'm working on. But the suicide of Mia Stoltzfus is an anomaly in a growing list of anomalies. Not just her suicide, but that she did it in a Lutheran church and she was married to an Amish bishop who was later murdered. I've been around long enough to know that when those kinds of irregularities begin to stack up, it's time to dig deeper.

I write down the address of the church and jot the name of the minister on my legal pad.

It's midnight when I close my laptop. As I climb into bed and pull up the blankets, I decide to swing by the church in the morning, on my way to Lewistown. As Tomasetti likes to tell me: Sometimes it's those seemingly random pieces of information that lead to something usable.

I sit bolt upright, disoriented, a gasp in my throat. For an instant, I'm not sure where I am. I reach for Tomasetti, find the place next to me vacant and cool. Then my mind clicks into place. I'm in Belleville. The motel.

What woke me so abruptly?

I stare into the darkness, listening. I'm aware of the symphony of crickets outside. The rumble of thunder from a distant storm. Sweat damp on the back of my neck. My heart beating too fast. That's when I realize the room is humid and hot, despite the air conditioner rattling beneath the window. I glance at the door, see the dim column of light, and realize it's standing open about a foot. I'd locked it before turning in. . . .

Adrenaline zips through me. I roll, reach for my .38 on the night table. I sense movement scant feet away. The rustle of clothes. The thud of feet against carpet. Someone rushing toward me . . .

Before I can grab the gun, a fist slams down on my arm. I swivel toward my attacker, sit up. Using the heel of my hand, I cuff him hard, make contact with a hard body, heavy clothing.

"I'm a cop!" I shout. "I'm armed! Stop!"

In the strobe of lightning that follows, I see the silhouette of a man. Tall and broad. Too close. Coming at me. My training kicks in. Leaning back, I raise both legs and kick him in the chest. He grunts, reels backward. His back strikes the wall.

I twist, lunge for my weapon, slap my hand down on it, fingers grappling. Not enough time to find my grip before his fist crashes down on my biceps. Electric pain zings up my arm. He sweeps my gun off the table. I hear it clatter to the floor. My .22 mini Mag is on the table, out of reach. I grab the lamp with both hands, draw back, swing it. He reaches for me, growling like an animal. A roar tears from my throat with the effort. But my position is bad. My aim is off. The shade crunches against the side of his head.

"Police officer!" I shout. "Get off!"

I barely get the words out when gloved hands snake toward me. I scramble back, but I'm not fast enough. Fingers close around my neck, the clamp of a vise, cutting off my air. I wrap my hands around his forearms, dig in with my fingers, try to pry them off. Simultaneously, he yanks me to my feet as if I weigh nothing. His strength stuns me. He wheels me around, thumbs digging into my throat, and shoves me to the ground. My back strikes the floor hard enough to send the breath from my lungs. He comes down on top of me, the weight of him crushing my chest, pinning me. I release his arms, punch his face with my fists. He doesn't relent. I slap and claw at his face. Find an eye with my thumb, shove it into the socket.

Howling, he rears back.

"Get off, you son of a bitch!" I snarl.

A sharp slap against my temple sends stars flying in my peripheral vision. He clinches his hand to my throat, cutting off the blood flow to my head.

"Go back where you came from," whispers a harsh voice.

I see the silhouette of his head against the light slanting in through the door. It's too dark to make out details. He's close enough for me to smell wet hair and stale breath and a body that isn't quite clean.

Stars pinwheel before my eyes. I writhe beneath him, bring up my knees and ram them against his back. I slap and scratch at his arms, his face. My hand tangles in his shirt and I yank hard, tearing fabric. I seek his eyes with my thumbs. My efforts are futile. He's stronger than me with the benefit of weight. I wonder if he's going to kill me. If I pass out, will he keep squeezing? I think of Tomasetti and panic leaps in my chest.

I pry at his fingers as they dig into my throat, peel one off, bend it back hard, try to break it. Snarling, he straightens, pulls my head and shoulders off the floor, then bangs me down hard. Once. Twice. The back of my head thumps against the carpet, jarring my brain, scattering my thoughts. My vision blurs, dims.

"Leave town," he growls.

Let go of me.

I open my mouth, try to speak, but nothing comes.

"Next time you won't walk away."

He releases me. I fall back against the floor, sucking in breaths, choking, my head spinning. Vaguely, I'm aware of him getting to his feet. I turn my head, seeking my .38, only to see him kick it beneath the bed.

"Don't make me come back," he says in a gruff voice.

I roll, try to get my feet under me, but my legs aren't strong enough. Instead, I scrabble toward the bed, aware that he could come back before I reach my weapon.

A sound at the door draws my attention. I look over my shoulder in time to see him disappear into the night.

Every investigation has a defining moment. A piece of evidence or snippet of information or middle-of-the-night epiphany that convinces a cop he's on the right track. Someone trying to warn me away qualifies and for the first time since arriving in Pennsylvania, I'm certain of two things: Jonas Bowman didn't murder Ananias Stoltzfus and the person who did doesn't want me poking around.

It takes twenty minutes for the sheriff's department to

arrive. It took me nearly that long to pull myself together. Once my head cleared, I got dressed, found my gun beneath the bed, my cell on the floor behind the night table. All the while I tried to get my head around what just happened and who might be responsible. When I first wakened and realized someone was in my room, I'd assumed it was a random break-in. Some junkie or thief looking for cash. It didn't take long for me to realize this was a targeted attack with a specific goal.

Go back where you came from.

This was not random. It was a clear message, intended to intimidate and scare me off. The messenger has no way of knowing his efforts did nothing but strengthen my resolve. The question now is this: Who wants me gone desperately enough to risk breaking into my motel room and attacking me in the middle of the night?

Someone with a lot to lose, a little voice replies.

I'm standing outside my cottage, looking at the smashed windshield and slashed tires on the Explorer, when the deputy pulls up, lights flashing. It's after four A.M. now. A family in one of the other cabins has ventured onto their porch to see what riffraff has brought the police to this peaceful little paradise.

The deputy gets out of his vehicle and starts toward me, the beam of his flashlight blinding me.

I raise my hand to shield my eyes and identify myself.

"Ten-twenty-three," he says into his shoulder mike, letting his dispatcher know he's arrived on scene. "We got a call about a break-in."

He's around thirty years old and built like a tank. Dark hair shorn to the scalp. Thick neck corded with muscle. The tattoo of an eagle and shield peek out at me from the sleeve of his uniform.

I tell him what happened.

He asks a few basic questions as he looks around the room. "Did you see where he went?"

"I saw him go through the door and that was it."

"Ten-eighty-eight." Suspicious activity found. "I need a unit." He turns his attention to me, lifts the beam of his flashlight to my neck. "You need an ambulance?"

"I'm fine."

"Any idea who it was?"

"No clue."

"You here alone?"

"Yep. It's just me."

He looks at me closely, as if he doesn't quite believe me, and I get the sense he's wondering if this is some kind of domestic dispute I don't want to talk about.

"What are you doing here in Belleville?" He asks the question in a friendly way, but he's curious about me, wondering why I'm here.

I tell him.

"I heard there was a cop from out of town asking questions." He nods as if his curiosity has been sated. "You think what happened here tonight is related to that?"

"He didn't ask for money or my purse. He did, how-ever, suggest I leave town."

His eyes sharpen on mine. "You get a look at him?"

I give the best description I can. Male. Six feet. Two

hundred pounds. It probably describes half the men in the county.

The deputy relays the description to his dispatcher, then leaves the room and walks to my Explorer. "Damn." He whistles. "Did a number on your vehicle."

I wince at the sight of the smashed windshield and four flat tires. "He must have done this before he broke in," I say.

"Must have been a pretty sharp instrument." He shines the beam on me again, this time keeping it out of my eyes. "Lucky he didn't use it on you."

It's a telling statement. If the intruder wanted to kill me, he could easily have done so.

"Is there an auto repair shop in town?" I ask.

"There's a good one over in Lewistown," he tells me. "They'll tow you. You can pick up a rental car there, too, if you need it."

He saunters to the door of my room and kneels to examine the lock. "Looks jimmied."

I follow, study the jamb over his shoulder. Sure enough, the paint is scuffed, the wood gouged. "Looks like he popped the latch bolt out of the bore," I say.

"This motel is pretty old." He glances at me over his shoulder. "Of course, we don't get much crime around here."

He rises and looks at me a little more closely. "You sure you don't have any idea who might've done this?" he asks. "Maybe you ticked someone off and they followed you back here?"

A cast of names scrolls through my brain. The people I've come into contact with. The ones who weren't exactly happy to learn I was looking into a cold case that apparently isn't that cold.

"The only person I know who *didn't* do it, is Jonas Bowman," I tell him.

Frowning, he motions toward the office in the main building. "I'll make a report, Chief Burkholder. We'll step up patrols in the area. In the interim, I suggest you watch your back."

CHAPTER 15

Big Valley Lutheran Church is a nondescript redbrick building with a crisp white spire, steep dormers, and arched stained-glass windows. A stately-looking sign in front proclaims ALL ARE WELCOME in big block letters.

It took me most of the morning to get the Explorer to the repair shop in Lewistown for a replacement windshield and four new tires. The work will take a couple of days, so the manager drove me over to the car rental agency, where I picked up a midsize sedan.

I'm feeling cranky and sore as I park in the lot behind the church and take the pavestone walkway to a side door marked OFFICE. The interior is hushed and smells of paper dust and lemon oil. I pass by the restrooms, spot another sign for the office, and head that way.

The reception desk is vacant, but I hear someone in a back room. "Hello?" I call out.

A silver-haired woman wearing a skirt, blouse, and cardigan, her arms piled high with padded envelopes and a few small cardboard boxes, comes through the door, and looks at me over the tops of her bifocals. "Can I help you?"

"I'm looking for Pastor Zimmerman," I tell her.

Two boxes slip off the stack in her arms and thump against the floor. "Oh, dear."

"I've got it." I round the desk and pick them up. "Where would you like them?"

"My office. This way." She marches past me and makes a right into an adjoining office. "Do you have an appointment?" she asks.

"No, but I just need a few minutes of his time." Taking in her rigid posture, I suspect she's hall monitor and visitor screener rolled into a single formidable package.

"I'm guessing he's in the courtyard out back." She motions to a folding table. "You can put the packages there." Then she jabs a finger toward another door. "Take the hall to the courtyard. Last door on the right."

I thank her and make my exit. The courtyard is an outdoor patio that's crowded with planters and greenery. Containers of geraniums and petunias burst with color. Hanging planters overflow with feathery asparagus ferns. There's a birdbath ahead and a row of birdhouses secured to the brick wall at the back. Half a dozen hummingbird feeders dangle from the eave. It's a pretty, calming place that smells of growing things and earth.

A scholarly-looking man with white hair and a neatly trimmed goatee tips a watering can into a terra-cotta planter the size of a barrel. Clad in khaki slacks and a blue shirt with a clergy collar, he looks serene and focused as he pinches off an unwanted stem.

"I like the snapdragons," I say by way of greeting.

He looks up from his watering and smiles. "You know your flowers."

"A few. My mom was a gardener."

"Everyone thinks I spend too much time with my plants." He chuckles. "I do. But then I'm of a certain age. Seems like it's either flowers or birds. I chose both."

I smile, liking him.

He sets down the watering can. "I'm Pastor Zimmerman." He gives me a curious once-over as he approaches. "You seem troubled this morning." He sends a pointed look to the bruises blooming on my throat. "Can I help?"

We shake hands and I introduce myself. "I'm looking into the Ananias Stoltzfus case."

"You're a private detective?"

"I'm a police chief. From Ohio. And a friend of the Bowman family."

"Ah." He grimaces. "I heard they found the bishop's remains. God rest his soul." Some of the good humor leaves his eyes. "Hard to believe an Amish person is responsible, isn't it?"

"I think his guilt is still to be determined."

He picks up the can and tips it to an exotic-looking fern. "It doesn't bode well for Mr. Bowman that they found his rifle at the scene."

"That's one of the reasons I'm here."

For a moment, the only sound comes from the chatter of barn swallows in a nest beneath the eave. Then he asks, "Are you a churchgoing woman, Chief Burkholder?"

"I'm thinking about it," I say honestly.

"Lutheran?"

"Anabaptist."

His brows shoot up. "Mennonite?"

"Formerly Amish," I tell him. "I left when I was eighteen."

He smiles. "You should find a church that you like and go." He says the words without judgment. "God takes on so many of our burdens. As I'm sure you know, we live in troubled times."

"Yes, we do."

He looks out across the courtyard, taking in the dozens of plants, but not quite seeing them now or appreciating their beauty. "You're here because you heard about what happened to Mia Stoltzfus."

I nod. "I don't know if her death is relevant to what happened to her husband, but it's enough of an anomaly to make me curious."

"A lot of people have asked me about that day, Chief Burkholder. Still do. Most are just nosy, you know. One gal drove all the way from Philadelphia, claiming she was writing a book of all things." He shakes his head. "I don't like talking about it. One thing I can't abide is morbid curiosity."

He turns to me, his gaze meeting mine, assessing. For the first time, I see the weight of his profession reflected back at me, and I'm reminded of the Amish *Diener,* the men who devote their lives to serving their community. I see the same burden of responsibility in this man's eyes, too.

"It sounds like you have a legitimate reason for asking," he says quietly.

"I'm trying to find the truth. Figure out what happened and why. A man's life depends on it."

"In that case, come on." He motions to the pavestone path that winds through the courtyard. "I'll finish my watering while we chat."

We take the path to a concrete-and-stone trough filled with a brilliant array of flowers, zinnias and daisies and a dozen other varieties I couldn't begin to name. I stand back and watch while he puts the watering can to use. "I never used to garden. Never had a green thumb. But after that day . . . those few minutes I spent with Mia, I suppose the Lord knew I needed healing and, as He always does, He showed me the way and gave me this gift of growing beautiful things."

We move to a row of wire baskets lined with coconut husk hanging from the rafter of a pergola. "I'd only been pastor a couple of years when it happened. I came in early that day. Worked in my office for a time and then I went into the chancel. I found her lying on the floor, near the altar." He makes a sound I can only describe as grief. "Poor child of God. She looked so alone. Blood everywhere."

"Was she already gone when you arrived?"

"She was alive, actually." He grimaces. "Barely. We weren't chained to our cell phones back in those days, so I covered her with my jacket and ran to my office and called the sheriff's department. Then I came back . . . to see if I could help. So she wouldn't be alone." As if lost in the memory, he pauses. "I did what I could. Applied pressure. Spoke to her. Held her hand. Stayed with her until help arrived."

"Did she say anything, Pastor?" I ask.

He pulls a small pruner from his pocket and snips a stem from a hibiscus. "We Lutherans practice confession and absolution. We put much emphasis on the holy absolution. The pastor, of course, is pledged to keep the confessed in confidence because those sins have been removed. That seal cannot be broken."

"Are you telling me she asked for confession and absolution?"

"Make of that what you will, Chief Burkholder. I'm bound by the seal of the confessional."

"Had you ever met her before?"

"No."

"Do you think it's odd that an Amish woman, an Anabaptist, would come to a Lutheran church and ask the minister for confession?"

"I do. As you well know, the Amish have their own ways. That said, we're all the children of God. Mia Stoltzfus was obviously in a dark place. Did she come here seeking comfort?" His expression tells me that while he has learned to live with what happened that day, the unanswered questions still bother him. "Do you have an opinion on that, Ms. Burkholder? I mean, you were Amish. Is there some scenario in which an Anabaptist woman would eschew her own religion for another?"

I think about my own community, growing up. How the Amish as a whole view the preachers, the deacon, and the bishop. How we view our English neighbors. "One of the most basic Amish tenets is that of separation from the rest of the world."

He nods, as if he'd already drawn the same conclusion. "I can only hope that in her final minutes, she found peace."

"Pastor, was there a note?"

"There was a little scrap of notebook paper on the altar next to her. I was so shaken up I didn't even notice it at first. But while I was sitting with her, waiting for the ambulance to arrive, I found it."

"Do you remember what it said?"

"It was in *Deitsch,* so I've no clue." His brows draw together. "She had a little journal with her, too."

"A devotional?" I ask.

"More like a diary, I think. Just some writings. Also in *Deitsch.*"

"Do you know what happened to the journal?"

"I pointed it out to the police and they took it."

I consider the tragedy and strangeness of the situation, but for the life of me I can't fathom any sort of link to the murder of Ananias Stoltzfus.

"Do you remember how she was dressed?" I ask.

The pastor uses the last of the water and sets down the can. "She was wearing typical Amish clothes. A dress. Head covering. She'd removed her shoes. Seeing her lying there bleeding and all alone was one of the most profoundly heartbreaking sights I've ever seen." His voice quavers with the final word, but he covers it with a cough and glances at his watch. "Ah, Betsy's probably wondering where I am. . . ."

I extend my hand to him for a second shake. "Thank you for talking to me."

"I hope the information is helpful in some way."

He walks me to the door and opens it for me. I'm midway down the hall and heading toward the exit when a final question occurs to me.

"Pastor Zimmerman?"

He stops before making the turn into his office and raises his brows.

"Do you know what happened to the note?"

"I supposed the police picked it up. Perhaps they passed it along to the family. I don't know."

I thank him and make my exit.

Puzzlement nibbles at the periphery of my brain as I take the sidewalk to my rental car. I'm not sure what to make of the story Pastor Zimmerman relayed about Mia Stoltzfus. One of the most important Amish charters is separation from the unbelieving world. In terms of religion, they are sectarian. Why then would the wife of an Amish bishop—a devout Anabaptist—end her life in a Lutheran church and ask a Lutheran minister for confession and absolution?

My best source of information is going to be the Stoltzfus family. The problem is that neither Mary Elizabeth nor Henry is particularly inclined to speak with me. Amish families can be protective of their own, especially when it comes to outsiders asking unpleasant questions. If there was some sort of scandal or indiscretion, they'll likely take the silent route.

A second source of information is the *Diener*, the three men who traveled to Painters Mill and asked for my help. The only physical address I have on hand is for Mahlon Barkman, the minister, who lives northeast of Belleville, so I head that way.

Barrville is a pretty area crisscrossed with meandering country roads and dotted with Amish farms. I pass two buggies on the way and get waves from both drivers, which bolsters my mood. The Barkman farm is small, with a hint of dilapidation that adds an interesting layer of character. The two-story house is set close to the road, with a massive weeping willow tree just off the front porch. I turn in to the gravel driveway and idle toward the rear. A garden the size of an Olympic swimming pool takes up the entire side yard, close enough that I can make out half a dozen rows of corn, staked tomato plants weighted down with fruit, and a lower growth of peppers and some type of melon. An older woman sits at a picnic table that's heaped with a variety of produce, bushel baskets, a cook pot, and crates.

I pull over and start toward her. "*Wie geht's alleweil?*" I say. How goes it now?

"*Ich bin zimmlich gut.*" I'm pretty good. She's snapping green beans and placing them in a big Dutch oven.

"I'm looking for Mr. Barkman," I tell her.

She doesn't stop what she's doing, doesn't even look at me. "*Sitz dich anne un bleib e weil.*" Set yourself there and stay awhile.

It's a pleasant late afternoon. Humid, but with a breeze coming down off the mountain. I take the bench seat across from her and start snapping green beans.

She eyes my technique. "You must be that police from Ohio."

"Yes, ma'am. I'm Kate."

"He told me you'd probably stop by." She's a fast snapper—faster than me—despite fingers that are twisted with arthritis.

When she runs out of green beans, she looks at me. "I'm Laura." Her eyes flick to my hands. "You've done this before."

"Too many times to count."

Her mouth twitches. "Well, you just keep on snapping. He'll be up shortly."

We've worked in silence for a few minutes when the barn door rolls open and Mahlon Barkman appears. I see him do a quick double take upon spotting me, and then he hobbles toward us.

"It's good to see you, Kate Burkholder." He offers his hand for a quick shake and settles in next to his wife. "How do you like our neck of the woods here in Big Valley?" he asks.

I pick up another bean. "It's beautiful."

"A beautiful valley full of good people." He looks at the beans, like a card shark intent on choosing just the right one, and he begins to snap. "You've talked to Jonas?"

"Yes."

"He made bail," he informs me. "This morning."

"I'm glad." Though it would have been nice for someone to let me know.

"The Amish pulled together, the way we do," Mahlon says. "Nathan took the money to the bondsman first thing this morning. Jonas was out in a couple of hours."

I see him studying the bruises on my neck. His eyes are sober when they meet mine. "You've been hurt. Here in Big Valley?"

As if sensing the rise of tension, his wife stops snapping and gives me her full attention.

I give them a condensed version of the ambush. "He suggested I leave town."

"That's worrisome." The old man picks up a bean, his expression troubled. "Does it have something to do with your looking into the death of Ananias Stoltzfus?"

"I think someone doesn't want me poking around."

Husband and wife exchange worried looks.

"I spoke to Pastor Zimmerman at the Lutheran church this morning." I grab a handful of beans and set it on the table in front of me. "How well did you know Mia Stoltzfus?"

"Well enough to know she was a good woman," Mahlon tells me.

"She was a quiet thing," Laura adds. "Worked hard."

"Do either of you have any idea why she committed suicide?" I ask.

The Amish woman shakes her head. "It was such a bad time. For all of us. Mia was part of our sewing circle for a while. A sweet lady." She looks down as if remembering and smiles sadly. "Wasn't much good at sewing for a woman her age. Of course, no one ever said so. It was just one of those odd things."

Having grown up Amish—and being resistant to the expected skill of sewing myself—I'm well aware that it's held in high esteem by the women.

"Was Mia depressed or unhappy?" I ask. "Was she having any problems?"

"The woman never spoke a negative word in her life," Laura says. "Mia had a smile and a kind word for everyone. Enjoyed her baking."

"Did she get along with her husband?" I ask.

"Never complained," Laura tells me. "But then Amish women don't, even when they have cause."

"Ananias was a good husband, I think." Mahlon scoops up a pile of snapped beans and drops them into the Dutch oven. "Strict with the congregation, but he always let her have her say. He made a good living. Provided well. Worked hard."

"Did you ever hear any rumors about them?" I ask. "Maybe some problem between them or a family issue? Anything like that?"

"Nothing out of the ordinary." The Amish man chuckles. "Ananias messed up his preaching service a time or two. Once, during *'Es schwere Deel'* he forgot to close with a reading from the Bible."

It's not the kind of information I'm looking for; a preaching misstep certainly doesn't rise to the level of offending someone enough for them to commit a violent act.

Laura stops snapping, sets her gaze on mine. "There was always something a little odd about the bishop. I don't mean that in an unkind way. It's just that he was different is all."

"How so?" I ask.

"He had that funny accent," Mahlon puts in. "They both did, I guess, especially when they spoke *Deitsch*."

"Said he was from Minnesota, but I have a cousin lives up there and they don't talk that way." Laura grabs another handful of beans from a bushel basket and tosses them onto the table.

"Where in Minnesota?" I ask.

"Harmony, I think. A lot of Amish up that way."

The Amish *Diener*—the ministers, deacon, and bishop—are almost always lifelong members of the church district. It's unusual that Ananias and his wife were from another state and yet Ananias was still nominated and elected.

"How long had they been living in Mifflin County?" I ask.

The couple exchange a puzzled look and then Mahlon shrugs. "They'd been here as long as I can remember."

That's when it occurs to me this couple are quite a bit younger than Ananias and Mia Stoltzfus. The bishop was eighty-six years old at the time of his death, and that was eighteen years ago. It's going to be difficult to find someone closer to his age who knew him well.

"Is there anyone who's still around who was close to either of them?" I ask.

"Mia used to work for a woman by the name of Amanda Garber," Laura tells me. "Amanda and her husband owned a nice little bakeshop in town years ago."

"Best cherry pie I ever ate," Mahlon says.

Laura tosses a bean at him. "Amanda left the fold a while back. She's Mennonite now. Lives down to Ramblewood if I'm not mistaken."

I jot the name and town in my notebook. "Do either of you know anything about a threatening letter Jonas sent to Ananias shortly before he disappeared?"

"Never heard of a letter," the minister says. "But I can tell you this: Jonas has a hot head. A hot head is the quickest shortcut to trouble I ever seen."

CHAPTER 16

For the first time since I arrived in Belleville, I feel the utter coldness of the Stoltzfus case. The distance of it like miles separating loved ones. I think about the years that have passed and I wonder what else lies dormant beneath the decades.

Ramblewood is an unincorporated area thirty minutes northwest of Belleville. I pass through picturesque countryside, including the Rothrock State Forest, where I'm rewarded with stunning views of the valley below.

Amanda Garber lives in a small house in Meadows Park off of Whitehall Road. I knock twice, using the heel of my hand a third time, but no one comes. I'm about to go back to the rental car for pen and paper to write a note when the door creaks. At first, I think the door rolled open on its own. Then I look down and see a tiny, white-haired woman staring up at me.

"Takes me a while to get to the door these days," she says in a voice that's surprisingly robust. "Everyone's in such a hurry."

She's barely four feet tall. Blue eyes filled with attitude take my measure. Her face is a mosaic of leather patches stitched together by capillaries. She's wearing a blue print dress with a crocheted shawl over hunched shoulders, and a Mennonite-style head covering. She leans heavily on a four-prong cane.

"Mrs. Garber?" I say.

"It's *Ms.* Garber now. And whatever you're selling, I ain't buying." She starts to close the door.

"I'm not selling anything." Quickly, I introduce myself. "I'd like to ask you some questions about Mia Stoltzfus."

The door stops mid-close. Through the space, she looks at me with more interest. "Mia?" Her voice goes soft. "That girl's been gone for years. Why on earth are you asking me about her?"

"I understand she worked for you."

"Worked for me, my eye! I loved her like a sister." She cackles. "She made being Amish all those years bearable and that ain't no easy task."

I switch to *Deitsch,* hoping the shared language will help convince her to invite me inside for a chat. "I'm looking into the death of Ananias Stoltzfus," I tell her.

Her eyes narrow. "You speak pretty good *Deitsch* for an *Englischer.*"

"I left, too," I explain. "When I was a teenager."

"I was almost seventy when I jumped ship," she tells me. "Don't know why I waited so long." She pushes open the door and turns away. "*Kumma.*" Come.

I follow her to a small living room cluttered with a sofa and two recliners, a coffee table strewn with magazines and books, and a TV the size of a boat. The air is stuffy and warm, despite the air conditioner wheezing in the window.

"Ananias Stoltzfus, huh? Haven't heard that name in a blue moon." She wobbles to one of the recliners, braces the cane against the floor, and plops onto the cushion, her feet flying up. "I might have something to say about him and it likely won't be flattering." She motions me into the other recliner. "Sit."

I take a seat. "In all fairness, I should tell you I'm a friend of Jonas Bowman."

She leans forward, looks left and right as if someone might be listening. "Ananias Stoltzfus was a son of a bitch. Far as I'm concerned, that boy did the world a favor. The man was drunk on power and had the conscience of a fox in a coop full of chickens."

"Was there anyone in particular he had problems with?"

"Rubbed a lot of us the wrong way." Her mouth curls. "Problem was, everyone was too scared of him to open their mouths."

"What can you tell me about Mia?"

"She was a sweet thing. Worked at my bakery for four or five years. She was one heck of a baker. That woman and her desserts . . ." Her thoughts turn inward and some of the wrinkles on her face seem to smooth out. "I closed my shop going on ten years ago and I still miss her."

"How long did you know her?"

Her face screws up as if she's trying to remember. "They moved here in 1967 or so." She shrugs. "Mia had her babies shortly thereafter. Wasn't until her kids were older that she came to work for me. I think that was around 1982 or thereabouts."

I put the timeline to memory. "I talked to Pastor Zimmerman earlier."

She narrows her eyes. "So you know what happened to her."

I nod. "Do you have any idea why?"

For the first time, Amanda Garber isn't quite so keen to hit back with some colorful retort. "Why are you asking about her now? After all these years?"

"I'm not sure the police have the right man in jail."

"I see." But I can tell by the way her nose wrinkles that she doesn't care one way or another. As long as the old man stays dead . . .

"Ms. Garber, I don't have to tell you how unusual it was for an Amish woman to end her life in a Lutheran church."

She looks down at hands that are dotted with brown spots. "Mia was a good girl with a soft heart. A kind heart. But she got the melancholy sometimes. She never complained, but I saw it. I always got the sense she'd . . . been through something she didn't want to talk about."

"Like what?"

She shrugs. "Something traumatized that girl."

I nod. "Was her husband abusive?"

She shakes her head. "I didn't like the man. He was a tyrant and a bully and he sure didn't pull any punches when it came time to dole out punishment. But I don't believe he was beating her."

"What about infidelity?"

The woman tightens her mouth. "I might've heard a thing or two. If you were Amish, then you know it isn't the kind of thing to be talked about."

"But women talk, don't they?" When she doesn't continue, I prod gently. "Friends talk."

Her gaze meets mine and holds. For a moment, I see beyond the rheumy eyes and wrinkles and get my first glimpse of the young woman she once was. A spirit that was too strong to fit in, one that wouldn't be quashed by propriety.

"He was two-timing her. Mia let it slip one day. Told me he went over to Lewistown every so often. Had himself a loose girl there. Worked at some dive called the Triangle. Serving liquor to drunk men." She removes her glasses. "Mia made like it didn't bother her. Let him have his little *huah*." Whore. "But it broke her heart." She tuts. "Kept him off her, I guess."

"Do you know the woman's name?"

"Rosemary, I think it was. Don't know what became of her. Don't much care."

"Is that why Mia killed herself?"

She shakes her head, adamant. "It didn't help. But there was something else there, too. Something she didn't talk about. It broke her." She taps her chest. "Inside."

I ask her about Jonas Bowman and Stoltzfus's children, but she doesn't know any of them. "Is there anything else you can think of that might help me find the person responsible?"

She leans back in the recliner and contemplates me, as if trying to decide if I'm worthy of the information. "There's a story about Levi Schmucker was going around years ago. Can't vouch for the truth of it."

"Who is he?"

A light enters her eyes. A storyteller about to embark on a tour de force. "Levi lived down to Reeds Gap with his wife and kids. Worked at the mill out Strodes Mills way. Word got around that Levi was acting improper with his oldest girl. Bad medicine, you know?"

I nod, wondering where she's going with this. What it has to do with Ananias Stoltzfus.

"It was a hush-hush kind of thing. Somehow, Ananias caught wind of it and paid Levi a visit." She leans forward, places her elbows on her knees. The light in her eyes shifts, goes dark. "From what I understand, there wasn't much talking done that night."

"What happened?"

"Someone beat Levi Schmucker to a pulp. Laid open his head. Broke his arm. Busted his teeth. Heard he spent the night in the hospital up in Lewistown."

A slow boil of disbelief churns in my gut. Of all the things I expected her to say, this isn't it.

The old woman isn't finished. "Levi claimed he fell. But two days later, he quit his job and left town without a word."

"Are you saying Ananias Stoltzfus assaulted him?"

"I'm saying the bishop got his message across. He was just mean enough to get the job done. For once, all that mean was justified." She leans back in the chair. "He carried that big walking stick, you know. Needed it for his rheumatism, or so he said. Maybe he used it for other things, too."

"Is Schmucker still alive?" I ask. "Is he still in the area?"

"Last I heard he was living in a nursing home up in Lock Haven."

"Does he have family?"

"What do you think?"

I ask a few more questions, but Amanda Garber is no longer in the mood to talk. "All this talk of ghosts." She waves me off. "It's exhausted me."

"Thank you for your time." I shake a limp, cool hand and start toward the door.

I'm midway there when a final question occurs to me. "Ms. Garber, did Mia ever talk about her life in Minnesota?"

"Minnesota?" She looks at me as if I'm a conspiracy theorist.

"Mahlon and Laura Barkman told me they were from Minnesota," I tell her.

"Mahlon Barkman is dumber than a bucket of rocks," she huffs. "He couldn't find Minnesota if it was a dot on his ass." She shakes her head, the way a teacher might at a student who'd failed a test he should have aced. "I can't speak for Ananias, but Mia was from Germany. Bavaria, I think it was."

"Germany?" I stare at her, flummoxed, wondering if she's mistaken. I'm no scholar on the Amish or the European history of the Anabaptists, but to the best of my knowledge, there are no Amish left in Europe.

"That's why her *Deitsch* was different," she says.

"Mia mentioned Germany a few times. Asked me not to speak of it. She was homesick. Missed it something fierce. I upheld her wish. Until now, anyway. I reckon she won't mind."

The old woman shrugs. "The stories she told. Seemed like such an exotic place." She sighs, remembering. "Her *datt* owned a bakery, there. That's where she learned to bake. Everyone loved her *Zwetschgenkuchen*. Never could replicate the recipe, but it sure wasn't for lack of trying."

CHAPTER 17

Twenty-one years before

I was in a dark place the afternoon I eschewed my usual worship Sunday singing for some time alone. I'd been in a dark place a lot the summer of my fourteenth year. That morning, I'd suffered through three hours of preaching and another two of yakking adults gorging themselves on date pudding and pie. I was on my way to the Tuscarawas Bridge, where I knew some of the English kids would be hanging out. I hadn't yet crossed the threshold of associating with them, but I was just awkward and angry enough to step over that line, if only to see someone else—namely my parents—as unhappy as me.

I was walking along the shoulder of Dogleg Road, a quiet stretch of barely-there asphalt that cut through corn and soybean fields and crossed over a tributary of Painters Creek. I was lost in the maze of my thoughts when the clip-clop of shod hooves alerted me to the approach of a buggy. I didn't want to see anyone, especially if they were Amish. I sure as hell didn't want to talk to anyone. I kept walking, head down, hoping they didn't stop.

"Where you headed?"

Jonas Bowman pulled up alongside me and slowed his horse to keep pace. He held the leather lines in both hands and leaned forward slightly so that he could see my face. He was smiling. Happy to see me, I realized, and I wondered what it was like to feel something so honest and simple.

I hadn't seen him in a while. I didn't play baseball anymore. He was eighteen now and spent most of his time working at the cabinet shop with his *datt*. I missed him, but it was a small misery compared to everything else. I missed a lot of things, but then that was what life had become for fourteen-year-old me.

"Nowhere," I told him.

"Why didn't you stay for the singing?"

A "singing" was where Amish teens got together, usually after worship, sang the "fast" tunes, and socialized. The girls sat on one side of the table, the boys on the other, and they took turns announcing the songs.

"I've had enough singing for one day," I told him.

We didn't speak for a minute or two, but the buggy kept pace. I didn't make eye contact, but I managed a couple of covert glances. He seemed older. More self-assured. His voice was deeper, too. All of it unsettled me in a way I didn't like or understand.

"Haven't seen you around much," he said.

"I've been busy." It was a lie. I was no busier now than those innocent days when we used to meet at old man Delaney's field and play our hearts out on that baseball diamond.

"Do you want a ride home?" he asked. "I can drive you."

"No." It wasn't true. I wanted to get into that buggy. I wanted to sit next to him and talk about something that wasn't important, but seemed like it. I wanted to laugh the way we used to. I didn't understand why I couldn't do any of those things, and my own foolishness exasperated me because I couldn't seem to be nice to the one person I actually liked.

Abruptly, he sped ahead a few feet and turned the horse, causing me to stop. I set my hand on the horse's neck and looked at Jonas over my shoulder to see him climbing down from the buggy.

"What are you doing?" I asked.

"Getting you to stop and talk to me," he drawled.

I rolled my eyes, looked away. "Maybe I don't have anything to say."

"Now there's a tall tale. Used to be you'd talk my ear off."

The sun beat down. I could feel a trickle of sweat between my shoulder blades. His eyes were shaded by the brim of his hat, but they were dark and watchful. Wondering what was wrong with me?

After a moment, he motioned toward the clouds roiling above the treetops to the west. "You're going to get rained on."

I didn't bother looking. I didn't care one way or another if I got rained on. I didn't even care if I got struck by lightning.

His brows pulled together, like a kid trying to figure out an arithmetic problem. "We're going to play base-ball tomorrow afternoon at the diamond out to old man Delaney's. You want to come?"

My heart quickened at the prospect. It seemed like years since I'd played. Oh, how I missed those days. . . .

"I can't," I told him.

"Why not?"

A dozen phony reasons scrolled through my brain. "I've got to help Mamm."

Puzzlement played at his expression as he reached beneath his hat and scratched his head. He was so much taller than me that I had to look up to meet his gaze. His eyes were dark, so different from my own. Looking at him used to be easy. Now, his gaze was harder. Not un-kind, but somehow more discerning. When he looked at me, it was with the eyes of a man, not the boy he'd been. What did he see when he looked at me?

"You used to be a pretty good hitter," he said easily.

I steeled myself against the rush of pleasure. I *had* been a good hitter. Fast, too. Why couldn't I just say yes and go?

"You still got the baseball I gave you?" he asked.

"I threw it in the trash." That was a lie, too, but I let it stand.

He looked away, rubbed sweat off the back of his neck. "You afraid of getting beat or what?"

The old competitive spirit jumped in my chest. In that moment, I remembered the *tink!* of the ball against the bat. The solid impact running up my arms. The way the ground blurred beneath me when I ran the bases.

The exhilaration of knowing no one could throw far enough or run fast enough to get me out.

"Never had you pegged as a coward, Katie Burkholder." He pointed at me. "I reckon we'll find someone else."

"Baseball's for little kids, anyway."

He stood a couple of feet away, but it might as well have been a mile. He was frowning because I'd insulted him. I couldn't seem to stop. What was wrong with me? Why couldn't I be nice?

"I'll let you get back to your walk." He touched the brim of his hat and turned away.

Feeling like a heel, I watched him walk away, a small part of me hoping he would look back. That he would turn around, beg me to play, and this time I would agree. Of course, he didn't, and I could feel something unwieldy build in my chest. Something I didn't understand and didn't want to unleash. I stood there, unmoving, watched him put his foot on the buggy step to climb inside.

"I might be able to make it," I blurted.

"Don't put yourself out," he said without looking at me. "You weren't that good, anyway."

I felt the insult like a knife sinking into my back and going deep. Tears burned my eyes, but I willed them away. Chest tight, hands clenched, I crossed to him.

"I said I'd play," I snapped.

I expected him to laugh, the way he used to. But when he turned, he looked at me the way he'd looked at those English boys the day they'd stolen our baseball diamond. With dislike. Disapproval. Worst of all, he looked at me as if I were a stranger. The pain was so intense I couldn't catch my breath.

A hundred words bombarded my brain. *I'm sorry. I want to play. I don't know what's wrong with me. I want everything to be like it was before Daniel Lapp ruined my life.*

I don't remember crossing to him. The world around me blurred. I couldn't feel my feet or hear the crunch of gravel beneath my shoes. The sun faded to gray. The next thing I knew my arms were around his neck. Somewhere in the backwaters of my mind, I heard someone crying. Shock rattled me when I realized the sobs were coming from me.

Vaguely, I was aware of Jonas stumbling backward. His hands flying up as if to shield himself. His back hit the side of the buggy, ending his retreat. I bumped against him and the contact was electric. He said something, but I didn't hear the words. I was crying openly now. Pain pouring out.

"You're not making any sense," he said.

I didn't know the first thing about kissing, but I set my mouth against his. My forehead bumped the brim of his hat and knocked it to the ground. He didn't seem to notice. For a second, I thought he would push me away. I wished he would because I knew I shouldn't be doing what I was doing.

He didn't push me away. Instead, his arms went around my shoulders. He tilted his head and kissed me back. Tentatively at first and then harder, so much that his teeth clicked against mine. I felt as if I'd jumped off a cliff and tumbled into a free fall.

"Katie."

I heard my name as if from a great distance. I didn't stop. The pain had ebbed and this was the cure. Then I felt his hands on my biceps. He shoved me to arm's length, gave me a little shake.

I opened my eyes to see Jonas staring at me, breathing as if he'd just run a mile, nostrils flaring, forehead dotted with sweat.

"What are you doing?" He released me as if my skin burned his palms.

The pain rushed back with such ferocity that a sob caught in my throat. I didn't let it out. Feeling ugly and awkward and embarrassed, I stepped back, looked down at the ground.

"You don't even know how to kiss," I managed.

For the span of several heartbeats, he didn't move. I could hear my breaths hissing. My heart beating out of control. Tears heating the backs of my eyes. *Don't cry. Don't cry.*

In the periphery of my vision, I saw him bend to retrieve his hat. Without speaking, he slapped it atop his head, climbed into the buggy, and left without a word.

CHAPTER 18

The memory of that long-ago day weighs bitter and sweet in the periphery of my thoughts as I roll up to the Bowman home. I was the girl I didn't want to be that summer. Awkward and hurting and misunderstood. Damaged beyond repair—or so I thought. I was a stranger I didn't know or trust—or even like. Only later did I realize my acting out was nothing more than an all-too-human reaction to pain. To the violence that had been perpetrated on my soul by Daniel Lapp. It took a long time for me to forgive myself for some of the things I did that summer. For what I did to Jonas.

I sit in the rental car and watch Jonas, Reuben, and Junior load cabinets into a truck emblazoned with the logo of a local construction company. The boys and their father work in tandem, knowing exactly what to do and how to do it. Choreography. As the truck pulls away, I get out and walk to the workshop.

I hear the generator rumbling at the side of the building, the whine of a saw as I go through the door. I find Jonas standing at the table saw, feeding a board to the blade. Junior stands next to him, watching with rapt attention while his father makes the cut. Beyond, Reuben is bent over a workbench, sliding two intricately dovetailed pieces of wood together. Effie is busy with a push broom, a big pile of sawdust on the floor next to an industrial-size dustpan.

"Looks like you got those cabinets finished on time," I say by way of greeting.

All eyes turn to me. Jonas pauses the cut, looks at me over his shoulder. I see the quick jump of pleasure in his eyes. "Katie."

Junior's face splits into a grin. "Mr. Gleason g-gave us a hundred-dollar b-bonus!"

"I'm not surprised," I tell him. "Those were some nice-looking cabinets and you were one man short."

Too shy to accept praise, the boy looks down at the length of wood in front of him and runs a chubby hand over the surface.

"They're for a big house up in Harrisburg," Reuben announces.

"A f-fancy mansion," Junior puts in. "Mamm let us stay up late so we could finish and then Datt came home this morning and we worked all day."

Jonas finishes the cut, then straightens and starts toward me. His eyes flit to the marks on my throat, but he doesn't mention them.

"You made bail," I say.

"All fifty thousand dollars of it." He looks away, but

not before I see the flash of shame in his eyes. "The Amish pulled together. Everyone put in what they could."

"They'll get it back," I tell him.

"I know, but . . ." He lets the sentence trail as if not quite sure how to finish.

"Have you had supper, Katie?" asks Effie.

"As a matter of fact, I haven't."

"Mamm made chicken and noodles with mashed potatoes," Junior proclaims. "It's my favorite."

"Everything's your favorite." Jonas brushes sawdust from his son's shoulder.

The boy ducks his head.

"Will you eat with us?" Effie asks.

"Wouldn't miss it," I tell her.

Jonas brings his hands together. "Kids, go wash your hands. Tell your *mamm* to set another plate."

Supper at an Amish home is a utilitarian affair that's looked forward to with a great anticipation, especially after a long day of physical labor. It's the time for a hearty meal and a bit of conversation—usually regarding work that needs to be done and who will be doing it. Suppertime symbolizes the importance of family and everyone's place in it. This afternoon, I'm part of the tradition, and despite my effort to maintain a prudent emotional distance, a sense of nostalgia moves me.

At the counter, Dorothy pulverizes boiled potatoes with a hand masher, putting enough muscle into it that her forehead is damp with sweat. Effie stirs noodles in a steaming Dutch oven on the stove. As a female guest, I'm relegated to setting out plates, flatware, along with glasses of tap water for the adults and milk for the kids. As we work, a breeze eases in through the window above the sink, cooling an otherwise hot kitchen. With the backdrop of clanging dishes, and Dorothy and Effie deliberating the prospect of a baby quilt for a neighbor, I'm swept back to a simpler time, and I find myself missing my own family.

"Katie?"

I glance over to see Effie pull out a chair. "You can sit here next to Mamm."

I set the final glass of water on the table and take my seat. Jonas sits at the head of the table with Junior and Reuben to his left. Dorothy sets a steaming bowl of chicken and noodles on a hot pad in the center and slides into the chair to his right, next to me. Once everyone is seated, heads are bowed. As is the case with the majority of Amish families, the prayer before meal is silent and heartfelt.

Everyone serves themselves and plates are heaped with mashed potatoes, chicken and noodles, and green beans. There's rustic-looking bread that's a little too brown. Homemade butter in a bowl and apple butter on the side. For several minutes, the only sound comes from the scraping of forks and spoons against plates.

Throughout the meal Junior entertains us with stories from the woodshop. His first half-blind dovetail. The can of stain he spilled on a table they'd just finished, and the client who thought it was the prettiest piece of walnut he'd ever seen. He talks animatedly about the accident six months ago that severed the tip of Reuben's pinky finger.

"Show her!" the boy exclaims.

I can tell by Reuben's expression he's no fan of being the center of attention, but the opportunity to show off a wounded-in-action scar is too good to pass up. Chewing, he holds out his hand. Sure enough, the tip of his left pinky finger and nail are missing.

"The bone was sticking out," Junior says breathlessly. "The doctor in town told us to find the missing finger and put ice on it and bring it to the hospital."

"We looked everywhere," Effie adds. "We couldn't find it."

"We think the cat ate it!" Junior cries.

Jonas clears his throat to hide his laugh. I take a sip of water to stanch my own chuckle.

Dorothy isn't amused. "Oh, for goodness' sake, Katie doesn't want to hear those kinds of stories while she's eating. Missing fingers and flesh-eating cats."

But she's laughing, too, and soon all of us are laughing so hard we've got tears streaming from our eyes.

I've much to discuss with Jonas about the investigation, about the case against him. I want to ask him about the bones found in the water well. About Amanda Garber and Mia Stoltzfus. Levi Schmucker. Most of what we need to discuss isn't for young ears, so I keep my impatience at bay.

When the children are finished and leave, I help Dorothy with the dishes, and while she makes coffee, I sit down across from Jonas.

"I couldn't help but notice those marks on your neck," he says slowly. "What happened?"

Dorothy turns and looks at me from her place at the sink, her expression telling me she'd noticed them, too.

"Someone ambushed me at the motel last night," I tell them. "They busted out the windshield on the Explorer and slashed the tires."

The Amish woman gasps. "What? Oh, no. Katie."

Jonas tightens his mouth. "Did the police arrest him?"

"He got away," I tell him.

His eyes sharpen on mine. "Do you know who it was?"

"It happened too fast. It was dark. All I know is it was a male." I meet his gaze, taking in the concern, looking for something else, anything askew, not finding it. "He suggested I leave town."

Jonas makes a sound of disgust. "The elders shouldn't have asked you to come here."

Dorothy sets cups of coffee in front of us and then takes the chair next to her husband. "You think it has something to do with your asking questions about Ananias Stoltzfus?"

"I think someone's afraid I'm going to uncover something they prefer to keep buried."

Dorothy looks from her husband to me as if she isn't sure if that's good or bad.

"You have to stop." Jonas grimaces. "It's too dangerous."

Dorothy pats her husband's hand. "He's right. Maybe we ought to rethink all of this and try to come up with another way."

"All it means is that I'm on the right track." The couple exchange a grave look, so I add, "In case you've forgotten, I'm a cop. I know how to handle myself. I'm armed. If it happens again, I'll be ready."

When neither of them responds, I pick up my cup and sip. "What I'm about to tell you isn't public knowledge, so I'm going to ask you to keep it to yourselves. Will you do that?"

"Of course," Jonas replies.

Dorothy nods.

I tell them about the human hand bones found in the well. "The police sent the remains to the lab for DNA analysis, but they believe they belong to Ananias Stoltzfus."

"*Mein Gott.*" Dorothy presses her hand against her breast. "Reuben was right."

Jonas's brows knit. "But the bishop's body was found in the field. How could his hands end up here?"

I lay out the most likely theory for the removal of the hands. The couple don't press, but even they know the explanation doesn't quite fit.

"How long have the bones been in the well?" Jonas asks.

"I don't know." But it begs even more questions. Did the killer remove the hands at the time of the murder and throw them into the well? Or did he, realizing he could frame Jonas for the crime, return to where he'd buried the body at a later date, remove the hands or bones, and throw them into the well?

"Whoever put them there wants the police to believe I killed Ananias," Jonas says.

I divide my attention between them. "Who knows about the well?"

"That area is overgrown with brush and trees, but not hidden." He considers a moment and shrugs. "Anyone who's been on the property."

"Have you had any trespassers?" I ask. "Have you seen anyone near the well? Recently or years past?"

Jonas shakes his head. "No."

I tell them about the anonymous tip. "Someone knew those bones were there and called the police."

"The person who did it," Jonas says.

"Or an accomplice," I add.

Dorothy looks down at the barely touched coffee in front of her and shakes her head. "Whoever did this is an evil person," she whispers. "I'm afraid for Jonas." She raises her eyes to me. "You, too, Katie."

"My best advice is to stay alert," I tell them. "Keep the doors locked. I know it's against the rules, but I'm going to bring a cell phone. That way, if there's an emergency, you'll have it."

"We don't need a—" Jonas begins.

I cut him off. "Put it in the kitchen drawer and forget it's there. Unless you need it."

It's clear the offer does nothing but frighten her even more.

For a moment, the only sound comes from the hiss of the gas lamp overhead and the steady drip of a leaky faucet in the sink. "Did either of you know Mia Stoltzfus?" I ask.

"Met her a few times," Jonas tells me. "Years ago."

"At worship." Dorothy's expression turns solemn. "Word has it the burden of being the bishop's wife was too much for her."

"Do you have any idea why she committed suicide in a Lutheran church?" I ask.

The couple exchange a grim look. "No one could ever figure that," Jonas tells me.

"Do you know anything about their pasts?" I ask. "Where they came from?"

"All I know is they were from Minnesota." Jonas looks at his wife. "Came here before we were born."

I think of my conversation with Laura and Mahlon Barkman, who told me they were from Minnesota, and Amanda Garber, who believed Mia was from Germany.

"Is there anyone around who was close to Mia or Ananias?" I ask. "A friend or family member who knew them? Or spent time with them?"

The two exchange thoughtful looks and then Jonas shakes his head. "Just his two grown children," he tells me. "Most of the folks who knew them are gone now."

He went over to Lewistown every so often. Had himself a loose girl there.

Amanda Garber's voice replays in my mind. "Did you ever hear any rumors about Ananias and any sort of impropriety?" I ask.

Dorothy drops her gaze to the tabletop, deferring to her husband.

Jonas looks away.

I wait, but he doesn't answer. A lot of the Amish are reluctant to speak ill of their brethren. Usually, I don't push. Tonight, knowing what's at stake, aware of the ache of bruises at my throat, I make an exception.

"Jonas, you're facing some very serious charges," I

remind him. "Whatever you do, don't hold out on me. Do you understand?"

He raises his gaze to mine. "He was our bishop, Katie. As much as I disagreed with him . . . as angry as I was with him for silencing my *datt* . . . I never heard of any improper behavior."

Dorothy pats her husband's shoulder and rises. "All of this talk of death and bones and cut-off hands." She shudders. "It's too troubling. I'm going to bed." She offers me a kind look. "I'll pray extra hard for you, Katie."

And she leaves the room.

It's after nine P.M. now and the house is quiet. Jonas and I sip coffee, lost in our troubled thoughts.

"You have a nice family," I tell him.

"I'm blessed." He offers a self-deprecating smile. "Don't know what I did to deserve them."

He holds my gaze. In the depths of his eyes, I see remembrance, a stir of the past we share. Tattered and faded, but not forgotten.

"Why didn't you tell me about the threatening letter you sent Ananias Stoltzfus?" I ask.

"It was a long time ago."

"How long?"

"Years." He shrugs. "I didn't know it was important."

"You mean while you were sitting in jail, charged with his murder?" I shake my head in exasperation. "You threatened him days before he went missing. You've been formally charged. What am I supposed to think?"

"Someone has the letter?" he asks. "After all these years?"

I tell him about my meeting with Henry Stoltzfus. "I haven't seen it, but he assured me his sister kept a copy." I consider the repercussions of such a letter and wonder if Mary Elizabeth gave it to the police. "Do you remember what it said?"

"I don't recall my exact words," he says. "I sent the letter to remind him that God would judge him harshly when his time came. Something like that."

"If the police have the letter, the prosecutor will probably use it against you."

"I don't know anything about the police or what they might do. But I *do* know the Bible and I can tell you the English police will not be the ones to judge or mete out punishment. Only God."

"The police won't be taking the Bible into consideration," I say dryly.

Scowling, he rises and goes to the cupboard, removes a corked bottle from an upper shelf.

"Is there anything else you haven't told me?" I ask.

"Probably." He returns to the table. Seeing my frown, he softens. "I've told you everything."

He sets the bottle on the table between us.

"What is that?" I ask.

"I think you *Englischers* refer to it as salvation."

"Booze?"

He pulls two mismatched glasses from the cabinet and returns to the table, sets one of them in front of me. "Dandelion wine."

"You're not breaking any rules on my account, are you?" I ask.

"The *Diener* have no problem with drinking homemade wine," he tells me. "It's from the land. Made by our own hand. As long as there's no drunkenness."

"In that case." I do the honors of uncorking and pouring. "If you get caught, you can always blame it on me."

Nodding, he raises his glass. "To old friendships."

"And finding the truth."

We clink our glasses together and drink.

It isn't the first time I've sampled Amish wine. It isn't the first time Jonas and I have drunk it together. This particular vintage isn't very good. Too sweet, with a grassy flavor and an unpleasant tang that stings the tongue and lingers.

Jonas shudders. "Never liked it much."

"It'll do in a pinch."

The silence that follows isn't quite comfortable, but I let it ride. I sip the wine and listen to the cry of a barred owl through the window. I try to stay focused on the topic at hand—the mystery surrounding the death of Ananias Stoltzfus. Despite my efforts, the history we share looms large.

"Amanda Garber told me Mia Stoltzfus was from Germany," I say after a moment.

"Never heard such a thing." Jonas's brows knit. "Mia *did* talk funny. Had that strange accent when she spoke *Deitsch*."

"What about Ananias?"

"Now that you mention it, the bishop had a unique way of speaking, too. Especially *Deitsch*. Course he was from up north." He swirls the wine, looks at me over the rim. "Do you think that means something?"

"I'm not sure, but it's come up a time or two. Might be worth a closer look."

I finish my wine and pour another couple of fingers into the glass. I tip the bottle toward Jonas's glass, but he shakes his head.

"Do you have a theory about what happened to him?" I ask.

He knocks back the remainder of his wine and then leans back in the chair, considering. "I had a lot of time to think about it while I was locked up, and I still can't figure it. Thing is, most of the Amish here in the valley are of the mind that Ananias was a *good* bishop. Yeah, he was strict. And there were a few of us who thought he enforced the rules with a heavy hand. But we were a minority. I can't see someone killing him for it."

"Did Ananias have much interaction with the English?" I ask.

"No more than the rest of us. We do plenty of business with the English. We visit with our English neighbors. We help them when they need it. You know how it is. We're separate, only we're not."

"I talked to the pastor at the church where Mia Stoltzfus committed suicide," I tell him. "He told me she asked for confession and absolution."

"That doesn't seem like something an Amish person would do." His eyes narrow on mine. "Do you think what happened to Mia, what she did, has something to do with the murder of Ananias?"

"I think it raises a few questions." I consider that a moment. "Did Mia Stoltzfus have any enemies? Any problems with anyone? Amish or English?"

"Not that I know of, but she was older than me. Seemed nice enough. Katie, I didn't really know her at all."

We fall silent again. This time, the silence is laced with the weight of our thoughts as they relate to the investigation. The puzzle of it. The unanswered questions. The ugliness of the end result.

"It seems like no one knows anything," Jonas says.

"A lot of investigations are that way at first," I tell him.

He offers a wry smile. "Are you telling me not to be discouraged?"

"I'm telling you we're just getting started."

He nods. "So what's next?"

"I'll keep poking around. Asking questions. Push if I have to."

"You were always good at pushing, no?"

I nod. "Sooner or later, something will give. It always does."

I finish my wine. I want more, but I don't reach for the bottle. I try to focus on the business at hand, but once again the past hovers.

"You don't wear a ring." Jonas motions toward my ring finger. "Do you have someone at home? A husband who's there alone and missing you?"

"I have someone at home," I tell him.

"You are married?"

I want to believe these are questions between old friends catching up on all the life events that have happened in the years since we last spoke. But it's too intimate, and I feel the creep of unease at the back of my neck. Maybe because Jonas and I were a lot closer than friends and I don't want that to get in the way of the investigation.

"Not yet," I tell him.

"Children?"

"We're thinking about it," I say simply.

If he's aware of my discomfort, he doesn't let on. "You seem happy."

"I am."

"And yet here you are. You've put your life on hold to come here and help me," he says. "When I'm little more than a stranger to you."

"We spent some of our formative years together."

"Played a lot of baseball."

Old man Delaney's field flashes in my mind's eye and I smile. Too late, I realize I've opened a door I would rather have remained closed. "Besides," I tell him. "I'm a cop and formerly Amish." I shrug. "That makes me qualified."

"I think there's a saying among the English," Jonas says after a moment. "Something about the elephant in the room."

I smile, but don't meet his gaze. I know if I do, he'll see my discomfort. He'll wonder about its source, same as me.

"Sometimes it's good to get things out in the open," he says. "Clear the air."

"Whatever happened between us was a long time ago, Jonas. We were kids."

"But that's why you're here, no?"

"I'm here to help you." I force my gaze to his, hold

it. "I think it's best if we concentrate on that and not dredge up ancient history. It'll just muddle things up."

He leans back in his chair and nods. "All right."

Needing a moment, I rise and take our glasses to the sink. As I wash and rinse them, I relay Amanda Garber's story about Ananias's middle-of-the-night visit to Levi Schmucker.

"I knew Ananias was a hard man . . . but that?" Jonas shakes his head in disbelief. "Katie, the bishop striking a man with a cane? Beating him with enough force to break a bone? It's almost too crazy to believe."

"I'm going to find Schmucker." Back on track. Safe ground. The past tucked back into its corner where it belongs. "If that actually happened, we'll know something important about Ananias we didn't know before."

"That he was a violent man?"

"If that's the case, I have to wonder if that behavior was a pattern. Did he dole out similarly harsh punishments to others? Did someone he hurt hold a grudge? Did someone decide they didn't have to take it? Stop it?"

"Katie, do you want me to—"

"I want you to keep a low profile," I tell him. "Stay here with your wife and kids. Let me do my job."

Frowning, he crosses his arms over his chest. "You were always full of vinegar. Too much in the eyes of some. Too much fight even when you were outnumbered. Some things don't change, eh?"

"You should know, Jonas. You were the one who stood up for me when no one else would."

He looks away, but not before I see the memory etched into his features, the raw affection for me, the same discomfort I felt earlier.

Moved more than I should be, I reach into my pocket for my keys. "Just FYI? I'm still a sore loser, too," I tell him, and start for the door.

CHAPTER 19

A cop never knows when a seemingly mundane parcel of information will turn out to be important. Chances are the rumor about Ananias Stoltzfus taking a cane to Levi Schmucker is just that: a rumor that's grown with time and been embellished upon over the years. An Amish bishop would never resort to violence to discipline a member of the church district. The Amish are pacifistic; submission and nonviolence are key tenets. The Amish will not defend themselves even if they are physically assaulted. Nor will they protect their property. During times of war, they are conscientious objectors.

In light of the myriad anomalies surrounding Ananias and Mia Stoltzfus, the allegation merits follow-up. The Amish are human, after all. We human beings are fallible, vulnerable to our imperfections, weaknesses, and emotions. That includes even the most ardent believers.

After leaving the Bowman place last night, I went back to the motel and spent a couple of hours with my laptop. I located Levi Schmucker at the Mennonite Faith Home for the Elderly in Lock Haven, which is about an hour northeast of Belleville. I should have slept well, but after the incident the previous night—and despite being in a different room with a functioning lock and security chain—I couldn't sleep. I ended up propping a chair against the door and kept my .38 unholstered, my .22 mini Magnum in easy reach. This morning, I'm running on coffee.

Faith Home for the Elderly is located on the west side of town just south of the university. It's a three-story, midcentury-modern-style building with mullioned windows and mud-colored brick. The grounds and landscaping are well tended. As I walk inside, I pass a bench where an elderly woman carries on a lively conversation with herself.

The interior falls somewhere between a public school and hospital. A brightly lit nurses' station and set of elevators face the entrance. Beyond, two long corridors lined with doors sweep toward the rear. I head toward the nurses' station, where a middle-aged woman in pink scrubs finger-pecks a keyboard.

"I'm looking for Levi Schmucker," I tell her.

She hits a final key and turns a smile on me. "Are you family?"

I'm not sure what the guidelines are with regard to visitation. Hoping there won't be a problem, I remove my driver's license and shield and lay both on the counter. "I'm visiting from Ohio and working on a case in Belleville," I tell her.

"Oh." She seems intrigued. "We don't get many police officers visiting our residents."

"I won't take up too much of his time," I say, keeping it vague and light. "I just need to ask him a few quick questions."

"Mr. Schmucker is in his room this morning." She squints at her computer screen, clicks the mouse. "I'll ask one of the NAs to take you in." She gestures toward a sitting area. "Someone will be with you shortly."

They don't keep me waiting. I've just checked in with my dispatcher when an African American man in blue scrubs calls my name. The badge clipped to his shirt tells me he's a nursing assistant and his name is Brent.

"You're here to see Mr. Schmucker?" he asks.

"Yes."

"You're in luck. He just finished with his PT and had breakfast." He gestures toward one of the corridors. "I'll take you."

According to the information I found online, Levi Schmucker was born in 1938, which would make him eighty-four years old. As we walk along the tiled hall, its walls affixed with chrome handrails, we pass half a dozen rooms, the occasional wheelchair, and I find myself hoping his memory is still intact.

"Here we are." The nursing assistant pushes open one of the doors and gestures me inside. "Good morning, Mr. Schmucker!" he says cheerily. "You've got a visitor."

I walk into a hospital-like room that smells of disinfectant, menthol analgesic, and urine. Two twin-size beds with safety rails and dual wheeled dinner trays take up most of the space. In the corner, an orange Naugahyde recliner squats next to a laminate coffee table and lamp. Someone tried to make the room feel cozy but didn't quite manage.

My heart sinks at the sight of the man sitting in the wheelchair next to the window. He's neatly dressed in navy trousers, a blue shirt, and stocking feet. The sunshine streaming in reveals a bald scalp mottled with age spots, a yellowed beard that hangs off his chin like a sock, and talonlike hands that rest on a towel in his lap.

Eyes set into a face that's creased like saddle leather take my measure. "Who is it?" the old man grumbles.

"Kate Burkholder," I tell him.

"Don't know no one by that name."

The nursing assistant touches my arm. "I've got to get back to work. If you need anything, just ask whoever's at the nurses' station."

I thank him and then he's gone.

The old man stares at me. "Who are you?"

I tell him. "I'm working on a case, Mr. Schmucker. I'd like to ask you a few questions about Ananias Stoltzfus."

The flash of shock on his face tells me his memory is intact. "Ananias Stoltzfus?" He whispers the name with trepidation, his eyes flicking to the door as if he's expecting the man to burst into the room and accost him. "He's *here*?"

"He's not here," I assure him. "Just me. I need a little information from you."

The old man's mouth opens, his lips quivering. "I don't want to talk to him. He's not welcome here."

I can't tell if he's hard of hearing or if his memory

is muddled. I press forward. "I understand you and Bishop Stoltzfus had a disagreement. There was an incident between you. Can you tell me what happened?"

"He's not my bishop. I ain't Amish no more. Washed my hands of it." The old man angles his head, his eyes seeking the call button, but it's too far away for him to reach.

Sensing that I'm not getting through—that I'm about to lose him—I switch to *Deitsch*. "Can you tell me what happened when Ananias Stoltzfus came to your house to talk to you about your daughter?"

Schmucker opens his mouth, his lips slick with saliva. "*See leekt.*" She lied.

"You're not in any trouble," I assure him. "I just want to know what happened between you and the bishop."

"I didn't do it. I didn't do anything."

. . . *Word got around that Levi was acting improper with his oldest girl.*

Looking at the old man, I bank a hard rise of disgust, and I have to remind myself the story could be gossip. I'm here about Stoltzfus, not to revisit an event that may or may not have taken place.

"The bishop came to you . . ." I let the sentence trail, hoping he'll fill in the blanks.

"Her *mamm* lied. *Lied.* The bishop came. Brought that big cane with him."

"What did he do?" I ask.

The old man stares at me, his face contorted as if he's watching some horror unfold right before his eyes, and he knows the monster is coming for him.

"I didn't do the things she said," he tells me.

"What did the bishop do to you?"

"He didn't believe me."

I'm aware of the old man's hands shaking on the towel in his lap. His left foot starting to jiggle. "Tell me what he did."

"He took me out to the barn. So we could talk man-to-man, he said. When we was alone, he . . . came after me. With that cane. Beat me with it. Busted my teeth." He looks down, lifts his right hand. "Broke my arm. Laid open my head. That old man beat me silly for something I didn't do."

"Did he say anything?"

"He told me to pack a bag and leave. Said if I came back, he'd kill me." His lips tremble. "I believed him."

I stare hard at him. "Did you ever go back to Belleville?"

"No! I swear! I didn't go back!"

"When's the last time you were there?"

"That night."

"Did the bishop hurt anyone else that you know of?" I ask.

The old man doesn't answer. His eyes drift to the window, and he stares at something unseen.

"Mr. Schmucker, did you go to the police?" I ask.

No response.

"Did you tell anyone what happened? Your wife? A friend? Anyone?"

He looks at me, but his eyes are blank, his mind seeming to disconnect. It's as if he doesn't hear me.

"Were there any witnesses?" I ask. "Did anyone see what happened?"

Nothing.

I spend a few more minutes posing the same questions in different ways, but Levi Schmucker doesn't respond. The old man sags in his chair, his chin against his chest, hands quavering, and ignores me. It's as if recalling his experience with Ananias Stoltzfus exhausted him.

I'm back on the road in less than an hour and on my way to Belleville. My conversation with Schmucker replays in my head and I pick apart the exchange word by word. The idea of a bishop beating a member of the congregation is so outrageous I can't even get my head around it. No bishop would resort to violence. Ever. The notion of the Amish meting out street justice is a Hollywood fable. Even if the story of the beating is true, is it related in any way to the murder of Ananias Stoltzfus?

If Schmucker was telling the truth I have to wonder: Did Ananias mistreat any other members of the congregation? Did one of them reach a breaking point? Did they snap, go to the bishop's home or lure him to the woods, and shoot him to death? Or am I wrong about all of this and his murder is about something else I'm not seeing?

I'm so preoccupied, I barely notice the verdant hills to the north or the postcard-perfect valley laid out before me. I find myself thinking about anomalies and it occurs to me almost all of them revolve around not only Ananias Stoltzfus, but his wife, Mia, too.

Said he was from Minnesota, but I have a cousin lives up there and they don't talk that way.

I can't speak for Ananias, but Mia was from Germany.

. . . Lutherans practice confession . . . We put much emphasis on the holy absolution.

Midway between Lock Haven and Belleville, I pull over at a scenic overlook, google Harmony, Minnesota, and learn it's located in Fillmore County. I locate the county assessor's office and make the call. I'm transferred a couple of times and end up speaking to a clerk who, after some back-and-forth and a lot of key tapping, informs me that neither Ananias nor Mia Stoltzfus owned property at any time in Fillmore County.

"Are you sure?" I ask, but the woman has already ended the call.

I puzzle over the information, wondering if the property was in the name of another family member. It would be unusual for an established Amish couple to rent. Or maybe they lived in a neighboring county or the clerk wasn't thorough and overlooked the information.

Next, I call the Fillmore County Sheriff's Office. I reach an investigator with the Criminal Investigations Division, but she tells me my request will be handled more expeditiously if I talk to someone in Patrol. I'm transferred to Deputy Lina Leonard. I identify myself and after some polite chitchat, I get to the point.

"I'm working on a cold case and looking into the background of the victim," I tell her.

"Happy to help, Chief Burkholder."

She sounds young. Judging by the background noise, she's in her cruiser, on patrol. I give her the fundamentals of the case. "Stoltzfus claimed he and his wife, Mia, were from Harmony. I need to speak with anyone in the Amish community who can confirm that."

"Not to throw a monkey wrench at you, Chief, but most of the Amish up here don't use phones, so it's not like I can call someone."

"I was hoping a deputy could get a message to the bishop or deacon or one of the ministers and have one of them call me back on one of their pay phones if they have them."

"I'm your man. And they do." She laughs. "I patrol the area that's mostly Amish. I've gotten to know a few of them."

"Do you know who the bishop is?"

"I think that's Elmer Hostetler. I've met him a couple times over the years. He's one of the elders."

I pause, thinking. "Do you happen to know how old he is?" I ask. "Stoltzfus would have lived in Harmony in the early to mid-sixties. It would be beneficial for me to speak to someone who was around at that time."

"Not sure. He's gray-haired. Maybe seventy or so?"

"He'll probably do."

"Okay, Chief, I'll ask around and get back to you. How soon do you need this information?"

Now it's my turn to laugh. "Yesterday?"

"Gotcha. Give me a couple days. I'll see what I can do."

CHAPTER 20

Every murder victim has a story to tell. Any cop worth his salt knows that finding that story and understanding it is central to solving his case. Some stories are easy to unravel; the victim *wants* to tell you what happened and leaves traces of his life behind. Others are a labyrinth of secrets tucked into dark places and not easily revealed. Ananias Stoltzfus falls into the latter category. That's unusual, because an Amish bishop is not some shady individual who's been engaging in unsavory activities.

What is his story? Why can't I seem to unravel it?

A victim should never be blamed for their demise. When it comes to murder, there's one individual responsible: the killer. Even so, victims can unwittingly play a role. They put themselves at the wrong place at the wrong time. They associate with dangerous or unstable individuals. They partake in risky behavior. They use poor judgment. Or any combination of the above.

Initially, I believed Ananias Stoltzfus was a kindly old man. An Amish bishop who, in the eyes of a few, was too strict. The more I learn about him, the more I've come to believe he was not benevolent. The bishop was judgmental, vindictive, and possibly violent.

It's afternoon when I pull in to the gravel lane of the Hershberger farm. I'm not quite sure how to approach Mary Elizabeth; I spent most of the drive trying to come up with some angle that will compel her to open up to me about her parents. The truth of the matter is she's not going to like the questions I want answered.

I park in the gravel near the picket fence and go through the gate. I've just knocked on the door when it swings open.

Mary Elizabeth Hershberger isn't happy to see me standing on her front porch. She's too well-mannered to say it, but I see the displeasure in her eyes. "Thought that was you."

"I may have some new information about your father. Your *mamm,* too. If you have a few minutes, I'd like to ask you some questions. It won't take too long."

I hear dishes clanging in the kitchen behind her. The Amish woman looks like she's thinking about slamming the door in my face. Instead, she nods and steps onto the porch.

"It's not often that husband of mine offers to help with the dishes, so this is probably a good time." She gives me a tired smile. "Let's just keep this short."

She brushes past. I follow her down the steps and along a narrow flagstone path where a bed of purple phlox blooms wildly. She stops and turns to me. "What is it you think you know about my parents?"

"I didn't realize your *mamm* was from Germany," I say.

"Germany?" She laughs. "Where'd you get that nonsense?"

"I spoke to your *mamm*'s best friend. Amanda Garber."

She gives me a knowing look, crosses her arms over her bosom. "There's a piece of work for you. She's *narrisch,* you know." Insane. "Mamm and Datt were from Minnesota," she tells me.

"Are you sure?" I ask. "I was told she was born in Bavaria—"

"Of course I'm sure. Why on earth would my parents lie about where they're from?"

"Amanda seemed to think your *mamm* was troubled by something that had happened in the past."

"My *mamm* was just fine. She was happy with her life. Her family. And her husband."

"Mary Elizabeth." I say her name gently. "I talked to Pastor Zimmerman at the Lutheran church."

Her gaze snaps to mine, her eyes narrowing. "Well, now, it looks like you found yourself some juicy gossip, doesn't it? But then that's what your kind does. Dig up all that dirty laundry. Make up lies. Start rumors."

"I'm trying to find out what happened to your father."

"I know what you're trying to do," she hisses. "You're trying to get Jonas Bowman off the hook for what he did."

"Mia ended her life in a Lutheran church, Mary Elizabeth. She asked the pastor for absolution. I don't believe an Amish woman would do either of those things."

"Are you saying she wasn't *Amisch*?" She chokes out a sound that's part laugh, part outrage. "My *mamm* had the melancholy, is all. Like her *grohs-mammi* before her. That's all it was and now you're trying to twist it around. I won't have it. My parents were good, decent Amish folk. I won't have you trying to ruin their good name for that no-gooder of yours."

"Don't you want to know what happened?" I ask.

Anger flashes in her eyes. I see her mouth working, as if she's chewing something that's stuck in her teeth. "I know what happened. My father was shot to death by an evil person. A criminal." She says the words brutally, her voice shuddering with the final word. "It was awful. And here you are, trying to blame it on him. On my *mamm* of all people. Anyone except the person who did it."

"Pastor Zimmerman said your *mamm* had a diary with her the day she died. Do you have any idea what happened to it?"

"Mamm didn't keep a diary. If she did, I didn't know about it."

I nod, not sure I believe her, press on. "Do you know a man by the name of Levi Schmucker?"

"Never heard of him."

"What about the letter Jonas wrote to your father?"

"You talked to my brother."

"Do you still have it?"

"I gave it to the police years ago." An odd light enters her eyes. "Got a copy, though. You sure you want to see it, Chief Burkholder? Might tear down that goody-goody image of Jonas Bowman you got stuck in your head."

I get a bad feeling in my gut. "I'd like to see it."

Turning away, she walks to the house and disappears inside. I stand beneath the shade of the elm, taking in the beauty of the phlox, but not really seeing it. Mainly, I'm hoping whatever's in the letter isn't too damning.

The screen door slams. I look up to see Mary Elizabeth trot down the steps. Her feet are heavy on the ground as she crosses to me.

"This might set you on the right track." She shoves a single sheet of paper into my hands.

I slip on my reading glasses, recognize Jonas's handwriting immediately, and I read.

We have the Ordnung to guide us. If somebody doesn't obey the rules, they are punished. As bishop, you have the right to punish your church people when they've strayed. What should happen to you when it is you who wrongs us? Be assured, an evil person will not go unpunished. Whoever sheds the blood of man, by man shall his blood be shed. Your day of judgment is near. When you are gone I will pray for your soul.

I look up at Mary Elizabeth. "Where did you get this?"

"It was in my *datt*'s desk. I found it a few days after he disappeared."

I read the letter again, feel the press of dread on my shoulders. The letter itself isn't incriminatory. Combined with the other evidence against Jonas, there's no doubt it could be used against him.

Sunshine filters through the treetops when I pull into the Bowman driveway. I park at the rear to see that the buggy is gone. I go to the back door to leave a note and the door swings open.

"You look like you've had a hard day," Jonas says.

"That's one way to put it," I tell him. "You got a few minutes?"

"Sure." He opens the door wider for me to enter. "Dorothy went into town for groceries. Took the kids." He steps back. "Come in."

I follow him through the mudroom to the kitchen. He motions me into a chair and then goes to the refrigerator and pulls out a pitcher. "She made mint tea before she left. Want some?"

It's a uniquely Amish tea; the memory makes me smile. "I'd love some."

He pours it into glasses, sets one in front of me, then takes the chair across from me. "I'm afraid to ask if you have news," he says. "Your expression is grim."

"I saw the letter you sent Stoltzfus."

He nods. "I barely remember it."

"It's damning." I relay the contents to the best of my memory. "The police have it. The prosecutor will probably use it against you."

"I have the truth on my side."

"The justice system isn't perfect."

"God will see me through."

I don't have the energy or the heart to tell him that sometimes God doesn't get it right either. Even after everything that's happened, he'd probably argue the point. "I went to see Levi Schmucker today."

He arches a brow. "He must be pretty old by now."

"Not so old that he couldn't remember that Ananias Stoltzfus beat the hell out of him." I tell him about my visit. "It was a vicious beating. Busted his teeth. Broke his arm. Put him in the hospital."

"I didn't care for Ananias or his tactics, but . . ." His troubled expression lands on mine. "Is it possible Levi is lying?"

"It's possible. Or he could be exaggerating. If he was, indeed, molesting his daughter, he might be trying to deflect. That's not what I'm getting at."

He raises his brows. "Then what?"

"What if Ananias Stoltzfus wasn't who he claimed to be?" Even to me the notion sounds far-fetched. Unlikely at best, conspiratorial at worst.

"I don't know what you mean," he says.

"There are a lot of things about Ananias and Mia Stoltzfus that don't mesh with their being Amish, certainly not with his being a bishop," I say. "I've been told his wife was from Germany. She committed suicide in a Lutheran church. She asked the pastor for absolution. The couple spoke *Deitsch,* but with an accent. Ananias messed up his preaching, not once but several times. He beat a man nearly to death with a walking stick. Jonas, none of those things are the actions of an Amish person."

He blinks at me. "Then who is he?"

I ponder the question a moment. "I need to know if there's anyone who knew Ananias or Mia. Even if it's someone who's moved away. Or elderly. Is there anyone I can talk to?"

"I don't know of anyone else. Ananias was old and all of this happened eighteen years ago." His expression turns troubled again. "Even if we discover he was not Amish or who he said he was, how does that help us find the person who killed him?"

"Maybe it was someone from his past or somehow related to his past. Maybe he has a history we don't know about."

Thoughts churning, we sip our tea in silence for a few minutes.

"So what's next?" he asks.

I shrug. "I put a call in to Minnesota," I tell him. "I'm waiting for a call back. Maybe someone there knows or remembers something about the Stoltzfuses or their past."

He nods, staring down at the glass sweating on the table in front of him. "Maybe we've reached a dead end."

Seeing the stress etched into his features, the circles beneath his eyes, I'm reminded of how much he has at stake. His freedom. His business. His family. His life.

"Not yet," I tell him.

When he raises his gaze to mine, it's disconsolate. "Maybe my going to jail is part of God's plan."

"That's bullshit." I soften the words with a half smile.

"You've done more than I would have asked, Katie.

You're away from home. Your family. You've been hurt. I can't ask you to stay on. Or do more than you already have. We've reached the end of our options. Maybe you should just go home. Forget about this mess and get back to your life."

"There's only one problem with that," I tell him.

He raises his brows in question.

"I'm not a quitter. You should know that about me. I can't abide injustice. I can't abide a killer thinking he beat the system. I sure as hell won't tolerate an innocent man going to jail for something he didn't do."

He looks down at the glass, his jaw working, saying nothing.

In that moment a hundred memories assail me. The mess I'd made of my life the last summer we were together. The intensity of the feelings we shared. The tumult of our relationship. The mistakes, most of them mine. Everything that happened between us—both good and bad—in the final days before he left.

"Last time I was here," I say quietly, "you mentioned the elephant in the room. I didn't let you finish."

"Probably a good call on your part." He smiles, but it's for my benefit. There's a profound sadness in his eyes he can't hide. He shrugs. "Ancient history."

I smile, too, and I'm surprised to feel that same sadness reach into my chest and twist. "Maybe 'ancient' isn't quite the right word."

We stare at each other, unspeaking, and yet we're communicating clearly and in a way that speaks of a closeness the years haven't erased.

"I'm sorry for what happened," I tell him. "I never got to tell you that."

The history between us is the last topic I want to revisit, ancient or not. But I'm a far cry from the confused and rebellious girl I was. The one that was in love and didn't have the slightest clue how to handle it or what it meant.

"It wasn't your fault," he says.

"Maybe. But I knew better. I knew what I was doing. I knew it was a mistake. That it was serious. I knew you would be blamed for all of it. You got into a lot of trouble."

A minute quiver runs the length of him as my words register. I expected him to wave off the statement. Make some joke. Laugh it off. Chalk it up to inexperience and immaturity. But he doesn't do any of those things. Maybe because we both know what happened that summer was as genuine and pure as it was wrong.

"It was a bittersweet time," he says quietly. "For both of us. You were too young. I was—" He bites off the word. The smile that follows is sheepish and reluctant. "I wasn't exactly kicking and screaming to get away from you."

"You lost a lot."

"You lost something, too, no?" He studies me with such scrutiny that I can barely hold his gaze, but I do. "We both did."

"You paid a big price," I tell him. "So did your family."

"Bad timing, no?" He cocks his head, his eyes probing

mine. "A few more years and things might've worked out differently."

I'm not sure I agree, but I don't say. He wanted to marry me. I was too young, too screwed up, to know what I wanted let alone make such an important life decision.

"The years teach a lot of lessons the days never know," I tell him.

It was one of my *mamm*'s favorite sayings. As a fifteen-year-old Amish girl with the weight of the world on her shoulders and a duffel bag full of anger in her heart, I had little understanding of its meaning. As a grown woman, I've never appreciated it more.

The sound of shod hooves against gravel and the music of children's voices come to us through the screen door, telling us Dorothy and the kids have arrived home.

And the moment is gone.

I call Deputy Vance on my way to the motel. I can tell by his tone he's not happy to hear from me. I make a halfhearted attempt to soften him up with small talk and a not-so-funny joke. He doesn't bite.

"I need your help," I say.

"Nothing personal, Chief Burkholder, but I think I've done my share of helping."

"I know this isn't an ideal situation," I begin, but he cuts me off.

"You're going to get me fired."

"There's no one else," I tell him. "I'm not getting much cooperation from your department."

"Let it go through the channels."

"Kris, you know as well as I do that Jonas Bowman didn't murder Ananias Stoltzfus. He didn't leave his muzzleloader at the scene. He didn't cut off a dead man's hands and toss them into his own well."

"Murderers aren't exactly the brightest bulbs in the pack."

"Will you at least hear me out?"

Vance says nothing, so I trudge on. "I've discovered some things about Stoltzfus that don't sit well. The more I uncover, the more convinced I am that he's not who he claimed to be."

"What are you talking about?" he asks irritably.

I give him the rundown of incongruities, starting with Mia's suicide and her request for absolution and ending with the beating of Levi Schmucker. "I grew up Amish. I can tell you those are not the actions of an Amish bishop."

"Maybe he was just an asshole."

"You guys should have looked into it."

He groans. "Look, I wasn't exactly involved in the case, Chief Burkholder. What the hell do you want from me?"

I pause, close my eyes briefly. "I need a DNA sample from those remains."

He has the gall to laugh. "You'll have to talk to the sheriff about that. I'm not part of chain of custody," he says. "I spend my time writing tickets and rounding up cows, for God's sake."

"Kris, if I can get my hands on that DNA, I'll send

it to the lab and have it run through some databases to see if we get a hit."

"What are you looking for?"

"A definitive ID for one thing. I know it's a long shot, but—"

"I'm not going to risk my job on a long shot, Burk-holder."

"Will you at least look into it?" I think about To-masetti, wonder if he has the connections to help, if he knows anyone on a federal level who might be able to step in and grease the wheels.

"Look, I'm not going to make any promises, but I'll see what I can do."

"Fair enough. Thank you."

He's anxious to end the conversation, so I jump into my next question. "One more thing. Do you have any idea what happened to the diary that was found with Mia Stoltzfus when she committed suicide?"

"I don't know anything about a diary."

"Do you know who might—"

He hangs up on me.

I've devoted most of my adult life to law enforcement and solving crimes, which sometimes includes putting someone in jail. How ironic that the one time I'm try-ing to prove a man's innocence and keep him *out* of jail is the one time I can't pull all the loose ends of the case together.

It's nearly midnight. I'm sitting at the table in my room at the Kish Valley Motel, thinking about old bones and the story those bones have told so far. I've been at it for a couple of hours and I'm doing my best not to be discouraged. I'm failing at that, too.

A DNA sample from the human remains found in the field or the water well could be tremendously helpful. Not only in terms of matching, but also running it through some databases to find out exactly *who* those bones belonged to. Chances are, that won't happen; the lab will likely only make the match and not take the testing any farther. That's when it occurs to me that at some point, I've come to believe Ananias wasn't the man he proclaimed to be. If I'm right and that's the case, who was he really? And why was he doing his utmost to conceal his identity?

Frustration sits in the chair across from me, a foul apparition, mocking me. I resolve to call the sheriff's department first thing in the morning and formally request that the DNA results be run through several databases. They may or may not agree to do so. I'm not going to hold my breath.

I google "Minnesota Amish" and tap a key, landing on the blog of a well-known scholar on the Amish culture. He writes about the settlement in Harmony, Minnesota, and I read with interest. I'm midway through when something pings my brain. I stop reading and backtrack, read the passage again.

Founded in 1972, Wadena is the oldest Amish community in Minnesota. Harmony was founded by the Swartzentruber Amish in 1974.

My conversation with Amanda Garber flashes in my brain. *They moved here in 1967 or so.*

If the Harmony, Minnesota, settlement was founded by the Swartzentruber Amish—in 1974, no less—how is it that Ananias was elected bishop? He wasn't Swartzentruber. According to Amanda, he arrived in Belleville in 1967.

"The timeline doesn't add up," I whisper.

It's possible that Ananias and Mia lived in Harmony before the church district was formally established. But in order for a bishop to be elected, there must be an organized church district, even if the term is used in a loose sense. In addition, it would be extraordinarily unusual for a bishop to move. Usually, when a bishop is struck by the lot, it is a burden he bears the rest of his life.

So what happened in Harmony?

And what does it mean in terms of the case here in Belleville?

There's one other source of information that might be helpful. A publication titled *Raber's New American Almanac,* which is a comprehensive list of Amish bishops and ministers by state. If I can get my hands on a copy or have someone look it up for me, I should be able to determine if Ananias was, indeed, a bishop in Minnesota. One of the *Diener* here in Belleville may have a copy. Possibly the library or another Amish elder.

My cell phone buzzes. A burst of pleasure in my chest at the thought of Tomasetti. But when I glance at the display, I see a local number I don't recognize.

I answer with, "Burkholder."

A hiss of air and then a whispered male voice. "I got proof Jonas Bowman killed Ananias Stoltzfus."

A couple of thoughts strike me at once. The caller is trying to disguise his voice. And there's no ping of recognition. No accent. Nothing familiar.

"Who is this?" I ask.

"Nelson Yoder knows the truth. He was there the night Stoltzfus was killed. *He knows everything.*"

"What does he know?" I ask.

"Bowman wasn't the only one who wanted Stoltzfus gone. They all did."

"Who?"

"Everyone hated him, including Yoder. Don't let them lie to you. They're covering for Bowman."

"Tell me who you are," I say.

Nothing.

"Why should I believe you?" I ask.

The hiss of a breath and then, "Because I was there, too."

"Who is this?" I demand.

A resonant click sounds and the call ends.

Exasperated, I toss the phone, watch it clatter onto the table. I sit there a moment, not sure what to make of the call. Is it an anonymous tip that warrants follow-up? Or is someone yanking my chain? Trying to convince me Jonas is guilty? That there's a witness? Deflect my attention to Yoder? Something else?

Nelson Yoder knows the truth.

If the bishop knows something about the case, why didn't he mention it? Why would he travel to Painters Mill to ask for my help? It doesn't make sense.

Cursing beneath my breath, I pick up my phone and look at the incoming number. Local. I hit the Call button. It rings a dozen times, but no one picks up. I go to my laptop, enter the number into a reputable reverse phone lookup site. To my surprise, the call originated at an Amish pay phone right here in Belleville.

CHAPTER 21

If Ananias Stoltzfus had secrets, he did a damn good job of keeping them hidden. I've discovered a slew of peculiarities about the bishop and his wife, but zero in terms of anything concrete that might explain what happened to him or why.

Between the phone call and frustration stemming from my lack of progress, I didn't sleep much last night. I researched Ananias and Mia Stoltzfus. Harmony, Minnesota. I looked at Mary Elizabeth Hershberger. Henry Stoltzfus. I even spent some time delving into the lives of the three elders who brought me into the investigation. Nelson Yoder, the bishop. Nathan Kempf, the deacon. And Mahlon Barkman, the minister. There isn't much out there. No criminal records. No legal issues or lawsuits. No drama. Even in terms of the Amish, they lead quiet lives.

I wrote down everything I could remember about the call.

*I got proof Jonas Bowman killed Ananias
Stoltzfus.*

*Nelson Yoder knows the truth. He was there the
night Stoltzfus was killed.*

*Bowman wasn't the only one who wanted
Stoltzfus gone. They all did.*

*Everyone hated him, including Yoder. Don't let
them lie to you. They're covering for Bowman.*

I said: Why should I believe you?

. . . I was there, too.

The statements are not random. They're bold and
specific. The caller claimed Yoder hated Stoltzfus. That
there were others who wanted him dead. He admitted
to witnessing the murder. It's a troubling notion, but is
it possible the murder was some kind of concerted effort? With the days slipping by and my making little in
the way of progress, I'm bound to follow up.

Nelson Yoder and his wife live in a heavily wooded
area high on the ridge. As I make the turn into their
driveway, a sign welcomes me to Yoder's Harness Repair. I take the sidewalk to the front door, which opens
to a reception area furnished with a sofa, chairs, and
a coffee table piled with magazines. A woman stands
at the counter, her nose buried in a paperback novel.

Through the doorway behind her, I see the bishop sitting at a sewing bench, running a big black sewing machine.

"Can I help you?" asks the woman.

I introduce myself. "I'm looking for the bishop."

She calls out to him in a loud voice, and I'm reminded that he's hard of hearing. *"Mir hen Englischer bsuch ghadde!"* We have a non-Amish visitor.

The old man finishes his stitching, then struggles to his feet and hobbles to the doorway. "I'm hard of hearing, not dead." He turns his attention to me. "Kate Burkholder. You come with news?"

"Just a few questions, Bishop."

He motions me in. "Come on back. I think I can work and talk at the same time, but we'll see."

I follow him into a room that was once a bedroom, before the house was converted into a business. Twelve feet square. Two windows without curtains. He indicates a metal folding chair, then slides onto the bench. Giving me only part of his attention, he feeds a wide leather belly band into the sewing machine.

"Albert Miller is expecting his harness this afternoon, so I need to keep working. He's not known for his patience, even if his repairman is the bishop." He glances up at me, smiling, then goes back to his work. "If he spent more time saddle soaping, and a little less time talking, the leather wouldn't need repairing."

I smile politely. "Do you happen to have a copy of *Raber's New American Almanac*?"

"You might check with Deacon Kempf," he replies.

"I'm wondering if there's anything new you remembered about Ananias or Mia Stoltzfus that you haven't told me, Bishop."

He glances at me over the tops of his wire-rim glasses, his eyes sharp, then back down at his work and continues feeding the leather into the sewing machine. "Not that I recall."

"Last night, I received a call from a man who claims he was there the night Jonas Bowman murdered Ananias Stoltzfus."

The old man deftly swivels the leather strap, takes the stitching down the other side, pulling it toward him now. "Who is this man? Why didn't he go to the police with what he knows?"

"He wouldn't say." I pause. "He said you were there, too, Bishop."

The old man stops sewing and gives me his full attention. "Now you're investigating me, Chief Burkholder?"

"I'm asking you a simple question." When he says nothing, I put it to him. "Were you there the night Ananias Stoltzfus was killed?"

His expression tells me he's not accustomed to being questioned. Certainly not by a woman or non-Amish. "Of course I wasn't there," he snaps. "That's a reckless, irresponsible question."

"Maybe it is," I tell him. "I had to ask."

For a minute, the only sound comes from the rhythmic clank and hum of the sewing machine. I watch, let him stew, take the time to get my words right.

"Is there anything else you want to tell me about Ananias or Mia Stoltzfus?" I ask. "Anything at all?"

Irritation flares in his eyes. "I heard you were hard-headed and difficult."

"Two things that have served me well."

He looks past me, where his wife is standing at the counter, pretending to be immersed in the book.

"Close the door," he says.

I rise and click it shut, then settle back into the folding chair.

"Being struck by the lot and becoming bishop is a weight to bear, Kate Burkholder. It is a blessing and gift. But it is also a burden that has broken many a strong man."

I nod my understanding of that.

"My *dawdi* had a saying about speaking out of turn." He switches to *Deitsch*. "Blessed are the ones who have nothing to say and cannot be persuaded to say it."

I wait.

"It's not easy to speak ill of a man, especially when he was your bishop. But that's exactly what I'm going to do." Grimacing, he leans forward and shuts down the sewing machine. "The meting out of punishments is a weight to bear," he says. "There is no enjoyment. Only duty. The call to do God's will."

I say nothing.

"Shortly after Ananias became bishop, there was a young Amish man in the congregation who worked at the mill in Lewistown. It was too far for him to drive his buggy every day, so he borrowed a car from an English friend. He didn't own it, mind you, but drove it nonetheless. Ananias warned him, but the driving continued. A few weeks later, Ananias put him under the *bann*. In the end, that young man left."

It's not an unusual story. But it's exactly the kind that could cause hard feelings. "You disagreed with the decision to *bann* the young man?"

"No. That young man had been warned and refused to comply. I would have done the same." The bishop seems to look inward, remembering, his lips turned down as if he's realized a bad taste. "But I was there the day Ananias excommunicated him. There were tears; this young man cried. He begged. Could something have been worked out?" The bishop shrugs. "Who knows?"

He raises his eyes to mine. "My point, Chief Burkholder, is that Ananias Stoltzfus enjoyed hurting that young man. He relished the tears. The begging. I saw the pleasure of it in his eyes. It was the kind of look a man gets when he has lust in his heart. That was the day I realized Ananias Stoltzfus was cruel."

"What did you do?" I ask.

"I did nothing. I was young and inexperienced. Naïve." He sags in the chair as if he'd failed a challenge he should have aced. "I didn't have the courage to do the right thing. At the very least, I should have consulted with the *Diener*." He looks down at his hands, but not before I see shame in his eyes. "I saw darkness in Ananias. I knew that darkness would cause problems. That one day there would be a reckoning."

"Bishop Yoder, do you have any idea who killed him?"

He bristles. "You're a fool, Kate Burkholder."

I sigh. "So I've been told."

He looks at me the way a teacher might look at an

unruly student in need of a good paddling. "By the teachings of Christ, violence is prohibited. The taking of a life is the darkest of sins."

"The Amish may be pacifists," I tell him, "but they're human, too. They have the same frailties as the rest of us."

"*Sell is nix as baeffzes.*" That's nothing but trifling talk.

It's a standoff. For the span of a full minute, neither of us speaks. The time gives our respective tempers a chance to cool.

"Were there any other displays of cruelty?" I ask.

He picks up the leather strap and runs his thumb over the stitching. "There was talk."

He raises his eyes to mine. In their depths I see a quicksilver glint. Shame? Guilt? Something else?

He looks away, snips the thread, and pulls the leather from beneath the presser foot. Leaning against his chair back, he gives me his full attention. "Mia came to me," he whispers.

Surprise cuffs me, a blow against my cheek, hard enough to jar. "What about?"

"She told me Ananias had . . . strayed." The old man's face darkens. "She was distraught. I counseled her. She told me other things, too, Chief Burkholder. She said Ananias had beat a man nearly to death. She said the devil had crawled into his soul. And that she was afraid."

"What did you do?" I ask.

"I went to Ananias. He denied all of it. He said Mia was having a mental relapse. He said it had happened before."

"Did you believe him?"

The old man turns his head and looks out the window, as if wishing he could be anywhere but in this room talking to me. Or maybe wishing he had the power to go back in time and change what has already been done. "No. Two days later she was gone. Killed herself in that church."

"Did you speak to anyone else about what you knew? Or about what Mia had said?"

He shakes his head. "She was gone. I didn't know if any of it was true, so I never spoke of it. I knew God would see us through whatever darkness lay ahead."

The Amish eschew power and yet the bishop wields a vast amount. A good bishop is cautious about how that power is exerted—if at all. If Nelson Yoder believed Ananias Stoltzfus was abusing the authority of his position and tearing the church district apart with his strict rules, tyrannical leadership, and cruel punishments, how far would he go to bring the other man's reign to an end?

It's a question I'm loath to ask, let alone answer.

Ananias Stoltzfus enjoyed hurting that young man. He relished the tears. The begging. I saw the pleasure of it in his eyes.

The road back to town is narrow and steep, short straightaways interrupted by switchbacks and hairpin curves. I'm so immersed in my thoughts I barely notice the beauty of the terrain or the dapple of shadow and light on my windshield.

That was the day I realized Ananias Stoltzfus was cruel.

I'm driving too fast, but I'm the only one on the road. I negotiate a banked curve with ease, then speed up for a ruler-straight stretch.

She told me Ananias had . . . strayed . . . beat a man nearly to death. She said the devil had crawled into his soul. And that she was afraid.

I catch a glimpse of a vehicle nestled in the trees to my right. As I pass, a pickup truck rockets out. I yank the wheel left, mash the brake. Steel clanks against steel as the front end crashes into the passenger door. I'm jerked right. My airbag explodes, punching my face and chest hard enough to daze. The passenger-door window bursts. Glass cascades over me. My rear tires skid, lose purchase. The other vehicle keeps coming, tires screaming, shoving me left.

The guardrail looms to my left. I wrench the wheel right. The guardrail strikes my door. Wood splinters. Steel groans. I glance right, catch a glimpse of a grille; then the rental car lurches violently and plummets.

My car tilts crazily. Saplings scrape the undercarriage. Gravity throws me against the door. My head strikes the window. Then I'm upside down, the safety harness digging into my chest. Glass breaking all around. A kaleidoscope of brush and debris flies outside the windshield. The car comes to a halt. I'm hanging sideways. The hiss of steam in my ears. The creaking of steel.

"Shit. *Shit*." Hoping the car doesn't roll again, I look around, try to get my bearings. The windshield is a shattered slab of ice crystals. A green canopy overhead. Through the passenger-side window beneath me, I see leaves and grass and dirt.

The top half of my body has come out of the shoulder harness. The seat belt burrows uncomfortably into my pelvis. I'm so shaken, it takes me several seconds to process what happened. I hang suspended, try to settle. My hands shake violently when I set them on the wheel. The smell of something burning tells me I don't have time to waste.

Holding the wheel with my left hand, I use my right to unbuckle the harness. Gravity slams me to the passenger-side door. I land on my knees. Bracing against the interior roof, I use my right foot to punch out what's left of the windshield, and I slip through.

I'm on a steep incline, branches tangling in my hair and clutching at my clothes. I look up the hill, realize my vehicle rolled about thirty feet, crushing dozens of saplings, landing against a tree on the passenger side. The hood is unlatched. A thin veil of smoke wafts out. I smell burning oil and radiator fluid.

I look around for my cell, go back to the car, peel back the windshield, and spot it on the ground. Reaching through, I snatch it up and get out. My hand is shaking so violently, I can barely punch in 911.

"Mifflin County Sheriff's Department," comes a female voice on the other end.

"I've been in a vehicle accident." Even as I say the words, it occurs to me that this was no accident. Someone ran me off the road. I look up the hill, but there's no one there. I look down the hill, assess its pitch, and I realize that if it hadn't been for one tree, the car would have continued rolling for another thirty or forty yards, picking up speed, ejecting or crushing me on its way down.

By the time the sheriff's department cruiser and rescue truck for the Belleville Fire Company arrive on scene, I've climbed up the hill and I'm standing on the shoulder of the road. I'm still shaking when the paramedic takes me to the rear of the rescue truck, sits me down on a pull-out bumper, and performs a cursory physical assessment. He's blinding me with a pen-size flashlight when a Mifflin County deputy sheriff saunters over.

"You're kind of popular around here, Chief Burkholder," he says.

He's a middle-aged guy with a wrestler's physique, a too-tight belt, and trousers creased with ruler perfection. I don't recall his name, but remember seeing him at the Bowman house the day the search warrant for the water well was executed.

"Tough on vehicles, too, evidently." He walks over to the road's white line and looks down the hill. "Rental car folks aren't going to be too happy with you."

I wince when the paramedic prods my knee. I look down to see that my jeans are ripped and blood has soaked through.

The deputy walks over to me and I'm able to read his name tag. Deputy Trombley. "You in a hurry today? Take one of those curves a little too fast?"

"No, but I suspect the guy who hit me did," I tell him.

His expression falls. "There was another vehicle involved?"

"A pickup truck." I motion toward the pullover from which the truck emerged. "Rammed my vehicle on the passenger side and proceeded to push me off the road."

The paramedic raises his gaze to the cop, looking concerned.

"Did you get a look at the vehicle?" Trombley slips a notebook from his pocket. "Make? Model? Color?"

Annoyed with myself for not noticing the things I've been trained to notice, I shake my head. "Dark. Blue or black." In the back of my mind, I recall the pickup truck I'd seen at Roman Miller's place and add, "I caught a glimpse of the grille when he came at me."

Tilting his head, the deputy speaks into his lapel mike. "Ten-fifty-seven," he says, using the ten code for hit-and-run. He crosses to the gravel pullover, pulls out his cell phone, and snaps a few shots of the skid marks on the asphalt.

The paramedic rises. "You're kind of banged up, Chief Burkholder. What do you say we get you down to Geisinger Hospital over in Lewistown?" he says. "Get that knee checked out. Make sure you're not concussed."

"I'm okay." To prove my point, I get to my feet. "I'll stop by the hospital later."

He glances over his shoulder at the deputy and lowers his voice. "If you don't ride with me, you'll likely have to ride with that guy."

It's not that funny, but I laugh. "I'll take my chances, but thanks."

He snaps his equipment bag closed and gets to his feet. "You be sure and ice the knee tonight. Tylenol for pain. Get yourself checked out as soon as you can."

As the rescue truck pulls away, I approach the deputy, who's walking along the shoulder near the pullover, snapping pics with his cell, looking down at the gravel. "There was definitely someone here." He motions to the place where the tires dug into the gravel. "Looks like he tore out pretty quick."

"He shot out fast. Came at me from the side." I look at the place on the road where the truck struck my vehicle, notice the two-foot-long skid mark. "I didn't see him until I was right in front of him."

"We get some drinking and driving up in these hills," the deputy drawls. "Workers on their lunch hour. Stop to have a beer."

"I don't believe that's what happened," I tell him.

He stops what he's doing and throws me a puzzled look. "You want to explain that?"

"This was deliberate," I tell him.

He chokes out a sound that's part laugh, part incredulity, but sobers quickly. "To what end?"

"I've been looking into the Ananias Stoltzfus case," I tell him. "After the incident at the Kish Valley Motel, I'd say this individual doesn't want me asking questions."

"Look, I'm not discounting what you're telling me, but I don't think we have any proof of that."

I look down at the skid mark. "I guess that depends on your perspective."

Frowning, he slants his head and speaks into his shoulder mike. "Ten-fifty-one," he says, requesting a tow truck.

It takes the rest of the morning to get the rental car uprighted and winched out. Sure enough, there's substantial damage where the truck's bumper or brush guard plowed into the passenger-side door. As the deputy and I worked to re-create what happened, he warmed to the notion that someone ran me off the road. When we finished and the car was towed, he offered to drive me to Lewistown and I accepted. I called the repair shop where the Explorer was and the manager assured me it would be ready in a couple of hours. It's a good thing, because I'm pretty sure the car rental agency wouldn't be thrilled to rent another vehicle to me.

It's almost four o'clock by the time the Explorer is ready. I've just pulled onto the street when a call comes in from Minnesota.

"Chief, this is Deputy Leonard with the Fillmore County Sheriff's Office."

It's the female deputy I talked to yesterday. I feel a quick jump of hope in my chest; I'd all but given up on any information coming from the Amish community in Harmony.

"I'm out here at Bishop Hostetler's farm," she tells me. "He's happy to talk to you if this is a good time."

"Put him on," I tell her.

Rustling sounds as her cell phone is passed to the bishop, and then an old man's voice rumbles over the line. "I had a cousin lived down to Pennsylvania," he begins.

"Kish Valley?" I ask.

"Lancaster County."

I clear my throat and switch to *Deitsch*. "Bishop, I understand Ananias Stoltzfus was the bishop in Harmony years ago. Did you know him?"

"How long ago was that?"

"In the 1960s, I believe."

"I'm eighty-two years old, Chief Burkholder. I've lived here in Harmony since 1974 when I left Ohio. I've never heard of anyone by that name, certainly not a bishop. Either he's mistaken. Or you are."

"Are you sure?"

"I'm not exactly a spring chicken anymore, but I remember my *Diener* just fine. Orla Weaver was bishop from the time I was knee high. He baptized me in 1963. He got me married off in 1965. He spoke at my *mamm*'s funeral in 1973. The next year, several Amish families—my own included—moved from Wayne County, Ohio, to Harmony." He pauses. "Orla went to the Lord in 1985. June, I think it was."

"Is it possible Ananias Stoltzfus was *Diener* in another community?" I ask. "Nearby?"

"If someone told you this Ananias Stoltzfus character was *Diener* in Minnesota, I might just think they were pulling your leg."

CHAPTER 22

For a full minute, I sit with my hands on the steering wheel, trying to figure out what it means that the bishop in Minnesota has never heard of Ananias Stoltzfus. If he's not from Minnesota, where *is* he from?

I can't speak for Ananias, but Mia was from Germany. Bavaria, I think it was.

Amanda Garber's words float uneasily in the back of my mind. If the couple were from Germany, why would they lie about it? Who were they? What were they hiding? Most importantly, does it have anything to do with the murder?

Of course, it's possible that all of this is a benign comedy of errors. Maybe Ananias Stoltzfus was from another part of Minnesota, the southeastern part of the state, for example, where most of the Amish live. Or maybe Bishop Hostetler is simply mistaken. I make a mental note to pay Deacon Kempf a visit to see if I can get my hands on a copy of *Raber's New American Almanac*. Even if I do, without DNA or fingerprints, a driver's license or some kind of ID, there's no way I can get the definitive answer I need.

My only other obvious source of information is Stoltzfus's children. Do they know anything about their parents' pasts? Their roots? Relatives? Mary Elizabeth wasn't exactly champing at the bit to talk to me. Henry Stoltzfus was downright hostile.

Facing a dead end—and the prospect of going back to Ohio without accomplishing what I set out to do—I opt to take my chances with Henry Stoltzfus. Putting the Explorer in gear, I pull back onto the road. I'm on the west side of Yeagertown and heading toward the highway when a battered metal sign hanging off the side of a building snags my attention. THE TRIANGLE BAR AND GRILL. My memory tings. I slow, trying to remember where I've heard it.

The car behind me honks, so I pull into the parking lot. I sit there a moment, staring at the peeling paint and hail-damaged sign. The place is a dump. There's no meaningful connection to anything I've been working on with regard to Ananias Stoltzfus. What the hell?

Amanda Garber's voice comes at me from the recesses of my memory. *Worked at some dive called the Triangle. Serving liquor to drunk men.*

She'd asserted that Ananias had a lover in Lewistown. She'd even remembered the woman's name. *Rosemary, I think it was. Don't know what became of her. Don't much care.*

I park next to an old Chevy truck and get out. As I head toward the entrance, I acknowledge this is probably a waste. If my timeline is correct, Rosemary has been dead and buried for a long time. What are the odds anyone will remember a woman who worked here two or three decades ago?

The Triangle is like a hundred other bars I've frequented over the years—dank, dark, and not quite clean. Eddie Money belts out "Two Tickets to Paradise." The window unit air conditioner blasts a cold blanket over my arms as I walk by, probably to disperse the smells of marijuana and grease that's gone rancid. A man the size of a woolly mammoth stands behind the bar, drying restaurant-style mugs. He's bearded and heavyset, wearing bib overalls, a white T-shirt, and staring at the TV mounted in the corner.

He spots me as I slide onto a stool, snaps up a cardboard coaster, and heads my way. "What can I get you?"

I want a beer, but I've got to drive so I settle for coffee.

"Coming right up."

There are three other patrons. A man wearing a mechanic's uniform sits in a booth against the wall, talking quietly into his phone. Two younger men in jeans and T-shirts are engaged in a game of pool near the back door, which stands open. The place is a dive and yet in an odd way, there's a certain character here, too. Or maybe I just want that beer. . . .

"Here you go." He upends the cup in front of me and pours from a carafe. "I got milk and sugar if you need it."

"Black's fine," I tell him.

He glances at the dozen or so cups he has yet to dry,

but doesn't move toward them. He's bored and would rather talk to me, which is probably a good thing since he's the only person around I can ask about the mysterious Rosemary.

"Ain't seen you in here before," he says.

"First time." I make a show of looking around. I want to tell him he has a nice place but it would be such an obvious lie, I don't.

As if reading my thoughts, he says, "I've got some remodeling planned. Thinking about installing central heating and air."

"You the owner?"

"Me and my two sisters." He grins. "I do all the work. They get all the money."

I sip the coffee, find it good and strong. "I'm told there was a woman who used to work here by the name of Rosemary."

He tilts his head, gives me a closer look. "Well, that would be Grams. She passed away . . . gosh, musta been eight years ago now." He hefts a laugh. "Raised me and my sisters since we were little, after my mom died. Woman never missed a day of work. She was in her nineties and still going strong. She was serving up a beer and collapsed right here at the bar. Dead before she hit the floor. Heart attack. Left the place to us three grandkids." He looks around and shrugs. "Beats the hell out of being laid off. Back in the day this was a hopping place. Before they shut down the mill, anyway." He shakes his head. "Hate to close up shop for good, but I can't keep her open without customers."

"How long has this place been here?" I ask.

"Grams opened it back in the 1940s. Bank next door was still open. This was a steel town back then. Folks had money."

"Bar must have a lot of history."

He laughs. "A little shady history, I guess."

I sip coffee, listening as Eddie Money gives way to an old Pink Floyd number. I miss Tomasetti. Wish he were here. I miss the farm. Mona and Glock and Pickles. I'm still craving that beer. . . .

What the hell are you doing here, Kate?

I don't think there's any information to be had here at this bar. Too much time has passed. Even if the woman in question were still alive and willing to talk to me, it's doubtful she'd have anything to say that would help solve the case. I've reached a dead end. Nowhere else to go. Time to call it quits and go home.

Good luck, Jonas. You're on your own.

I tell him my name. "I'm looking into a cold case out of Belleville. A homicide. I was told your grandmother had a relationship with the victim. I'm wondering if you could answer a few questions."

"Wow. Murder, huh?" He looks intrigued. "I'm Bob, by the way. Who was the victim?"

I tell him, adding what little I know about the purported relationship between his grandmother and Ananias Stoltzfus. "I hope I'm not putting a black mark on your grandmother's reputation."

A surprising amount of color infuses his cheeks. He chortles to cover his embarrassment. "Well, Grams was a little ahead of her time, if you know what I mean." He looks around and lowers his voice. "From what I hear, she liked her men. Almost as much as she liked her booze."

Smiling, I look down at my coffee. "I know you must have been a kid, but do you recall any of the men she was seeing? Anyone talking about it?" I comb my memory for the timeline. "I'm guessing it would have been back in the late 1980s or early nineties."

"Dang, that *is* a cold case." He makes a face. "Gramps died in 1970. Grams was here a lot after that. I don't recall hearing about a boyfriend. Never heard any talk about one."

"Did your grandmother happen to leave behind any letters? Old photos? Anything like that?"

"Grams didn't have much. Some crappy furniture. A few knickknacks. We didn't keep any of it. Just the bar. I know it ain't much, but this place was her life, I guess." He motions toward a couple of beat-up café doors behind the bar. "Only thing I got left is the memorabilia case in the office. It's old and dusty, but you're welcome to take a look."

I round the bar and follow him through the café doors, past a galley-type kitchen with a sink, an industrial-size grill glazed with a brown film, and a refrigerator that looks nearly as old as the building. Using a key, he opens the door to a small office. There's a metal desk piled high with paper and files. A 1980s-type calculator with tape. A bookcase. Framed photos on the wall to my left. Ahead, a glass-front memorabilia display case is mounted on the wall.

I look at the pictures first. Most are faded black-and-white prints. Old. People laughing and drinking, probably from the fifties and sixties. I see a small woman in a snug red dress. Curly brown hair spilling out of a wide-brimmed hat. A smile that speaks of attitude and confidence. I pull out my cell and snap a photo.

"That's Grams there," Bob tells me, motioning. "Nineteen sixty-five or so."

I can't help but think she really was ahead of her time. I look at the remaining photos, but there's nothing out of the ordinary. Just a woman who owned her own business enjoying her customers and success.

I move on to the memorabilia display case.

Bob flips a switch and light rains down on a hodgepodge of items. "That antique microphone belonged to Joseph Campanella. The actor, you know. He was a radio broadcaster here in Lewistown before he got famous. That ball cap belonged to Jack Palance. He was born over in Lattimer Mines." He motions. "See that shot glass? Rumor has it crime boss John Sciandra drank whiskey out of it when he got stranded here in a snowstorm back in 1940. Grams collected stuff like that. No one cares now, but back in the day it was some interesting shit."

I snap a couple of photos from different angles. "You guys have had some colorful clientele," I say.

"I'll say. Grams told me Jimmy Stewart came in for a drink and left her a hundred-dollar tip. That was a lot of money back in the day." He grins. "She needed the cash, so it didn't get added to the case."

At the top right side of the display case, I spot an

unusual looking badge or shield attached to a square of fabric. It's metal with a flat top and rounded base. There's an eagle at the top. The impression of a map, the geography of which I don't recognize. Directly below is the word "LAPPLAND" in capital letters.

I set my finger against the glass. "Do you know what that is?"

"No idea. Been there for as long as I can remember." He fishes in his pocket and brings out a ring of keys. "Let's take a look."

I watch as he unlocks the display case. Dust motes fly when he opens the door. The fabric base is attached to the display-case backing with a safety pin. He struggles with it a moment, then plucks it off and hands it to me.

"Looks pretty old," he says.

The badge is metal, but lightweight in my hand and slightly tarnished. I turn it over in my hand, but there's no other inscription. "Some sort of military decoration?"

"Looks foreign," he murmurs.

"Do you have any idea where your grandmother got this?" I ask.

"No clue." He gestures toward the case. "Chances are, if it's here, someone gave it to her."

That the old badge shares a display cabinet with items that obviously had some meaning to the woman who owned it niggles at me. "Do you mind if I take a photo?"

"Knock your socks off."

I set it on the desktop and snap the shot.

"Do you think a patron here at the bar gave it to her?" I ask. "Or a friend?"

He laughs. "Only thing I can tell you is that nothing went into that display case that didn't mean something to Grams." He jabs a thumb at the display case. "If it didn't have some sentimental value, she'd have pawned it."

CHAPTER 23

There is a moment in the course of an investigation when you know it's going to come together. It's a frenetic time. You don't know how all the information fits or if it will come to you in the right order. All you know is that the answer is buried somewhere in the slapdash pile of data churning in your head.

It's dark by the time I arrive back in Belleville. I swing by a mom-and-pop café for a sandwich and make a beeline to the motel. I fire up my laptop, grab the folder containing every hand-scrawled note and scrap of paper I've amassed, and I spread everything on the too-small table. Most of what I have are my notes from conversations, along with my thoughts and observations. I've downloaded a few background reports and several newspaper stories I pilfered from the internet. When the tabletop becomes too crowded, I drag the nightstand over, set the lamp on the floor, use it for work space as well. I put everything in chronological order. The newspaper stories about the suicide of Mia Stoltzfus. The disappearance of Ananias Stoltzfus. The things I learned from the *Diener* when they came to Painters Mill and asked for my help. The flurry of newspaper articles on the discovery of the remains and the arrest of Jonas Bowman.

It's impossible to lump a culture into a box and profess to know everything about it. It can't be done and anyone who claims otherwise is a fool. But there are cultural norms that can—and should—be taken into consideration, especially when it comes to the Amish. The culture is steeped in tradition. They are a religion centric sect and prefer to remain separate from the rest of the world. They are a patriarchal society and pacifistic in nature. The family unit is the core of Amish life. They're decent, hardworking people. They're good neighbors. Good friends.

All of that said, the Amish aren't perfect. They're human and they suffer with all the same failings as the rest of us. They lose their tempers. They make mistakes. They behave badly. They break the rules. Sometimes they break the law. Some of the behaviors Ananias Stoltzfus partook in went beyond human frailties.

It's eleven P.M. when I remember the sandwich. I unwrap it and eat without tasting, without pleasure. I wash it down with iced tea that's gone tepid. At midnight, I pull the yellow legal pad from my laptop case, uncap my pen, and I go to town on that paper, stream-of-consciousness. Sometimes nonsensical, but I let it fly.

My mind is humming, frustration bumping me from behind, urging me on. The need to know is a drug and I'm an addict jonesing for more.

I write:

> *No one in Harmony, Minnesota, remembers Ananias. The Amish would remember their bishop. Why don't they remember him?*
>
> *Levi Schmucker accused of molesting his daughter. Word got back to the bishop. Ananias beat him. A bishop would never resort to violence.*

I flip through several pages and come upon the notes from my conversation with Deputy Vance. *Hand bones found in Bowman's well. Hands missing. Info never made public . . .*

I think about the killer. Try to get into his head.

"Why did you remove his hands?" I murmur.

I answer my own question. "Because you didn't want him identified."

That still doesn't make sense, Kate, tsks a little voice. *There's got to be something else. . . .*

At one A.M. I make a pot of coffee. It's room coffee; it's awful. I don't care. I need caffeine. The answer is here. I'm not going to stop until I find it.

I down a cup, put my notes back in order, and go through them again. I reread everything I learned from my visit with Amanda Garber.

. . . always got the sense she'd been through something

she didn't want to talk about. Germany? Bavaria? . . . her Deitsch was different. . . . She was homesick. . . .

"Only there are no Amish in Europe," I say, my voice sounding strange in the quiet of the room.

I go to my laptop and call up my search engine to make certain I'm right. Sure enough, the last Amish congregation in Europe merged with the Mennonite church in 1937.

I take the last sip of coffee, get grounds that have gone cold. I glance down at my notes.

. . . where she learned to bake. Her datt *owned a bakery.*

I go to my laptop, hit a couple of keys, scroll aimlessly through my search for Amish communities in Germany. Nothing there. Nothing. Nothing. Nothing. I pause on a random page. Some bakery in Bavaria offering up a recipe for *Zwetschgenkuchen.*

I didn't write it down, don't know the proper spelling, but Amanda Garber's voice floats in the backwaters of my mind.

Everyone loved her Zwetschgenkuchen.

"Who the hell were you?" I lean back in the chair, astounded by the words I just spoke aloud. "Why were you lying to everyone?"

I feel another layer of information falling into place. Whoever removed the hands from the corpse in that field knew the answer. The killer wasn't afraid the body would be identified as Ananias Stoltzfus. He was afraid the body would be identified as someone else. . . .

"What were you hiding from?" I whisper.

Something unsavory scratches at the back of my

brain. A sharp claw, dirty and germy, digging into my brain. Something I don't want to know.

I reach for my notes. Ananias and Mia Stoltzfus moved to Mifflin County in 1967 or '68. He was elected minister in 1977. He became bishop in 1990. I scrabble through several pages. Levi Schmucker was beaten in 1991. Allegedly, Schmucker sexually abused his daughter. A normal course of action would be for a family member or friend or neighbor to call the sheriff's department. A bishop would counsel the individual, tell him he must confess to the congregation or else be placed under the *bann*. Instead, Ananias Stoltzfus took his walking cane to Schmucker. Put him in the hospital. Ordered him to leave town. The sheriff's department was never called. . . .

"You didn't want the police involved." I set down the notes, pick them back up. "That beating wasn't about Schmucker or what he did. It was about you, wasn't it?"

What were you hiding, old man?

I think about Mia. . . . *always got the sense she'd been through something she didn't want to talk about.*

What had disturbed Mia so profoundly that she couldn't live with it? That she couldn't live with herself? Bad marriage? Secrets? Infidelity? All of the above?

I think about the woman he'd taken as a lover. . . . *Grams was a little ahead of her time. From what I hear, she liked her men.*

Remembering the pics I took of the memorabilia display case at the bar in Lewistown, I glance around for my cell, find it on the bed. I pull up the photos and swipe. Useless memorabilia. Meaningless junk.

Shit.

I come to the photo of the badge Bob the bartender pulled from the case. The one with the eagle, the map, and "LAPPLAND" inscribed in all caps. I look around, find my reading glasses on the bed, slip them on, go back to my cell. I enlarge the image. I still don't recognize the geography of the map.

I spin back to the table, type "LAPPLAND" and "badge" into my search engine.

The Lapplandschild was a World War II German military decoration awarded to military personnel of the 20th Mountain Army which fought Finnish and Soviet Red Army forces in Lapland from 1944 to 1945.

A chill I can't identify sweeps up my spine. A glass of ice water splashed between my shoulder blades and pouring down. I stare at the photo and the dirty claw that had been scraping at my brain gains access. A boil being lanced. A release of pus. The stench of something vile.

For a moment, I can't quite catch my breath. My mouth fills with saliva. The acid burn of coffee roils in my gut. And in that instant, another unanswered question coalesces. I know what Ananias Stoltzfus was hiding. I know why his wife couldn't live with herself. I understand why he beat Levi Schmucker to within an inch of his life.

Messed up his preaching service a time or two . . .

. . . funny accent when he spoke Deitsch.

Wasn't much good at sewing for a woman her age . . .

Everything that hadn't made sense suddenly does.

I close my eyes, sick with exhaustion and too much coffee. I don't like the information zinging in my head. I push away from the table, get to my feet, sit back down. I feel like hell. A little wild on the inside. I don't know why; this is what I wanted, isn't it? *Isn't this what you wanted, Kate?* A solid theory? Part of one, anyway. But I feel like crying. I feel sullied. Unclean.

The alarm clock tells me it's 4:18 A.M. Too early to call Tomasetti. But I need him. I need to know if I'm right. I hate it, but I don't trust my instincts. I hate it even more that I'm so desperate to find the truth and grasping at straws. I'm afraid the answer that's come to me is so far out there it couldn't possibly be true.

I make the call. One ring. Two rings. I close my eyes, suddenly desperate to hear his voice. I'm about to hang up when his voice rasps over the line. "Everything okay, Chief?"

Tears burn the backs of my eyes. I want to blame it on dry eye or sleep deprivation or the fact that I've been staring at my damn notes and laptop screen for six hours, but it's not the truth.

"I miss you," I tell him.

I hear a rustle on the other end, picture him sitting up in bed, concerned, giving me his undivided attention. "You want to talk about something?"

"I think I need to."

"I'm all ears."

For an instant, I can't find my voice. I don't know where to start. I blink and I'm surprised to feel tears on my cheeks. "I slept with Jonas Bowman. I was fifteen. He was nineteen. I think I might've loved him, but I was so screwed up at the time, I never figured it out."

Several beats of silence and then, "All right."

"He didn't seduce me. I seduced him."

"Okay."

"I was a minor child. He . . . wasn't. That's why his family had to leave town. My *datt* found out and somehow the sheriff's department got involved."

"Even with a Romeo and Juliet law," he says slowly, "Jonas could have been charged with statutory rape or some variation thereof."

"That was the year . . ." I clear my throat. "That was the year after everything happened with Daniel Lapp. I was . . . messed up. Stupid. Confused."

"You were a teenaged kid who'd been through a severe trauma."

I let out a breath, hear it shudder. I know he hears it. I know he's going to ask before he does.

"You still love him?"

"No, but I care. Too much. I feel guilty for . . . what happened. To him. His family. The role I played. I want to make it right. I'm not sure how. It might be too late."

Another pause, part thoughtful, part baffled. He's usually grumpy first thing in the morning. He's the guy you don't talk to pre-coffee unless you want a smartass reply. He knows this is an important moment. He's being kind.

"It was a long time ago," I tell him. "But I needed to get it off my chest."

"Just so you know," he says. "I didn't ask."

"I know."

"I trust you, Kate," he says. "You know that, right?"

"I do."

He sighs. "That said, I'm pretty damn glad you're not in love with another dude."

"That would have really complicated things, wouldn't it?"

We laugh and some of the ugliness loose inside me scampers back into its hole.

"You sound exhausted."

"And weird, I know."

"So what's going on?"

I tell him all of it, leaving nothing out, ending with my happenstance visit to the Triangle Bar and Grill and my conversation with Bob the bartender.

"I know it seems unlikely," I say, "but it would explain just about everything."

"Text me the image of the badge," he says.

I put him on speaker, find the pic and send it. "I feel like all of this is pretty far out there."

"Timeline is right. In terms of his age, anyway." He falls silent and I know he's looking at the image. "Let me take a closer look."

"Thank you."

"There aren't many of these war criminals left, Kate. They're in their nineties or older now. Most are dead. But I know there are a couple of organizations that are working to identify remains, both perpetrator and victim. Do you know if there's DNA?"

"The remains found in the field are at a forensic lab in Erie. I don't know if they were able to extract DNA."

"They use the Erie Regional Laboratory," he says. "Let me make some calls."

"Do you have any contacts in Pennsylvania?"

"I'll figure something out."

"All of this seems like a long shot," I tell him.

He makes a sound that's not quite a laugh. "That might be a little optimistic."

"Even if the DNA identifies Stoltzfus as another individual, it can't tell us who killed him."

"No, but it opens up a new field of possibilities," he says.

"That doesn't necessarily involve the Amish community."

"Especially if your suspicions about him are correct."

The weight of the statement presses down like humidity before a storm.

"What's next?" he asks.

"I'm going to talk to his family again. See if there's anything they can tell me."

A too long pause and then, "Are you okay?"

The pang of missing him that follows is so powerful, I set my hand against my abdomen, close my eyes, take a moment because I know the pain of it will reverberate in my voice if I'm not careful. I don't want him to worry.

"I am now," I say. "Sorry to wake you so early."

"Hey, that's what I'm here for." But he laughs. "Do me a favor?"

"Name it."

"Be careful."

I smile. "Tomasetti, did anyone ever tell you you you worry too much?"

"Just you."

CHAPTER 24

It's true that cops don't sleep much in the early stages of an investigation. At least during those first couple of days, when time is like sand slipping through fingers. I'm not exactly working in a law enforcement capacity, but the sense of urgency pulsing in my veins is the same.

After speaking to Tomasetti, I slept for a couple of hours. A quick shower and a fast-food breakfast and I was on the road by nine. Despite the lack of sleep, I'm clearheaded and focused as I make the turn into the lane of the Stoltzfus farm.

My best sources of information are Mia and Ananias's grown children. Though both of them were born after the couple arrived in the Kishacoquillas Valley, they may know something that will confirm—or disprove—my theory about their father. They may have heard something in passing, have relatives I can call upon, or have kept mementos or documents.

Having worn out my welcome with Mary Elizabeth,

I opt to try my luck with Henry first. I'm midway down the lane when I notice someone working at the base of the corn silo. I pull over and park. I'm midway there when I notice the red spray paint on the corrugated steel.

Like father. Like son. Both in hell.

I find Henry Stoltzfus standing in hip-high weeds on the other side of the silo. He's dressed much the same way as last time I saw him. Gray trousers. A single suspender over a blue work shirt. Straw summer hat. Work boots.

I stop a few feet away from him and take in the bold red paint. The large letters. The slipshod writing. "Any idea who did it?" I ask.

He looks at me from beneath the brim of his hat, his eyes shaded, expression guarded. "No."

"It's pretty high up." I make a show of looking at the graffiti. "Must have used a stepladder."

"Dogs were barking last night." He motions behind him. "Grass is trampled."

"Did you call the police?"

He frowns at me, doesn't answer. "I figure I'll just paint over it." He motions to the cageless ladder that's come loose from the silo. "Fix that ladder while I'm at it."

A spray can of cold galvanizing compound lies on its side at his feet. Next to it, a wrench the size of a tire iron. A MIG welder and diesel generator sit on the ground a few feet away.

I recall Dorothy telling me about the fire at the old

mill owned by Mary Elizabeth and her husband. The broken window I saw when I was there. Coincidence? Or has someone targeted them?

"Has anything like this happened before?" I ask.

He picks up the wrench, bends to pluck a bolt from the box at his feet. "A time or two."

"Any idea why?" I ask. "Or who?"

He sets his shoulder against the ladder. "No."

He's trying to press the ladder against the corrugated tin and screw in the bolt at the same time—a task that requires more than just two hands. I go to the ladder, set my shoulder against the rungs, brace my legs, and push until the ladder is snug against the tin.

"Tight enough?" I ask.

An instant of hesitation and then he fits the mouth of the wrench over the bolt head and begins to tighten. "*Ja.*" He snugs the head down tight, grunting with the effort. "Need to put a nut inside, too."

"I'll hold it."

He makes eye contact with me an instant before passing behind me and going through a trapdoor and disappearing into the interior of the silo. I hear the tap and scrape of his wrench beneath my shoulder as he screws in the nut on the other side.

He emerges through the trapdoor a minute later. "Got it," he says.

I release the ladder. "Looks like it's going to hold."

"It better. I got corn to harvest and cattle to feed."

I step back, survey his work. "Is someone upset with you?"

Using a drill, he deburrs the next bolt hole. "Upset

with my *datt,* maybe. He was a firm-minded bishop. A weak man might not like that too much."

"Someone has a long memory."

"Finding the bones dredged up some old feelings, I reckon." He removes the bit, sets down the drill, turns to face me. "What brings you here?"

I pick up the box of nuts and bolts and hand him three of each. "I talked to an old friend of your *mamm*'s. Mia told her she was from Germany. Bavaria. Her father, your grandfather, owned a bakery there. That's where she learned to bake."

He takes them, drops them into his pocket. "My parents were from Minnesota."

"I talked to the bishop in Harmony. He's never heard of Mia or Ananias Stoltzfus."

He blinks, looks away, but his eyes swivel back to mine. "My parents left Minnesota over fifty years ago. Whoever you talked to either doesn't remember or has forgotten."

"I also talked to Pastor Zimmerman at the Lutheran church here in Belleville."

He glowers at me, shakes his head. "Of course you did."

"He said your *mamm* had a journal with her the day he found her," I say. "The sheriff's department returned it to the family."

"I don't know anything about a journal."

He works in silence for a couple of minutes. He finishes with the second bolt and steps back to assess his workmanship. "You didn't come here to help me with this silo," he says.

"But it's good to get help when you need it."

He looks at me from beneath his hat, saying nothing.

"Henry," I say slowly. "I think someone took that muzzleloader from Jonas Bowman's mudroom, killed your father with it, and left it at the scene so the police would find it and Jonas would be blamed. I think that same person planted evidence in the old water well behind Jonas's house." I motion to the graffiti. "Maybe it's the same person who did that."

He looks down at the wrench in his hand. Uneasiness quivers between my shoulder blades, but he tosses it into the old toolbox a few feet away. "I don't know what you want from me."

"I think what happened to your father has something to do with his past. In Germany. I think he may have done some bad things—"

"Bad things?" He stops working and frowns at me. "My father was an Amish bishop. I'll not have you stand on my land and speak ill of him."

"Your parents came here to start a new life. I think someone knows about your father's past in Germany and they killed him for it."

"I have nothing to say to you about that. I don't know who these people are you've been speaking to, but they're wrong."

"I know you loved and respected your *datt*. I understand that. But I need your help. I need Mary Elizabeth's help. If there's anything at all you've heard or know about, if there's anything you have in your possession—"

"My father was a strong leader. Ezra Bowman nearly caused a schism with all his backtalk and complaining. When he died, Jonas blamed my father. He lost his mind and killed him. And now here you are, blaming my father—and defending the man who killed him." He tightens his mouth and looks away. "I think we've talked enough."

"Henry—"

"No more questions." He raises a hand, cuts me off. "Get off my property and don't come back. You're not welcome here. You never were."

Turning away, he scoops up the wrench and disappears inside the silo.

CHAPTER 25

Twenty years before

The thermometer read ninety-two degrees the day I finished my chores early and went to the creek to cool off. For two hours it was just me and the sun, the smell of grass, and that rusty reel mower. By the time I finished it was late afternoon. I'd worked barefoot and my feet were stained green. Grass clippings clung to my sweaty legs. Mamm had taken the buggy and a bushel of sweet corn over to the neighbors, which gave me about an hour.

Mower stowed, I rushed inside for my bath towel and laundry-day dress, and set out across the pasture. Sweat dribbled down my temple as I entered the woods. A few yards in, the path widened and I caught sight of the water, dappled with shade. The earthy smells of growing things hovered as I made my way to the bank. I draped my towel and fresh dress on a branch, removed my *halsduch*, or cape, and hung that as well.

Swimming wasn't practical with my *kapp* and dress. But the cool brace of the water felt heavenly as I waded in. The bottom was gravelly against my feet. Cupping my hands, I bent to splash water on my face, scrubbing away the sweat and specks of grass.

"Well, isn't that a sight to behold. Katie Burkholder taking a bath."

Gasping, I spun to see Jonas Bowman sitting on a log, watching me with amusement. I hadn't seen him for a few weeks. I wasn't sure if I was avoiding him or if he was avoiding me, but somehow we'd managed.

"You're not supposed to be here," I said.

"Is that so?" he drawled.

I didn't reply. I couldn't stop thinking about the last time I'd seen him. That I'd behaved badly and now I was too embarrassed to face him.

"Need some help?" he asked.

I was standing in about three feet of water. My dress was soaked and clinging, the fabric cold against my skin. It wasn't proper. I turned away from him. "If you wanted to help, you could have come over earlier and cut the grass," I said.

"I would've if you'd asked."

He wore a baseball cap instead of a straw hat. No suspenders. I'd heard he was on *rumspringa* and enjoying his "running around" time to the fullest. He looked older. More man than boy now. He looked more serious, too. Something different about his eyes.

"Mattie told me you're w-working at the feed store," I said, hating that I'd stuttered.

"Helping Datt, too. Saving my money. We built a hog barn, you know. Going to buy some sows down to the auction in Kidron."

Leaning forward, he began to unlace his boots.

"What are you doing?" I asked.

"What do you think?" He didn't look at me. "It's a hundred degrees. I'm going to cool off."

"You can't come in here."

"Just going to get my feet wet."

I looked around, not sure what to do. I wanted to grab my towel and dress, and run home. But even as the thought flitted through my brain, I acknowledged that I wasn't being quite honest with myself. I might be terrified by the prospect of him coming into the water, but a small part of me thrilled at the idea.

Tossing his boots aside, he stood, his feet bare, jeans rolled up to his knees. He made a sound of pleasure as he entered the water.

I couldn't look at him. Instead, I swept my hands through the water, watching the white flash of them beneath the surface.

"You been playing any baseball?" he asked.

I glanced up to see him wading toward me. "I'm too old to play a kids' game."

"Yeah? Tell Barry Bonds that."

I had no idea who that was. I didn't care. His jeans were getting wet, the water reaching his thighs. "You're going to get your clothes wet," I told him.

"That's sort of the plan, I guess."

"Your *mamm*'s not going to be happy with you."

"What she doesn't know won't hurt her, will it?"

"It's not proper for you to be here."

He stopped a couple of feet away, looking at me as if I was some puzzle he couldn't quite figure out. "You weren't too worried about proper the day I saw you out on Dogleg Road, were you?"

My face heated. I dropped my gaze to the water. My heart was beating so fast I couldn't catch my breath. I thought about ducking under the surface and swimming around him, going to shore, grabbing my clothes and running.

"Haven't seen you around much this summer, Katie," he said quietly.

"I've been busy."

"Yeah? Doing what?"

Avoiding you. "Chores," I blurted. It wasn't true. In fact, chores were the farthest thing from my mind. The last thing I wanted him to know was that I'd spent most of the summer pining for him. That I missed him so much it hurt.

He stood there with his arms at his sides. Head cocked, studying me. I didn't have the courage to meet his gaze, though for the life of me I couldn't name what I was so afraid of. I'd known Jonas since I was six years old. He was the same Jonas I'd always known. Just last summer, I might've splashed his face or maybe reached down for a mudball and thrown it at him.

"There's a singing after worship next church Sunday," he said.

I watched a water spider skate across the surface.

"I could drive you home afterward," he offered.

"Mamm says you're too old for me," I murmured.

He shoved his hands into his pockets. Looked back toward shore. "My *datt*'s eight years older than my *mamm*. They get on just fine."

I looked down at my hands, pale blurs in the blue-green water. I watched the water spider. Listened to the chip of a cardinal. The next thing I knew, water spattered my face.

I wiped my eyes. Jonas laughed, lined up for another attack. I felt the grin emerge. Heard the laugh escape my mouth. Before he could move, I swept my hand across the water and got him good.

"Hey!"

For several seconds, we were kids again. Laughing and splattering in a competition to out-splash the other. I swept my hand in a wide arc, a perfect alignment for the mother of all splashes. But he caught my wrist and stopped me.

"Not bad for a girl who's too grown-up to play baseball."

He was looking at me funny. Blinking as if I'd done something to surprise him and he wasn't sure how to respond. His fingers were wrapped around my wrist and his skin was warm against mine.

He tugged me toward him. I knew better than to allow it, but I went. We stood a scant foot apart. Looking at each other. Nothing but water between us. I was aware of his hands moving to my biceps, gentle and yet insistent. I could barely look at him, and yet I couldn't look away.

Water gathered in his lashes and dripped from his chin, off the tip of his nose. "Let me drive you home after the singing."

"Mamm won't let me." The words were little more than a whisper. "I have to go."

"Me, too."

Neither of us moved.

I knew he was going to kiss me an instant before he angled his head and pressed his lips to mine. They were cool and wet and tasted of creek water and mint. I knew it was wrong, but I raised my face to his and he deepened the kiss. I felt his hands loosen and slide over my shoulders to my back. He pulled me closer and then his body was flush against mine. I felt the solid pressure of him in a place I'd never acknowledged and for the first time in my life I understood how men and women did the things they did.

I didn't mean to put my arms around him. I couldn't believe how large and hard his shoulders were. All of it was foreign and forbidden, but I wanted him even closer.

After a moment, he pulled away. He closed his eyes, pressed his forehead to mine. "I'll drive you home from the singing."

"I'll find a way," I whispered.

CHAPTER 26

There is a saying about assumptions and for the most part it holds true. When I arrived in the Kishacoquillas Valley to look into the death of Ananias Stoltzfus, I'd been operating on the notion that he was a kindly and much-loved bishop, a man revered by all. I believed that his untimely death had left a wound on the community and an ocean of broken hearts in its wake.

From the outside looking in, those things may have been true, at least in a topical sense. As bishop, Stoltzfus touched many lives in positive ways—baptisms, communion, and marriages. But a number of people who came in contact with him—for some transgression or perceived wrongdoing—were met with the kind of heavy hand that could alter the course of a life—or ruin it.

Ananias Stoltzfus enjoyed hurting that young man.
He relished the tears.
I saw the pleasure of it in his eyes.

Bishop Yoder knew what kind of man Ananias Stoltzfus was. He disagreed with many of his decisions. There was friction between the two men. Was it enough to drive Yoder to commit an act of violence? Did he take it upon himself to permanently remove the man who was hurting his brethren and sucking the lifeblood from the community?

Yoder isn't the only one who might have benefited from his death. Roman Miller—who has access to a dark pickup truck—was forced to leave the Amish and join a local Mennonite church. Levi Schmucker was accused of sexually abusing his daughter. He suffered serious physical injuries and was forced to abandon his family and leave town.

And what about Jonas? a little voice whispers.

His father was excommunicated and silenced. After Ezra's death Jonas blamed Ananias. Jonas wrote a threatening letter and they argued publicly. The rise of doubt that follows is a physical pain.

All of these men had motive, means, and opportunity. Is one of them a killer? Is there something else I'm simply not seeing? And how does any of it play into my suspicion that Ananias and Mia were lying about where they came from?

After visiting Bishop Yoder, I went to see Nathan Kempf. Though the deacon wasn't able to tell me anything I didn't already know, he did have a copy of *Raber's New American Almanac*. I took it back to the motel and spent a couple of hours substantiating what I already knew. Ananias Stoltzfus was never a bishop in

Harmony, Minnesota. Later, I stopped by Mary Elizabeth's place, but there was no one there. By and large, the afternoon was a bust.

It's dusk by the time I pull into the Bowman driveway. Lightning flickers on the western horizon as I park and head inside. The wind has picked up and the air smells of rain as I take the sidewalk to the porch and knock. The door opens and Junior grins up at me, a chocolate Fudgsicle sticking out of his mouth.

"Hi, Katie!" he says excitedly. "You're just in time. D-Datt says God is going to water the grass and m-make the tomatoes grow. Do you want a Fudgsicle? There are two left and I'm only allowed to have one."

Before I can respond, he takes my hand and pulls me into a living room aglow with lamplight. Dorothy sits in a rocking chair, next to the window, a needle and thread in hand, clothing ostensibly in need of mending piled at her feet.

"Hi, Katie." She looks at the boy, her mouth twitching. "God is going to make all those weeds grow, too."

Jonas stands in the kitchen doorway, leaning against the jamb. "And He made your hands just the right size to pull them," he says to his son.

Realizing he is the center of attention—and facing an afternoon of weed-pulling tomorrow—Junior rolls his eyes and slinks up the stairs.

Effie is curled on the sofa, tongue sticking out in concentration, an embroidery ring and swatch of fabric in her hands. I can see from where I'm standing it's a chicken-scratch pattern, the only kind of needlepoint I enjoyed as a kid.

"Looks like someone's going to get a pretty baby quilt," I say to her.

"Mrs. Kurtz is going to have her baby in two weeks." Effie raises the ring to assess her work and wrinkles her nose. "My stitches are crooked."

"I don't think the baby is going to notice," Jonas mutters.

In the beat of silence that follows, the first fat drops of rain ping against the window. I look at Jonas, wishing I didn't have to darken the scene with questions about murder.

"I need to talk to you," I tell him.

I can tell by his expression he knows the news isn't good.

Before he can respond, Dorothy rises and scoops up the clothes at her feet. "Effie, you can finish tomorrow. Let's go upstairs and get ready for bed. I've devotional to read and you could use a bath."

Effie deflates, her expression telling me she'd rather stay down here and eavesdrop, but she's too well-mannered to argue. "Junior smells worse than I do," she grouses. "Why doesn't he ever have to take a bath?"

Jonas wrinkles his nose. "In Junior's case, I think it's those beans he had for dinner."

Effie giggles.

"There's coffee on the stove, Katie." Dorothy gestures toward the kitchen. "You make yourself at home while you're here."

The aromas of cooked onions and meat hover in the kitchen when I enter. I take in the warmth of this house, the closeness of this family, and I try to ignore the doubt I felt earlier, the sense of things lost, of nostalgia pressing down on me.

Jonas goes to the lamp and turns up the gas. "You're limping," he says.

I tell him about the accident. "It was a pickup truck. Dark. Blue or black."

At the stove, he tips a percolator and pours coffee into two cups, cuts me a sharp look over his shoulder. "Are you okay?"

"Just a little bruised." I hold his gaze. "Do you know anyone who drives that kind of vehicle?"

He sets a cup in front of me and takes the chair across from me. "Roman Miller drives a truck."

The rumble of thunder that follows rattles the plates hanging on the wall. I listen to the storm, sip coffee that's a little too weak.

"The bishop in Minnesota has never heard of Ananias or Mia Stoltzfus," I tell him.

He sets down his cup, his brows furrowing. "How can that be? Ananias was bishop. For years. Is it possible the man you spoke with is mistaken?"

"Ananias also had a lover." I recap my conversation with Bob the bartender at the Triangle Bar and Grill. "In Lewistown. Her name was Rosemary. An English woman who owned a bar." I pull out my cell and show him the photo of her. "Have you ever seen her before?"

"No."

I set my phone on the table, thinking about my conversation with Nelson Yoder. "How well do you know Bishop Yoder?"

"I've known him for many years." He narrows his

gaze on mine. "He is a good bishop. A good man, I think."

"Are you sure about that?" I ask.

"What are you asking me exactly?" he snaps. "What does he have to do with any of this?"

"Evidently, Yoder didn't care for Ananias either, but then you already knew that, didn't you?"

Jonas looks away, says nothing.

"Yoder told me Ananias was cruel. He claims to have witnessed that cruelty firsthand. He said Ananias's tactics were tearing apart the community."

He stares down at the tabletop in front of him, his mouth tight.

"Jonas, do you think it's possible Bishop Yoder—"

"No." He slaps his hand down on the tabletop. "No."

I pick up my phone, scroll through the photos until I find the shot I took of the Lapplandschild shield. I show it to him. "Do you know what this is?"

Reaching into his shirt pocket, he pulls out a pair of reading glasses, slides them onto his nose, and studies the photo. "No."

The Amish attend school through the eighth grade. Most of their education focuses on reading, math, spelling, grammar, penmanship, and some history. "It's a wartime medal," I tell him.

He looks at me, incredulous. "Are you telling me Ananias fought in a war?"

"I think he was in the military. In some capacity."

"You know as well as I do an Amish man would not fight. He would not kill."

It's a true statement. The Amish are pacifistic; they

eschew any kind of violence. "I think he was a soldier." I tap my nail against the photo on the screen. "I think this badge belonged to Ananias. I don't know how or why, but he made some kind of contribution to the war. And he was rewarded for it."

"Why are you telling me all of these things?"

"I'm getting to that," I say. "How well do you know your history?"

He looks away. "Just what I learned in school. . . ."

Which means if he hasn't read up on world history as an adult, he probably isn't well versed. "I think Ananias and Mia were from Germany."

He stares at me, saying nothing.

I continue, "They were living in Germany during World War II. As you know, some German soldiers were guilty of terrible things. War crimes. When the war was over, some of those bad people fled the country to escape justice. I think Mia and Ananias were among them. I think they fled to the U.S. At some point, Ananias stumbled upon the Amish and realized it would be the perfect place to hide. They were already fluent in German. So they studied the culture, changed their names, invented a past. And they assumed Amish identities."

He stares at me, blinking, his expression shocked. "I don't know what to say to that."

"I know it sounds far-fetched, but it fits. It would explain a lot." I look down at the pic on my cell. "I think Ananias kept that badge because it meant something to him. But he knew he shouldn't. I think he gave it to Rosemary, his lover. Not realizing what it was, she displayed it in her bar.

"Ananias became bishop here in Mifflin County in 1977. In 1978, Levi Schmucker was accused of sexually abusing his daughter. Ananias didn't want the authorities sniffing around, so he went to Levi, beat the hell out of him, and ordered him to leave town. Problem solved." I stumble over the words, not sure of their plausibility, hating it because I have no proof of any of it.

Still, I press on. "Mia couldn't live with the lie. She couldn't live with what her husband had done back in Germany. That's why she took her life. She did it in a Lutheran church, she asked for absolution *because she was a Lutheran.*"

A rumble of thunder punctuates the statement. The air is so heavy, it's as if the storm has come in through the window and pulses in the room like a hot, sweaty fist.

"Ananias was an evil man," Jonas says.

I nod. "He did a good job researching his new identity, of lying and deceiving and fitting in, but he couldn't hide what he was. He couldn't rid himself of the darkness in his heart. Evidently, the people around him had noticed. I think someone discovered the truth about their bishop and took it upon themselves to end the charade."

We startle when my phone jangles.

I glance at the display. A local number I've seen before but don't recognize. I answer with my name.

"Chief Burkholder!"

It takes me a moment to place the voice. "Mary Elizabeth?"

"Our barn! Someone set it on fire!"

"You called the fire department?" I ask.

"Yes!" she cries. "They're coming, but we need help."

I get to my feet. "Is everyone accounted for?"

"Adrian's getting the horse and cattle out." She chokes back a sob. "All of my *datt*'s things! His trunk! It's all there! Everything that proves you're wrong about him! It's going to burn if we don't save it!"

"I'll be there as soon as I can. Stay calm. Don't go into the barn."

The line goes dead.

"Shit." I look at Jonas. "I have to go."

Already on his feet, Jonas strides to the mudroom, grabs two slickers off a hook. "Let's go."

"You stay—"

He shoves a slicker at me, then puts his fingers to his mouth and emits an earsplitting whistle. "Junior!"

The boy thunders down the stairs, his eyes darting from me to his father. "Datt?"

"There's a fire. At the Hershberger place. I'm going to help. Tell your *mamm*."

I'm already across the room and yanking open the door. I hear Jonas behind me and then we're down the steps, sprinting toward the Explorer.

CHAPTER 27

I zip through Belleville well over the speed limit. Rain hammers down on the roof in a deafening roar. Lightning splits the sky overhead. The thunder follows with such violence that the ground shakes.

Beside me, Jonas grips the armrest a little too tightly. "Maybe a lightning strike hit the barn," he says. "Caused the fire."

"Maybe." But it's the other possibilities that trouble me. I can't help but think of the fire at the mill in the back of the property. The broken window. The graffiti spattered on the silo at Henry Stoltzfus's farm.

Like father. Like son. Both in hell.

I glance away from my driving and look at Jonas. "Their farm has been vandalized in the past."

He nods. "I remember hearing about it. The mill."

"Henry Stoltzfus, too." I tell him about the spray paint. "Any ideas?"

He shrugs. "Maybe it has to do with Ananias Stoltzfus."

I blow the stop sign at Blue Run Road and hang a right. The Explorer hydroplanes, the rear end fishtailing. I slow as I approach the covered bridge. Little Kishacoquillas Creek has transformed into a raging torrent of churning brown water.

"We needed the rain," Jonas mutters, "but not this much."

I make the turn into the lane of the Hershberger farm. Mud and gravel ping against the undercarriage as I speed toward the house. I make the final turn to see the glow of a lantern ahead. Adrian is running toward the barn. A bucket in each hand.

"I don't see a fire," I say.

"Maybe he got it put out," Jonas replies.

I slide to a stop a dozen yards from the barn. Then I'm out of the Explorer. Smoke hangs like a pall, black and wet and choking. I start toward Adrian.

"Where's the fire?" I ask.

"Inside the barn!" he shouts.

"Is everyone out?"

"The cows!" he cries.

Jonas sprints past me toward the barn. I follow. The bellowing of cattle rises above the roar of rain against the roof. Jonas reaches the gate, struggles to open it. The silhouettes of a dozen head of cattle are backlit by the flames inside. The panicked animals push against the gate. Horns and bawling and the stench of terror. Jonas struggles with the chain, but it's too tight to unfasten.

I scrape rain from my eyes, look around wildly. I

run to the Explorer, hit the fob. The rear door yawns. I
yank out the fire extinguisher, go to my toolbox. I tear
it open, pull out the bolt cutters. I sprint to the gate.
Jonas glances over his shoulder. I open the jaws of the
bolt cutters, snap them down.

The chain springs apart. The gate flies open, strikes
me in the chest, nearly knocking me down. A dozen cattle stampede past. Jonas snatches the fire extinguisher
from me, charges into the barn. Flames shoot ten feet
into the air. Not a huge fire, but gaining momentum. He
fumbles the lever, aims, and sprays. The flames totter
and leap. A final burst of heat. A billow of smoke. And
then the fire goes dark.

We stand there a moment, breathing hard, looking at
each other, knowing a disaster was narrowly avoided.

"This wasn't a lightning strike," I say.

Jonas nods. "Someone did this."

The stink of wet ash hangs in the air. Residual heat
presses against my face. Pulling out my mini Maglite,
I shine the beam on a door that will ostensibly take me
into the main part of the barn. I go to it, slide it open, go
through. Jonas shadows me, on my right. Our feet are
silent on the dirt floor as we enter.

The aisle takes me to the raised wood floor at the
back of the barn. Smoke hovers, thick and acrid. Lightning flickers in the window ahead. I go to it, slide it
open to bring in fresh air. Adrenaline quivers in my gut
when I see movement in the pen below. The silhouette
of a man climbing over the pipe fence. Jumping to the
ground. Running away. Moving fast.

"Someone outside." I sweep my beam around, spot the stairway opening in the floor that will take me down to the pens. "Stay put."

"Katie—"

"*Stay here.*" I jog to the opening in the floor, flick off my flashlight, plunge down the steps.

I reach ground level. My feet sink into mud and manure as I cross through the pen. No sign of the man. I unlatch the gate, go through. I wade through mud; then I'm in the grass. The rain has slowed, but there's no moon. Not enough light to see. I'm loath to use my flashlight; it'll give away my position, but I'm blind without it. I flick it on for an instant, get my bearings, check for footprints, catch sight of a heel impression filled with water. He's heading toward the woods. I turn off the flashlight and push myself into a run.

I'm aware of my .38 pressing against my side as I race down the hill, my backup sidearm tucked into my ankle holster. I crash through brush and saplings, barely avoiding a pile of deadfall. At the base of the hill, I splash through a wet-weather creek. I reach an open area, flick on the flashlight. Catch sight of a figure as it disappears into the trees ahead.

"Stop!" I shout. "I'm a police officer! Stop!"

I freeze, listen for a response. Thunder and the pouring rain drown out any sound. I jog to the trees, tug out my cell phone as I enter, hit 911.

"Nine one one, what's your emergency?" comes a female voice.

Quickly, I identify myself. "I'm at Adrian Hershberger's farm." I give the address. "There was a suspicious fire. A prowler. Male. Heading toward the rear of the property—"

"Ma'am, do not approach the suspect. I've dispatched a deputy and fire department—"

I hit End, pick up speed, find my stride. I flick on the flashlight. Wet foliage all around. Rain glistening on leaves. A rise of fog. I glance down, spot a footprint. Not enough detail to know the shoe type, but he came this way, moving fast.

I maintain a brisk clip, weave through old-growth forest. Blackberry and raspberry catch at my slicker. I keep my eyes on my surroundings, watching for movement, straining to hear anything above the pound of rain. The wind has kicked up, the treetops a restless sea above.

The trail narrows, the path littered with deadfall, and overgrown with branches and foliage. Lightning flashes, a strobe far too close for comfort. Two seconds and a deafening clap of thunder shakes the ground.

I'm out of breath. My heart pounding. Too much adrenaline dumping at once. Rain pours down, dripping down my face. In my eyes. My hair is soaked. I slide the .38 from its nest.

All the while, I ponder who I'm following. Did he set the fire? A vandal with some bone to pick? Someone disgruntled with Ananias? With Mary Elizabeth or Adrian? Someone I've met? And where's Jonas?

I reach the peak of the hill. I shine my beam down the other side. It's steep and heavily treed with a creek at the base. I debate the wisdom of following this unknown individual. I don't know his intent or if he's armed. But while I may be a civilian here in Pennsylvania, I'm still a cop. I know if I stop now and leave this to the sheriff's department, he'll get away.

Movement thirty yards ahead snaps me back. A figure moving through the trees. Fast. A male. In good physical condition. Something familiar about the way he moves.

"Stop!" I shout. "I'm a police officer! I need to talk to you!"

The figure melts into the trees.

I start down the hill, ducking the occasional branch, moving too fast for the gradient, my feet sliding. I trip over a fallen log, nearly go down, catch myself just in time. I hear the roar of water before I reach the creek. The trees open. A behemoth structure looms, seemingly out of nowhere, as much a part of the forest as the trees. The old mill, I realize. Dozens of windows stare at me like black, watchful eyes. The hairs at my nape stand on end. My flashlight beam illuminates two stories constructed of brick and stone, hemmed in by trees and covered with vines.

The creek is too wide to cross. There's a dam to my left; water thunders over the spillway, rushing between a series of concrete piers. The only way across is to step from pier to pier. Not an ideal situation, but I know my suspect did just that and made it. Chances are, there's a road on the other side of the building where he's parked a vehicle. If he reaches the vehicle, he'll get away.

Rain pours down as I start across the piers. I set my beam on the opposite bank. One foot in front of the other. Water thundering all around. *Don't look down.*

I reach the other side, shine my light ahead. A loading dock abuts the building. Concrete steps to my left. Above, a rusty catwalk looks out over the water. I take the steps two at a time to the loading dock. Knee-high weeds jut from the crumbling concrete. Two overhead doors locked down and reinforced with chain-link fencing. A single footprint in a thin layer of mud. A man door stands open about a foot. I shove it open with my boot, go through.

Dark as a cave inside. The pound of rain on the roof is deafening. The smells of mold and creek water and rotting wood.

"It's Kate Burkholder!" I call out. "Come out and talk to me!"

I pause to listen, curse the din of rain, but there's no response.

I sweep my beam around the interior, get the sense of an abandoned factory that's frozen in time. Ancient wood beams overhead, some broken and slanting down. Moss growing on the walls. High windows boarded up. A rusty steel tank lies on its side, petrified sludge spread out beneath the spout. A Volkswagen-size piece of machinery of indecipherable origin. To my right, an open stairway leads to an upper level. Ahead, a brick arch leads to another room.

Senses on high alert, I pass beneath the arch, find myself in a cavernous room. There are several tanks of different sizes. A stone wall covered with creeping vines. Water cascading down from above. I shine my light upward, see the fire-damaged roof. I keep going.

"The sheriff's department is on the way!" I call out. "You're not in any trouble. Come out and talk to me!"

A loud *clang!* sounds from behind me. I spin, rush back to the room where I entered. I see movement at the top of the stairs.

"Stop!"

I dart to the stairs; they're steel with pipe rails. I take them two at a time to the top. Windows to my right. Glass broken out. Rain and wind pelt me as I ascend the steps. At the top, I go through a doorway. Wood floor littered with debris. Machinery to my left. Not many places to hide. Where the hell did he go?

I sidle toward the machinery. My .38 in my right hand. The butt slick against my palm. Maglite in my left. Wrists crossed. "Come out and talk to me!"

A figure emerges from the shadows. I shift my light, blind him. Recognition kicks. "Keep your hands where I can see them," I say.

Henry Stoltzfus raises his hands, shields his eyes from my beam with his left. "Don't shoot me."

No weapon in sight. That doesn't mean he doesn't have one tucked into his waistband. It doesn't mean he's not dangerous.

"Are you armed?" I ask.

"No."

I don't lower my pistol. "What are you doing here?"

He stares at me. Eyes wide. Mouth open.

"What were you doing at the Hershberger farm?" I ask.

No answer.

"Did you start the fire?"

He raises his gaze to mine. "I did what I had to do."

If I were in uniform, I'd get him on the ground and cuff him to secure the situation and keep both of us safe. Of course, I'm not in uniform; my zip ties are in the Explorer.

"Do not move," I tell him.

Never taking my eyes from his, I set my Maglite on the floor, the beam pointed toward him. Keeping my .38 steady, center mass, I work my cell from my pocket and hit redial with my thumb.

"Nine one one, what's your emergency."

"This is Kate Burkholder. I'm at the old mill with Henry Stoltzfus. I think he's involved in the fire at the Hershberger farm. Send a deputy right away. It's an emergency."

The dispatcher speaks, but I hit End, drop my cell back into my pocket.

I look at Henry and frown. "This might be a good time for you to start talking." I have to raise my voice to be heard over the pound of rain against the roof, the roar of water cascading over the dam outside, and the spattering of water onto the floor through a hole in the roof.

"You can't possibly understand," he says.

"Try me."

"I didn't mean to hurt anyone," he tells me. "I didn't mean to hurt *you*. But I knew you were going to figure it out."

"Figure what out?" I ask, more gently.

He emits a sob, looks around as if searching for a route of escape. He shifts his weight from one foot to the other. Feet restless. Hands raised. Acting squirrelly.

"Don't do anything stupid," I tell him.

He squeezes his eyes closed. He's trembling now. His face is wet; I can't tell if it's from the rain or if he's crying, but he's struggling with some internal demon.

"Henry, I'm the best friend you've got right now," I say softly. "Stay calm. Let me help you."

His gaze meets mine. In its depths, I see a tangled mass of pain and desperation and hopelessness.

"My *datt* was not a good man," he whispers.

"I know what he was," I say.

"Such a bad thing. So many lies." His mouth trembles. "He betrayed us. All of us. He tried to betray God, but the Lord would not be fooled."

"Is that why you killed him?" I ask.

He blinks as if the question comes as a shock. "I did what I had to do." His voice is so faint, I'm not sure I heard the words correctly. "You have to understand. There was no other way."

He charges me without warning. Animal sounds tear from his throat. I step back, raise the .38. "Stop!" Slip my finger inside the guard. "Stop! *Stop!*"

He keeps coming.

I fire twice. Catch a glimpse of his face. Disbelief in his eyes. Teeth clenched. Lips peeled back. He plows into me hard, a linebacker crushing the opposition. His shoulder rams my midsection. Knocks the breath from me. Then I'm reeling backward, feet tangling.

"Stop!" I try to get my gun into position for another

shot, but he's too close. His arms locked around my abdomen, trapping my right hand.

My back crashes against the wall. Wood splinters. The screech of steel. A puff of cold air. Rain on my back. My foot finds air. And then I'm falling into nothingness.

CHAPTER 28

It's as if I've been sucked into a vacuum. No sound. No gravity. Just me and a free fall of terror and the knowledge that I screwed up. I tumble down. My forearm strikes something solid. An explosion of pain streaks from forearm to shoulder. A scream tears from my throat. The water slams into my back like a concrete slab. Cold closes over me, stealing light and sound and air. The churning of water all around.

The slicker tangles around my arms. I can't see or hear or breathe. The sensation of being sucked down. Panic engulfs me and for an instant, I struggle mindlessly. I don't know up from down or dark from light. My foot plunges into mud. I shove off and propel myself toward the surface. One arm slips free of the slicker sleeve. I kick. Swipe at the water with my uninjured arm. Another burst of panic and then my face breaks the surface.

Water roars all around. I try to suck in a breath, swallow water, end up choking. I've lost my flashlight and .38. I don't know where Henry is. If he means to harm me. I tread water, look around, try to get my bearings. Too dark to see anything. The one thing I do know is I'm being swept downstream.

I let the current carry me. Using my right arm, kicking my feet, I make my way to shore. My feet touch bottom. Swift water tries to pull my legs out from under me. But I muscle through, maintain my balance. Once I'm in shallow water, I fall to my knees and crawl up the bank.

"Kate!"

Jonas. I look up, see a flashlight beam through the driving rain. "Here!" I call out.

The yellow cone of light bounces and nears. I hear the crash of brush over the roaring water. Then I see Jonas skidding down the bank toward me. Yellow slicker shiny and wet. Hat gone. Eyes intense and focused on me.

"Where's Henry?" I ask.

"I don't know." He bends to me, grasps my hand in his, helps me to my feet. "Are you hurt?"

"He set the fire," I tell him. My legs wobble as he hauls me up the steep bank. "He tried to kill me. I fired my weapon; I don't know if I hit him." I look around, hating it that I'm shaking so violently I can barely stand. "I lost my gun. My flashlight."

"Henry pushed you into the water?" he asks.

I take his flashlight, shine the beam on the second story of the structure. Sure enough, there's an opening where the wood splintered and both of us went through.

"The wall gave way," I tell him.

"You're hurt." He looks down where I'm cradling my injured arm.

"We need to find Henry," I tell him.

The wail of a siren rises over the roar of water, the din of rain. I look toward the front of the mill, see the flashing lights reflecting off the treetops.

"Maybe you ought to leave that to the police," he tells me.

I don't argue.

CHAPTER 29

Twenty years before

I was fifteen years old the last time I saw Jonas Bowman. It was worship Sunday at Leroy Miller's farm. I'd suffered through three hours of preaching in a sweltering barn and another two of the old folks "piecing" on pie and coffee and catching up on the latest gossip. As usual, a "singing" was planned for afternoon; as usual, I had no inclination to attend.

The problem was, I'd agreed to let Jonas drive me home afterward. I wasn't sure why that was a problem; my parents would be none the wiser if he dropped me off at the end of the lane. I had no idea what was wrong with me. I thought about him all the time. I missed him and yet I didn't want to spend time with him. I couldn't even be nice to him.

I'd caught glimpses of him throughout the morning. But with the women seated on one side of the barn and the men on the other, we didn't speak. Didn't even make eye contact. I didn't, anyway. But I caught him looking in my direction a time or two. By the time worship was over, I was feeling sulky and out of sorts. The last thing I wanted to do was ride home with him.

We'd seen each other several times over the summer. We didn't talk about it or make plans to meet, but somehow it always seemed to happen. He'd helped my *datt* dig postholes for the cross fence at the back of our property. Twice, we'd met at the creek. Once, at the covered bridge. Those stolen moments had become important to me, the more spontaneous, the better.

Mamm knew something secret was afoot. On more than one occasion, she reminded me that Jonas was too old. She couldn't explain why Datt—who was six years her senior—wasn't too old for her. When you looked at it that way, the four years between Jonas and me didn't seem like that much.

I was almost to the Tuscarawas Bridge when the clip-clop of hooves—and the electric blare of music—drew my attention. I turned to see Jonas in his buggy pull up beside me. I kept walking. He slowed the horse to keep pace.

"You stood me up," he said.

I looked straight ahead, trying not to acknowledge the tension climbing up the back of my neck. "I forgot."

I kept walking, but I was keenly aware of him, keeping pace, watching me. The music floating in the air like birdsong.

"You could have at least told me you didn't want to ride with me," he said. "I looked for you."

I kept my eyes on the road in front of me. I didn't

want him to know that I was secretly happy to see him. I knew if I looked at him, he would know.

Finally, I mustered my best frown and looked at him. "That radio is going to get you into trouble."

"Since when do you care about getting into trouble?" Leaning forward, he turned up the music. "I like this one."

It was a beautiful song with a wailing guitar and a woman's voice that sounded like poetry or some exotic foreign language.

"It's awful hot to be walking in the sun," he said.

"I'll get into trouble if I ride with you."

"No one has to know," he drawled. "I'll drop you off at the end of your lane."

"So you said."

But I stopped walking. He halted the horse and climbed down. For an instant, we simply looked at each other. I didn't remember him being so tall. For the first time in my life, I smelled men's cologne. In that instant, the music faded and the only thing I could hear was the pounding of my heart. Then he took my hand and helped me into the buggy.

A sense of freedom and excitement engulfed me as we flew down the road. I'd never felt so grown-up. I waved at Mrs. Fisher as we passed their farm. Any other time, we might've stopped to chat, but Jonas kept going, the radio blaring. I didn't say anything when he passed the turnoff for the farm where I lived. I had an idea where he was taking me, but it was the only place in the world I wanted to be.

A mile farther, he made the turn onto Rockridge

Road. The asphalt gave way to gravel and he kept going. Another quarter mile and the road dead-ended.

"Whoa." Jonas stopped the horse, then climbed down to loosen the lines so the animal could graze.

It was a pretty spot. Tall elm trees offered welcome shade. A profusion of wildflowers in the ditch. Raspberry bushes growing along the fence. I was thinking about climbing down and checking for ripe berries— maybe taking a few home—when he came back and climbed in beside me. Reaching under the seat, he pulled out a cooler and handed me a beer and got another for himself. I caught a glimpse of the other items in the cooler. Cookies wrapped in wax paper. Some kind of cheese. Crackers. Only then did I realize he'd planned a picnic—and I'd foiled his plans by standing him up.

Embarrassed that I'd noticed the food, he closed the cooler.

"There's a baseball game Friday out to John Hershberger's place," he said. "Wanna go?"

I sipped my beer, thinking, knowing my parents wouldn't let me go, wondering if I could sneak out. I didn't look at him because I was afraid he'd see just how desperately I wanted to go. "Maybe."

"You never used to be so complicated," he said.

I slanted a look at him, trying to figure out if that was an insult. "I'm not complicated."

"First you say yes, then you stand me up. What am I supposed to think?"

I didn't have an answer. For several minutes we didn't

speak. I listened to the music, loving the voices and instruments and lyrics, and I daydreamed about escaping with Jonas into a world that wasn't as muddled as the one in which we lived.

"You ever been to the Icebox?" Jonas asked.

The Icebox was a swimming hole on Painters Creek. A mysterious place where the water was so deep no one had ever touched the bottom. Stories abounded; the most memorable was about the English boy who'd drowned when the creek flooded. The Icebox turned into a whirlpool and sucked his canoe into the abyss. To this day, his screams can be heard in the woods at night.

"I've been there," I told him, leaving out the fact that I hadn't had the guts to get in the water.

"Elam Yoder told me his grandfather saw the whirlpool back when that kid was killed," he said.

I felt my eyes widen. An imagination is the one thing I'd never lacked. The thought of all that water swallowing a boy alive made me shiver. "I don't see how the water can be that deep."

"That's not all he said." Watching me, he tipped his bottle and drank. "A couple weeks ago, Elam and his friends were there, swimming, and he decided to find out just how deep that hole really is. So he got this big rock, tied a rope to it, and went into the water where there's a drop-off. He let that rock take him down, held on to the rope as long as he could, but he ran out of breath before he reached the bottom."

My imagination surged with the mystery of it, the danger. "Did he see anything?"

"He said there was a big cave down there. All sorts of strange currents." He lowered his voice. "Said he saw that canoe, too, and it creeped him out."

I stared at him, feeling that tingle for adventure take hold. "Have you ever been there?" I ask.

"Twice."

"Did you try to reach the bottom?"

"What do you think?" He laughed. "I'm a good swimmer, Katie. I tried, but I couldn't do it. Never seen water so deep. The deeper you go, the colder it gets."

A small part of me didn't believe all the stories. But it was fun to imagine such a dangerous and exciting place right here in Painters Mill.

"It's early yet. Plenty hot." Squinting against the sun, Jonas looked out across the land. "Want to go?"

Despite my efforts otherwise, I was intrigued. I wanted to see the Icebox again. I wanted to explore its depths. I wanted Jonas and me to be the ones to reach the bottom before anyone else could.

"How far is it from here?" I ask.

"Couple miles down the road. We can be there in five minutes."

I looked down at my dress and shoes, knowing swimming wasn't a very good idea. But, oh, how I wanted to explore that storied body of water. I could always hang my clothes in the sun to dry afterward. Mamm might not notice. I could always tell her I slipped on a rock while wading. . . .

"You brought all that food." I smile at him. "Maybe we can have our picnic there."

Jonas smiled back. "I brought two towels, too."

"You thought of everything." I got to my feet. "I bet we could find a couple of big rocks. . . ."

He took my hand. "Come on."

We never reached the bottom of that deep pool of water. We had sex right there on the sandy bank, atop the afghan his grandmother had knitted some forty years ago. It was a first for both of us. Awkward. Earth-shattering. Beautiful.

I won't get into the sordid details, but we got caught. One moment we were entwined in each other's arms, half dressed, awestruck by what had just happened, trying to come to terms with what it meant in terms of our lives and the future. Then we heard the sound of buggy wheels against gravel—and my *datt*'s voice calling my name—and we flew into a panic. We barely had time to yank on our clothes. One look at my *datt*'s face and I knew he knew. It was the most mortifying moment of my young life. Only later did I learn that Mrs. Fisher had gone to my *datt* and told him she'd seen us together. Because of our age difference, the bishop got involved. When the sheriff's department paid the Bowmans a visit and had a conversation about statutory rape, Ezra Bowman decided to move his family to Pennsylvania.

Three days later Jonas was gone, and I never saw him again.

CHAPTER 30

Some nights are a bottomless pit of darkness filled with nightmares and the kinds of monsters your parents assured you didn't exist. I'm almost surprised when I see the eastern horizon lighten with the first vestiges of dawn, and not for the first time I'm reminded that light always transcends the dark.

I'm standing on the loading dock at the rear of the old mill, smelling of pond water and mud, trying in vain not to shiver. My forearm aches with every beat of my heart. My clothes and hair are damp, cold, and uncomfortable. Despite all of it, I'm damn glad to be alive.

The occasional bark of a police radio emanates from the front of the building. Voices echo inside as the sheriff's department wraps up their investigation. Upon their arrival, I spent two hours in the back seat of a departmental SUV, being pelted with questions by a short-tempered lieutenant and an investigator with the Pennsylvania State Police. In light of the circumstances—namely my admittance that I'd fired my weapon in self-defense—both men were particularly interested in locating my .38. I explained to them I likely dropped it in the creek when I fell. Though I'm a peace officer from a neighboring state, and I maintain a concealed-carry license in Ohio, which has a reciprocity agreement with Pennsylvania, they weren't happy with me.

After I gave my statement, a young EMT wrapped my forearm and set me up with a sling to tide me over until I can get to the clinic in Lewistown for X-rays. He didn't think it was broken, but thought I might have a hairline fracture. Six hundred milligrams of ibuprofen and I was on my way.

Henry Stoltzfus's body was recovered a short while ago, half a mile downstream. The deputy I spoke with said the cause of death wasn't evident. Much to my relief, there was no sign of a gunshot wound. He may have drowned or sustained an injury in the fall. The official cause and manner of death will be determined only after an autopsy.

Lambent sunlight, heavy with morning dew, slants down through the treetops to play on the surface of the creek. The water has receded, but the telltale debris is still piled against the spillway, as if in testament to the violence of the night. I can't stop thinking about those last minutes I spent with Henry Stoltzfus. The desperation etched into his features. The hopelessness and despair. I've gone over every detail a thousand times. Let the scene play out a dozen different ways. I've analyzed my every move, critiqued my every response, my every word. Could I have done something differently that might've saved his life?

"Katie?"

I turn to see Jonas coming up the steps leading to the loading dock. Shirt untucked. Hat missing. Clothes muddy and damp.

"Tell me I don't look as bedraggled as you," I say.

A smile whispers across his features as he crosses to me. "The bishop sees me without my hat and I could be in trouble."

"You were a little busy pulling me out of the creek."

"You're okay?"

"Thanks to you."

His eyes fall to the sling, but he doesn't point out the obvious. "The deputy said Henry Stoltzfus is gone."

"They found him downstream." I'm too raw to say anything more.

To his credit, he doesn't press.

For the span of a full minute, we stand there, looking out across the water. On the other side of the stream, a turtle crawls onto a log to catch a ray of sun. Once again, I'm stunned by the lush beauty of this place. And I'm shocked all over again that so much violence could play out in such a pretty spot.

"I think Henry murdered Ananias," I say.

He cocks his head as the repercussions sink in. "He admitted it?"

I did what I had to do.

I weigh my response and nod. "In a roundabout way."

"Did he say why?"

I hit the highlights of our exchange. "At some point,

he must have figured out what his father was. Who he was. A charlatan. A liar. Maybe a killer." I shrug. "He saw it as a betrayal. And he snapped."

My datt *was not a good man.*

Henry's voice comes to me as clearly as if he's standing next to me. For an instant, I'm transported back in time. The sight of him charging. The discharge of my weapon. The seconds I spent beneath the surface of the water, not knowing if I'd make it out.

"To be raised Amish," Jonas says. "And find out that your parents lied about who they are. That they are not Amish. To learn that your father may have done terrible things." He shrugs. "Those are big lies to live with. To forgive."

"It must have thrown his entire existence into question. Everything he believed in."

"He would have let me go to jail for something I didn't do."

"He didn't approve of you or father's ideals," I tell him. "He thought you were bad for the Amish community and he wanted you out of the picture. He knew the history between you and Ananias. That there was bad blood, and he put that to work."

"But he was *Amisch.*" Of all the things Henry Stoltzfus did, that he betrayed the Amish doctrine seems to bother him the most. "I can't understand that."

"I've been doing this a long time, Jonas. People rationalize what they do. They make excuses. Lie to themselves. It's a protective mechanism, I think. That's a powerful thing, especially when someone is desperate." I shrug. "Maybe Henry justified what he did by convincing himself that getting you out of the picture would somehow heal or unite the church district."

He nods, but I can tell by his expression he still can't fathom how an Amish man could purposefully hurt—or kill—another human being. "And the rifle?" he asks.

"I suspect he'd seen it at some point in the mudroom. Had he ever been in your house?"

"We were never close . . . but we're Amish." He shrugs. "We've had worship at our place a time or two. It's possible."

"So he knew it was there. He either went into your house when no one was home, or at night, while everyone was sleeping. He used it to kill Ananias and left it at the scene, so it would be tied back to you."

His brows knit. "What about the hand bones?"

"He was afraid fingerprints would identify his father, not as the Amish man he claimed to be, but a German soldier with a shady past—or worse." I give another shrug. "We'll never know the whole story."

Jonas shoves his hands into his pockets. "I don't know how you did what you did, but I'm a thankful man. You went through a lot and even though you were hurt, you didn't stop." He slants a look at me and smiles. "You still play to win, no?"

"I've been accused of being persistent."

"A time or two." Thoughtful, he looks out across the water. "You'll be going back to Painters Mill. To that man you're going to marry. Your life as a police chief."

I offer my best smile. "All of the above."

His gaze shifts back to me and the space between us charges, like the air in the seconds before a lightning strikc. For a flccting instant, I'm that fifteen-year-old Amish girl again. The one who'd loved him with all my woman's heart and missed him so much I wanted to die.

"I'm a happily married man," he says after a moment.

"I know that," I tell him. "It suits you."

His eyes hold my gaze captive so that I can't look away. "I thought about you a lot over the years," he says quietly. "What might've been if my parents hadn't left when they did. I wondered how things might've turned out if I'd stayed. For a long time after I left, I wondered what it would be like to see you again."

"We were too young," I tell him.

"I almost came back for you."

"Jonas—"

He starts to speak over me, but I raise my hand and press my fingers against his mouth. "Some things aren't meant to be," I say quietly.

His expression intensifies, as if he's seeing me for the first time after a long separation, and he isn't quite sure I'm really there or if I'm the same person and he desperately needs to find out if I am. "I would have married you," he whispers. "I wanted to."

It's the last thing I expected him to say. I sure as hell didn't expect the words to touch me so deeply—or to hurt. My relationship with Jonas is ancient history. A sweet spot in my past that will forever remain just that. A memory that's been cleaned up by time. The messiness and pain erased. Time, the great healer.

"Everything worked out the way it was supposed to," I tell him.

"Tell my nineteen-year-old self that."

He leans toward me, reaches out to cup my face, but I gently grasp his wrist and stop him. We both know such an intimate touch would be considered inappropriate for a married Amish man. He may be willing to take the risk, but I'm not.

A smile whispers across his features.

And he walks away.

CHAPTER 31

I've closed my share of cases over the years. A few were major crimes that required in-depth investigation, dogged determination, and gobbled up hundreds of hours—everything I had to give. Most were lesser offenses that entailed the same, only on a smaller scale. No matter the type of case, the one thing I always appreciate at the end is the sense of closure. The satisfaction of knowing a bad guy is off the street. The gratification that comes with a solid resolution and the knowledge that you did your job.

While this wasn't an official "case," a murderer was taken off the street. An innocent man was cleared of wrongdoing. Though I didn't participate in a law enforcement capacity, I played a major role. Despite all of it, there's little in the way of closure. There are too many unanswered questions. Too many loose ends. Who was Ananias Stoltzfus really? Where was he from and what did he do? How much did Mia know? And how did Henry discover his identity?

They are questions that will likely take weeks or months to answer—if they're answered at all. The only thing I have at this point is conjecture. The one thing I am certain of is that Ananias Stoltzfus was not a good man and may have very well been an evil man. That his son took matters into his own hands and destroyed his own life in the process is a far cry from justice.

I'm standing at the entrance of the old mill, watching the paramedics heft the bag containing Henry Stoltzfus's body into the rear of an ambulance. It's nearly noon now. Jonas and I gave our statements. Henry's family has been notified. The crime scene unit pulled out twenty minutes ago. I should have left hours ago. I could have been showered, packed, and on my way to Painters Mill by now.

So why are you still here, Kate?

"Chief Burkholder!"

I turn to see Deputy Kris Vance stride toward me. The wariness is gone from his expression. Now that the case has been solved, he isn't concerned about associating with me or my pressing him with questions he shouldn't be answering.

"You need a ride back to your vehicle?" he asks.

We shake hands. "I'm parked at the Hershberger place just through the trees," I tell him.

"It's on my way. Save you a walk up that hill." He motions to his vehicle and we start down the steps. "It'll give me a chance to apologize."

"Your superiors didn't exactly make it easy for you to share information," I say.

"There is that. But I was a jackass. I'm sorry I wasn't

more helpful. You were right. We were wrong." His smile is contrite. "Lesson learned."

I smile at him over the top of his cruiser as we get in. "I won't hold my breath waiting for a call from the sheriff."

"Just between us, he's a bigger jackass than me." Grinning, he puts the vehicle in gear and starts down the muddy lane. "I thought you'd want to know: The state police will be sending the remains to the forensic lab for DNA testing."

"Positive ID would go a long way toward tying up a lot of loose ends."

"No one figured Henry Stoltzfus for the crime," he says. "All these years and he was right under our noses. Nice guy. Family man. Spotless record. He was never on the radar."

"At some point, Henry must have figured out who or what his father was." I shrug, trying to work through the logistics of it, coming up short. "He didn't like what he found and just . . . lost it."

"I suppose even the Amish have their limit." He makes the turn into the Hershberger place and parks behind my Explorer.

"In any case, Chief Burkholder, I mainly wanted to apologize for shutting you out of the investigation. You're a damn good cop and with your knowledge of the Amish, you would have been a good resource had we given you the chance."

I open the door, get out, and bend to look at him. "Keep me posted on that DNA?"

"You bet."

I slam the door, give a wave, and then he's gone.

I stand in the driveway, vaguely troubled, and watch him pull out. I fish the fob out of my pocket, walk to the Explorer, and open the door. But I don't get in.

I expect the Amish will be arriving shortly, to support Mary Elizabeth and her husband in their time of grief, to keep the farm up and running, and the household chores done. I'm probably the last person she wants to see, but I'd like to keep a line of communication open between us. In the coming weeks, much more information about her father will be forthcoming. At the very least, I can offer my condolences—and leave the rest to her.

I close the door of the Explorer and walk to the house, take the steps to the door, and knock. I wait, getting my words in order, but no one comes. I'm on my way back to the Explorer when I notice the barn door standing ajar, so I head that way.

I pause at the doorway, stare into the dimly lit interior. The smell of smoke lingers. I hear the cattle bawling at the rear. Dim light filters in through the windows ahead. To my right, stairs lead up to the hayloft. Gardening tools hang on the wall—a shovel, pitchfork, and hoe. Livestock stalls line the aisle on my left. I keep going, stop a few yards in, give my eyes a chance to adjust to the murky light.

"Mary Elizabeth?" I call out. "It's Kate Burkholder."

"What are you doing here?"

I glance left, see Mary Elizabeth in silhouette against the window behind her. Long dress and apron. The strings of her *kapp* hanging down. Black oxfords. Even with her face in shadow, I can see that she's been crying.

"I didn't want to leave without telling you how sorry I am about your brother," I say.

She winces at the mention of her brother, hangs her head. "Blessed are those who mourn, for they will be comforted."

"Matthew," I say.

That I'm familiar with the Bible passage seems to please her. She raises her gaze to mine, scrubs her hands over her cheeks to wipe away the tears. "The deputy I talked to said you were there. When it happened."

I nod.

"Did he say anything?" she asks. "Did he say why?"

I search my memory for something that will answer her question and yet won't add to her misery. "He said he didn't mean to hurt anyone," I tell her. "That he was sorry."

She squeezes her eyes closed, presses her fingers to the bridge of her nose. "How could he do what he did? To our *datt*? To Jonas. It's beyond me."

I don't have the answers she needs. What little I know about her father will only add to her despair. I'm not exactly in a position to comfort her. "I know it must be difficult," I say. "When you're ready, you might see if you can find your *mamm*'s diary. There may be some answers there."

She pulls a tissue from her pocket and blows her nose. "I don't see how an old woman's scribblings could drive a good man to kill."

"Sometimes we write about the things that hurt us the most," I tell her.

"My own brother." The Amish woman presses her hand over her mouth, but she can't suppress the sob that escapes. "He lured our *datt* to that old farm and shot him like an animal. Left him for the coyotes and vultures and God only knows what. He lied about it all these years." She uses the tissue to wipe her eyes. "To cut off a man's hands? How does anyone do such a thing? I can't bear to think of it."

The world around me grinds to a halt. The ground seems to shift beneath my feet. Something cold and sharp scrapes down my back. "Did Henry tell you that?" I ask.

She looks up at me, sniffs. "Tell me what?"

"That the hands had been removed?"

She shakes her head. "I must have read about it or heard it somewhere. Gossip probably. You know how the Amish are."

I stare at her, an internal alarm shrilling. It was the one detail the police didn't make public. Even if the information got out—which it did to me—hearing about the mutilation of a loved one isn't the kind of news you forget where you heard it.

I'm aware of the sliding door standing open a few yards behind me. The loft above and to my right. Stalls on my left. The sound of the cattle bawling and moving around outside.

Mary Elizabeth stares at me. Tears are wet on her cheeks and yet something cold shifts in her eyes. "You should have left," she tells me.

I lower my hand to the holster where my .38 usually rests. Of course, it's not there. I'm aware of the mini Magnum against my ankle. Not easily accessed. I set my other hand against the key fob in my pocket. My cell is in the Explorer, drying out after being submerged. I don't know if it's operable. Shit.

"You have the journal," I say.

"The police gave it to *me* after Mamm died," she whispers. "Not Datt. Not Henry." Her expression turns mournful. "I missed her so much. I wanted to understand why she did it." She shakes her head. "Reading it was quite a shock. God in heaven I wish I hadn't."

I stare at her, focused on the .22 strapped to my ankle. I don't know exactly what this woman knows or what she has done. I don't know if she's armed or what she's capable of. I have no idea where her husband is. The one thing I do know is that I'm in danger. All I have to do is kneel, yank up the hem of my slacks, slide the revolver from its nest . . .

"How my *mamm* suffered," she says. "The things he did. The horrors stuck in her head. Such ungodly things."

Keeping my eyes on Mary Elizabeth, I back toward the sliding door. "Henry knew," I say, buying time.

"He knew you'd figure it out." She tilts her head, looks at me as if I'm something to be pitied, an injured animal about to be put down. "No one wanted you hurt. We're not that way. We just wanted you *gone*."

I drop to a kneeling position, yank up the hem of my slacks. A sound from above startles me. I glance up to see a wall of hay lean. I reach for the .22 but I'm not fast enough. Dozens of bales plummet. I lunge, try to get out of the way. A bale strikes my shoulder. Another slams into my back. I sprawl to the ground. A tremendous weight pummels me. I'm flat on my belly. The world falls silent.

And it's just me and the dark and the knowledge that I've been buried alive and there's no way out.

CHAPTER 32

I lie still, dazed, adrenaline sizzling in my gut. I'm in a prone position, arms outstretched, my head turned, cheek pressed to the ground. I have dirt in my mouth. Dust in my nostrils. Crushing weight on my back. Darkness all around. I suck in a breath. Dirt hits the back of my throat. I cough, my chest heaving, fingers of panic digging in.

Dear God, I can't move.

I recall the hay tumbling from the loft. Dozens of bales coming down on top of me. I try to raise my head, but can't. I flex my arm, try to push myself off the ground, but there's too much weight pressing me down. A rush of claustrophobia assails me, primal and intense. I struggle mindlessly, grunting with the effort of trying to move. A scream tears from my throat. Dear God . . .

Easy does it, Chief. You got this.

Tomasetti's voice comes to me out of the dark. I go still, listen to it, focus on the words. *You got this.* Slowly, the panic loosens its death grip. I bend my elbow. Bring my hand to my face. I wipe spit and mud and bits of hay from my mouth. I take another breath, not too deep. I move my leg, try to bring up my knee, only manage to dig the toes of my boots into the dirt.

All the while, I listen for voices. The only thing I hear is the hard pounding of my heart, my pulse thrumming in my ears. I try to shift onto my side, but there's not enough room. I go still again, work my way through the chain of events, and I know this was no accident. Someone was in the loft and pushed the hay down on top of me. Adrian?

The thought prompts another barrage of panic. I fight it this time, force myself to remain still, reach for calm that isn't there. I concentrate instead on my physical condition. No pain. I'm not injured, but I won't last long without fresh air and with the weight of the hay crushing my lungs.

I have no idea how many bales came down. Each weighs fifty or sixty pounds. They're rectangular and likely scattered on impact. The strongest muscles in my body are my legs. If I can shove just one bale aside, I may be able to dig my way out.

I bend both arms, set my hands against the ground, try to push off, push-up style. Hay scrapes against my skin. My scalp. I shove as hard as I can. No go.

I shift to my left side, bring up my right leg, try to roll to get my knee under me. The bale on top of me shifts, but another comes down. At first, I think I've made the situation worse. Then suddenly, my knee is beneath me. I twist, push against the bale with my back. I feel another bale move. Groaning with the strain, I shove harder. Get my other knee beneath me. Loose hay rains down. In my eyes, my mouth, my hair. But I see light, too. I'm in a crawling position now. Arms shaking with exertion. Breaths puffing. Choking on dirt. I bring my knee forward, get my foot beneath me, shove off against the ground. The bale on top of me tumbles away. Cool air pours over my sweat-slicked face. I suck in a breath as I squeeze between two bales. I see the rafters above. The broken rail hanging down. And then I'm free.

I look around. Mary Elizabeth is nowhere in sight. No sign of Adrian. Keeping my eyes on my surroundings, I clamber down, jump to the floor. Land on my feet. I reach down, yank up my pants leg, tug the mini Magnum from its holster.

Every sense on high alert, I sidle to the wall beneath the loft. Eyes everywhere, my back against the wall, I edge toward the door. I'm midway there when Mary Elizabeth comes through. Her mouth falls open at the sight of me. The bag she'd been holding drops to the floor.

"Get your fucking hands up!" I level the mini Mag at her. "Get them up. *Now!*"

She raises both hands. All the while she stares at me as if I'm a ghost.

"Where's Adrian?" I demand.

She blinks. Shakes her head as if her eyes are deceiving her. "House." The word comes out like a puff of air.

"Get on the ground. On your belly. *Do it now!*"

When she doesn't move fast enough, I stride to her, grab her scruff, push her down. "Get down! Spread your arms! Do not move! Do you understand?"

The woman obeys. I don't have handcuffs. I don't have a phone. Or my regular service weapon. The one thing I do have in abundance is baling twine.

I look at Mary Elizabeth. "If you move, I will shoot you dead. You got that?"

Without looking at me, the woman jerks her head.

Holding the gun center mass, I back to the nearest hay bale. I reach into my pocket, remove the folding knife, and slice the string. Pulling it free, I go to her.

"Put your hands behind your back," I tell her. "Now."

"But, you can't—"

I rap the side of her head with my palm. "Do it!" I hear anger in my voice, feel the rage crawling over me, and I pull myself back from an edge I don't want to get too close to.

Kneeling, keeping one eye on the door, on the loft above, I loop the string around her wrist several times, pull it behind her back, and secure it to her other wrist. I yank both tight and triple-knot the twine. It's not an ideal restraint, compromising her circulation and likely chafing her skin. But it'll work just fine until the sheriff's department arrives.

Considering what this woman has done, the discomfort of a temporary cuff is the least of her worries.

To my surprise, my cell phone worked despite having been submerged in creek water. It takes the sheriff's department fourteen minutes to arrive on scene. I made good use of the time, snagging the zip ties from my toolbox in the Explorer and finding Adrian. I caught him in the house as he was coming down the steps. If the situation hadn't been so serious, I might've been amused by his expression at the sight of me. He didn't resist when I trained the mini Mag on his chest. I made use of the zip ties, marched him to the barn, put him facedown on the ground next to his wife.

That was two hours ago. Since, I've given my statement, first to Sergeant Gainer with the Mifflin County Sheriff's Department and then to an investigator with the Pennsylvania State Police. The general consensus is that I'm lucky to be alive.

I'm tired and cranky, the adrenaline having long since given way to fatigue. I'm sitting behind the wheel of the Explorer, contemplating a hot shower and eight hours of uninterrupted sleep, when Sergeant Gainer approaches my vehicle.

"Thought you'd be gone by now," he says by way of greeting.

"I'm working on it," I tell him.

"We got the Hershbergers booked in. DA is working on charges. Going to be a slew once we get things figured out. They'll be arraigned tomorrow morning if you want to be there."

"I think I'll pass," I tell him.

"Heading back to Painters Mill?"

The mention of home makes me smile. I think about Tomasetti. My team of officers. And in that moment, I've never been more homesick in my life. "First thing in the morning."

"The investigation is ongoing, Chief Burkholder, but it looks like they were planning to burn the barn while you were trapped beneath all that hay." He motions toward a nearby shed. "We found a gas can, rags, matches, and a bunch of canning jars filled with gas."

It takes a good bit of effort not to shudder. "They would have blamed it on the so-called vandal that had started the fire here last night as well as the one at the mill."

"I suspect it was Henry all along," he tells me.

"He wanted to divert police attention away from him and his sister," I murmur.

"Exactly." He nods. "He was probably our tipster, too."

"The hand bones in the well," I say.

"He wanted us to focus on Bowman, so he piled on as much manufactured evidence as he could." He grimaces. "Probably attacked you at the motel. Ran you off the road that day up on the mountain."

I nod, remembering, and I realize the physical description of my attacker fits. "He was desperate," I say. "He thought he could frighten me into leaving town."

"I reckon that's not the first time you've been underestimated." He gives me a self-deprecating smile.

I smile back, liking him. Almost.

"Going to take a while to sort through everything." He reaches beneath his cap and scratches his head. "We don't even know at this point which one of them shot and killed Ananias Stoltzfus."

"The answer to that might just lie with Mia Stoltzfus's diary," I tell him.

"Speaking of the diary." Gainer's expression turns grim. "We executed a search warrant earlier. I found the journal. Before logging and sealing it, I paged through. The thing went back decades. Some of it was written in

German. But there was enough English for me to see that Mia Stoltzfus made some very serious accusations about her husband."

"What kinds of accusations?"

"Things that happened, things he did. During the war." His expression turns queasy, as if his breakfast is thinking about coming up. "Let me tell you something, Chief Burkholder, that diary is a thing of nightmares."

I feel the same queasiness creep up on me. "Any idea how Mary Elizabeth got her hands on the diary?"

"I dug up the police report from the suicide of Mia Stoltzfus." He grimaces. "The diary should have been returned to the surviving spouse. Inadvertently, it was given to Mary Elizabeth."

Another piece of the puzzle snaps into place. "She knew what her father was," I say.

Gainer stares at me intently. "If any of what I read in that diary is true, it's enough to make anyone snap." He shakes his head. "We'll know a lot more once we sit down and talk to her. I suspect her brother was involved."

I think about my final conversation with Henry. Family dynamics. "He was protecting her," I say. "Even if Mary Elizabeth is the one who pulled the trigger, Henry helped her cover up the crime. He framed Jonas Bowman. In the end, he took the fall for his sister."

He nods, looking at me intently. "At the risk of screwing up my reputation as an asshat." A sheepish smile splits his face. "That was some damn fine police work you did. Thank you."

"I had an advantage," I tell him.

"You're Amish."

Now it's my turn to smile. "I knew Jonas Bowman."

He sticks out his hand and gives mine a firm shake. "Just don't go running for sheriff around here next election."

"Wouldn't dream of it," I tell him, and I drive away.

CHAPTER 33

I'm not very good at goodbyes. I avoid them when possible. I prefer the see-you-next-time kind of farewell even when both of us know we'll likely never see each other again. I considered skipping this one, but I didn't want to leave things unfinished a second time. As I make the turn into the driveway of the Bowman house for the final time, I'm glad I came, even though I know it's going to hurt. Such is the nature of life.

I park between the house and workshop. As usual, the shop door stands open. I exit the Explorer to the wail of a saw, the hiss of air through the lines, and the rumble of the diesel generator at the side of the building.

I enter to find Jonas and Reuben standing at a huge lathe, turning a wood spindle that will likely become the leg of a kitchen table. Junior sits cross-legged on the floor adjacent to six cabinet doors that are lined up against the wall. He's staining the doors a two-tone maple and merlot. One down, five to go. Effie stands at the rear of the workshop, broom in one hand and dustpan in the other, looking a lot more interested in the machinery around her than sweeping up sawdust. *Good girl,* I think.

"Katie!"

I turn to see Junior trotting toward me. He's grinning. A dribble of wood stain on his forehead. Sweat on his cheeks.

I motion toward the cabinets he'd been working on. "I like the two-tone."

"Datt didn't think the merlot would go with the maple," the boy tells me, "but Effie put both colors on a piece of scrap wood and Datt liked it just fine."

"So we decided to do the whole dining room set with those two colors."

At the sound of her voice, I glance over to see Effie approach. She's left the broom and dustpan behind and runs her fingertips over one of the naked cabinet doors.

"You have a good eye for color," I tell her.

"Datt says I can pick out the hardware, too," she tells me.

"Katie."

I glance over my shoulder to see Jonas and Reuben approach. It's only been a couple of days since I saw the boy, but he looks taller. I'm struck all over again by how much he resembles his father at that age.

"You're going home," says Jonas.

"I couldn't leave without saying goodbye." I discern the excessive cheer in my voice. It's silly, but I'm having a difficult time meeting his gaze, so I focus on the children, taking in their faces, wanting to remember them just like this.

"Datt, what about the . . ." Junior drops his voice to a whisper. "You know."

I look at the boy and raise my brows. "That sounds suspiciously like there might be a surprise in store for someone."

"You!" cries Effie, and slaps her hand over her mouth, giggling.

Finally, I look at Jonas. Feel the weight of his stare. The rise of emotion in my chest. Something inside me shifts and free-falls, and I know this is one of those moments. One that's fleeting, but will forever be remembered.

I smile. "They get their subtlety from their *datt*."

Jonas rolls his eyes. "Reuben, go get them."

I watch the young man walk to a beat-up workbench and pick up three large wooden candleholders. He handles them with reverence as he brings them to us and hands one to me.

"For you," he says. "From all of us."

"I turned them." Effie looks as if she's holding her breath. "My first."

"I s-stained them," Junior tells me.

"They're beautiful." I turn the candleholder over, admiring the workmanship. "I love them."

"We wanted to thank you," Jonas says. "For everything you did for us while you were here."

"It was Mamm's idea," Effie points out.

"I'll cherish them always," I say, hoping no one notices the frog in my throat or that I'm blinking a little too quickly.

I look at Jonas, hating it that I don't quite trust my

voice to speak. He stares back at me and in that moment we're teenagers again. The world has no weight, our dreams know no bounds, and our hearts are free.

I extend my hand to him for a shake. "Thank you."

He looks down at my hand as if he's not sure he should take it. But he does and his touch is electric. I feel calluses against my palm. The strength of his grip. The warmth of his skin against mine. A thousand memories passing between us.

"Katie!"

I glance toward the door to see Dorothy rush through, a brown paper bag in her hand. "I thought I heard the saws go quiet." She grins at her husband, then crosses to me and passes me the bag. "I made you some date-nut bread for the trip."

The aromas of cinnamon and maple waft from the bag as I take it. "You can bet I'll put it to good use."

I shake the hand of each of the children. I hug Dorothy and thank her for the bread. I take a final look at Jonas. "I know it's a tall order, but if it's not too difficult, stay out of trouble," I tell him.

"Same goes," he says.

And I walk away.

CHAPTER 34

The Amish have a lot of sayings about a lot of things. One that has stayed with me over the years has to do with family and goes something like: Home is anywhere you are with the ones you love. I hadn't thought of that adage in years, but as I pass by the sign welcoming me to Painters Mill, the words play in the periphery of my thoughts, and I feel the solace of this place fall over my shoulders with the warmth and comfort of an old coat.

I spent most of the drive thinking about Jonas Bowman, the past we shared, and how those formative years shaped our lives. Had the circumstances played out differently, I might've married him. We might've had children and a farm somewhere right here in Painters Mill. Of course, it would have been the wrong path for me. Him, too, probably. But that scant piece of time we shared as teenagers was precious nonetheless. Looking back, the ache is truly both bitter and sweet.

As I idle down Main Street, I consider stopping in at

the station to let Lois know I'm back in town, but I don't pull in. More than anything, it's Tomasetti I want. He is my family. My love. My life. The need to see him, touch him, hear the sound of his voice has a desperate edge that has me cranking the speedometer over the limit.

I fly through Millersburg and head north on Ohio 83. South of Wooster, I nearly blow the stop sign at the township road. I wind it down just in time to avoid skidding on gravel as I make the turn into our lane. Dust billows in my rearview mirror. My heart patters against my ribs when our old farmhouse looms into view. Fresh paint from a marathon weekend of painting last summer. The grass is freshly cut, phlox blooming wildly in the side yard. Next year, I think, a garden. Maybe a maple tree in the front to replace the spruce we lost last winter.

Tomasetti's Tahoe is parked in its usual spot. I glance left toward the bank barn to see an old pickup truck I don't recognize. It's hitched to a rusty stock trailer. The rear door is open, the ramp pulled out. No livestock inside. The barn's big sliding door stands open. I see light inside, telling me he's there.

I park behind the Tahoe. Leaving my overnight bag and laptop case, I start toward the barn. Midway there I break into a run. By the time I go through the door I'm breathless, not due to the exertion, but because I can't wait to see him.

Our riding mower is parked against the wall to my left. The smells of freshly cut grass and gasoline in the air. Garden tools—shovel, hoe, and rake—hang neatly on the wall next to the mower. A bag of fertilizer sits next to a bag of grass seed. No sign of Tomasetti. I turn, spot the light seeping out from the aisle to my left, so I head that way.

I find him standing outside one of the livestock stalls. The sliding door stands open. He's so absorbed in whatever's going on in the stall that he doesn't notice me until I'm nearly upon him.

He does a double take upon spotting me. His eyes land first on the sling cradling my arm; then his gaze meets mine and a grin emerges. "Now there's a sight for sore eyes," he says, starting toward me.

I smile. "Yard looks nice. You've been busy."

"You have no idea."

He reaches me, and I plow into him, put my arm around his neck. His arms wrap around me and he pulls me tight. "You're early," he murmurs.

"I missed you," I whisper into his ear.

Standing on my tiptoes, I press a kiss to his cheek. He shifts his head, and I find his mouth. I kiss him long and hard, embarrassed because I'm an inch away from crying and I'm not sure why.

"I like it when you miss me," he murmurs.

I pull away slightly and for an instant, we grin stupidly at each other. "Whose truck?" I ask.

"Ours," he says. "Got it for a steal. Couldn't pass it up."

I release him and glance toward the stall where a bare bulb rains down light. "Dare I ask?"

"Mr. Baker was looking to buy some feeder calves," he tells me. "Asked me to drive over to the auction in Kidron yesterday."

A cry that's part bleat, part kitten mewl sounds from inside the stall. I look over his shoulder, realize that the light is actually a heat lamp and shining down . . .

"Come here." Taking my hand, he leads me to the stall door. Fluffy yellow straw covers the floor. A small brown goat stands in the middle of the stall, nibbling hay from a feeder I've never seen before. Three tiny brown kids huddle beneath a big heat lamp in the corner.

"You bought goats?" I say dumbly.

"Goat, actually. She's a Nigerian Dwarf."

"In case you hadn't noticed, there are four of them."

"Mama had triplets this morning." He grins, but I can tell he's not sure if I'm pleased.

I walk into the stall and bend, run my hand over the adult goat's back. "Hi, Mama," I say quietly.

I go to the babies and kneel. They're tiny things, as soft as stuffed animals, and don't weigh more than five or so pounds each.

Tomasetti comes up beside me, kneels, and picks up one of the babies. I hear the mama goat behind me, shuffling around, poking her head between us to keep an eye on her newborn.

"I think you're making Mama nervous," I say.

"She and I got to know each other pretty well this morning."

"You helped her have her kids?" I ask, easing my arm from the sling.

"She's a trouper." Tomasetti places the kid in my arms. "Support its head and belly. Like that. There you go."

I look down at the tiny creature and I feel a quiver in my chest. "Tomasetti, you're not going soft on me, are you?"

"I roughed these little guys up pretty good earlier," he says, deadpan. "Showed them who's boss."

"You tough guys are all the same." I laugh. "We work too much to have livestock."

"They're easy keepers. Good milk producers, too," he says. "I know how you feel about goat cheese."

"You would bring up my weakness for goat cheese." Seeing that the other two babies have gone to their mama to nurse, I lower the one I'm holding to the ground.

I don't look at Tomasetti as I rise and leave the stall. I can't. I'm overcome with emotion and close to making a fool of myself. Over baby goats of all things.

He follows me to the aisle, holds back. I stand with my back to him, blinking furiously, feeling awkward and embarrassed, knowing his eyes are on me and he's wondering what the hell is wrong with me.

After a moment, he touches my arm. "Kate."

When I don't face him, he gently turns me to him. I let him, keep my eyes on the floor.

"I take it this isn't about the goats," he says.

I laugh, but it's an emotional sound, accentuated by the silence of the barn. My intake of breath sounds a little like a sob.

When I trust my emotions not to betray me, I raise my gaze to his. His eyes search my face. He knows there's something going on. He isn't sure what. Looking for its source.

"Tough trip?" he asks.

I think about it a moment, trying to pinpoint exactly what's got me so out of sorts, and in that instant, I realize none of this is about the trip or the things that happened in the course of the investigation. It's about us and the world we live in. The passage of time. The fragility of life. The wheel that never stops.

"You think you have all the time in the world," I tell him. "Sometimes you don't and if you don't pay attention, you risk losing something precious."

He cocks his head, looks at me more closely. "Where is this coming from?"

"I've spent a lot of time running away from . . . us," I tell him. "From what we have. There were times when I didn't appreciate it. I was wrong to do that to you. I think there was always a small part of me that felt as if I didn't deserve it."

He absorbs the words with a calm that is classic Tomasetti. "Why do you think that is?"

"I don't want to screw this up."

A smile whispers across his features, but it's not patronizing. It's thoughtful and compassionate and in that moment, I realize he gets it. He gets me.

"I'm still here." He raises his hand, sets his palm against the side of my face. "Somehow, I think we're going to muddle through."

The words bring me dangerously close to tears. "Bishop Troyer won't marry us," I tell him.

If he's surprised that I've asked the bishop about administering our marriage vows, he doesn't show it. "We'll find someone else."

"There's a Mennonite church. In Sugarcreek. I talked to the pastor."

"I'm not the only one who's been busy."

I set my hand over his. "We're not Mennonite, so Pastor Tom can't perform the ceremony in the church. But he can do it here, at our farm."

"I'm liking Pastor Tom more by the minute."

I laugh again, ridiculously pleased he has the ability to make me laugh when I'm feeling shredded on the inside.

"We've been talking about getting married for a while," he says quietly.

"And I always seem to come down with a case of cold feet."

He slides his hands down to the small of my back, then tilts his head and kisses me on the mouth. "Why the change of heart?"

"I didn't have a change of heart," I tell him. "I think I've just realized it's time."

"You know I'm going to hold you to it."

"I think that would be wise," I tell him. "I've been known to waffle."

"What do you say we get these goats bedded down for the night, and then we'll go inside and break open that nice bottle of Malbec I've been saving."

"That sounds like an offer I can't refuse."

ACKNOWLEDGMENTS

As with every book, I owe untold thanks to my publishing family at Minotaur Books. First and foremost, I wish to thank my wonderful editor, Charles Spicer, who always helps me take the book to the next level. Many thanks to my fabulous agent, Nancy Yost—I appreciate you and your friendship more than you know. To the rest of the team at Minotaur Books, my gratitude and heartfelt thanks for the support and for doing what you do so very well on my behalf: Jennifer Enderlin. Andrew Martin. Sally Richardson. Sarah Melnyk. Sarah Grill. Kerry Nordling. Paul Hochman. Allison Ziegler. Kelley Ragland. David Baldeosingh Rotstein. Marta Fleming. Martin Quinn. Joseph Brosnan. Lisa Davis. Laurie Henderson. Cathy Turiano. Terry McGarry. Omar Chapa. Rowen Davis. My sincerest thanks to all.

Read on for a look ahead to AN EVIL HEART—
the new novel by Linda Castillo,
coming soon in hardcover
from Minotaur Books!

PROLOGUE

The sky above the treetops blazed in hues of fluorescent orange and Easter-egg pink when Aden Karn backed his bicycle from the shed. Dropping his lunch box in the handlebar basket, he wheeled it to the road, threw his leg over the seat, and set off at a brisk pace. The ride to the pickup point where he met his English coworkers usually took about twenty minutes. For once he was early and he was glad for it. Autumn had settled over this part of Ohio in gentle increments this year, bringing a burst of color to the maples and walnut trees that grew alongside the road. Another week and the countryside would be aflame. According to his *mamm,* they were God's colors. This morning, he had to agree.

Sweat dampened his shirt as he flew past the old bank barn at the curve, tires humming against the asphalt. His English coworkers gave him flak for riding the bike, but it was a good-natured kind of ribbing; Aden didn't mind. It wasn't like he could leave a buggy horse tied all day while he worked. Sure, he'd gotten wet a time or two, a problem easily solved by the slicker tucked away in his lunch box. Some of the Amish were using scooters now in Holmes County, but Aden wasn't interested. He liked the quiet of the bike, the physical labor, the speed and freedom of it. Somehow, he felt closer to the earth—closer to God—when he was astride the bike, drinking in the bounty He had bestowed on His children.

Aden took his time as he pedaled along the township road. He passed by the mossy pond in Mr. Yount's pasture where the ducks skimmed across the water's surface, dipping their heads to nibble on pondweed, and flapping their wings. As he passed over the bridge, he came upon the sheep that grazed the orchard grass that grew thick in the low area. He'd watched the lambs grow over the summer. Farther, he whisked past the field of "cow corn" Mr. Dunlop had left to dry. He stood on the pedals and pumped hard as he climbed the hill at County Line Road. He cruised the downhill side a little too fast, enjoying the breeze, and he leaned in as he made the turn onto Hansbarger Road.

He was so embroiled in his thoughts he didn't notice the figure in the ditch until he'd sped past. Having caught a glimpse out of the corner of his eye, Aden braked hard, surprised, wondering if there was a problem. He stuck out his foot and stopped so abruptly the back tire skidded sideways.

Both feet on the ground, he turned and looked over his shoulder. Oddly, there was no vehicle in sight. Just the figure standing in the ditch, looking at him.

"Is everything all right?" he called out.

Only then did he notice the weapon. At first, he thought it was a rifle, but that was strange; it wasn't deer season. Then he noticed the shape—the spread of the limbs, the cam on the left, the cocking stirrup in front—and he realized it was a crossbow. He watched uneasily as the weapon came up. An instant of disbelief as the figure's head tilted, eye lowered to the sight.

He felt a pang of alarm and released the handlebars, raising his hands. "Hey! What are you—"

Thwank!

An invisible fist punched the air from his lungs. A shock of pain in his chest. A burning streak shot down his back. His knees buckled. The bike went sideways, the handlebars twisting, and clattered to the asphalt. Aden glanced down in disbelief as he caught sight of the bolt sticking out. Then his shoulder hit the ground. His temple banged against the asphalt. Around him, the world went silent. He lay still, blinking and confused, the roadway warm against his cheek, pain thumping from chest to pelvis.

He moved his leg and rolled onto his back, trying to make sense of what happened. The movement brought a riot of pain to his spine. Darkness crowded his vision. Groaning, he looked down at the bolt, realized it had gone clean through and was sticking out the back.

Dear God in heaven . . .

His bladder let go. He felt the warm spread of urine on his thigh, soaking his trousers. Too much pain to care. Too much fear. The knowledge that he was badly injured hit home. Panic swept over him. He opened his mouth, tried to suck in a breath. A horrible sound poured out of him.

The crunch of shoes against gravel drew his attention. He looked up, tried to speak. He raised his hand, fingers spread. "Help."

Dead eyes stared down at him, cold as iron, dark with intent. Not seeing. Gloved hands reached down. Face set. An impersonal task, unpleasant but necessary. Both hands gripped his shoulder.

He whimpered. "Don't."

An electric current of pain tore through him as the bolt was pushed deeper. Another, as he was rolled onto his belly. The groan that followed came out as a gurgle. Breaths tearing in and out, each one an agony.

Another explosion of pain as the bolt was yanked from his body. His arms and legs convulsed. Once. Twice. Darkness encroached, stealing the light. Night pressing down. Aden felt the hands on his shoulder again. Fingers digging into his arm as he was rolled onto his back.

He lay there, helpless and terrified, listening to his own ragged breaths, pain pulsing with every beat of his heart. Vaguely, he was aware of the crossbow being lowered to the ground. The toe of a boot jammed into the stirrup. The squeak of the bowstring as it was drawn tight. The click of the string engaging with the nock.

Please don't . . .

The crossbow was lowered. Emotionless eyes burrowed into his. "I can't abide you doing what you're doing," the shooter told him.

He knew what came next and the horror of it was too much to process. Terror infused his every muscle.

He tried to move, to run or crawl away, felt his leg shift and flop, useless. He raised his hands, grabbed the shooter's ankle, his fingers clasping the fabric.

"Don't," he pleaded.

The head of the bolt was placed against his mouth with excruciating gentleness. The sharp tip cut his lip as it was worked between his teeth. Steel clicking against the enamel. The salty tang of blood. The bolt invaded his mouth, depressed his tongue, and went deep. He gagged. Once. Twice. Horror and disbelief overtook him.

He tried to speak and retched.

He felt a boot on his shoulder, pressing him down, trapping him. The shooter's finger on the trigger. The bolt cutting the back of his throat. His mouth filled with blood. He coughed and gagged, his throat spasming. His hand yanked at the fabric of the trousers, twisted.

Please.

Thwank!

He looked up at the sky, but he could no longer see the sun.

CHAPTER 1

My *mamm* had a saying about life's small discomforts.

Vann es shmatza, hayva da shmatz un bayda es dutt naett letsht zu lang. If it hurts, embrace the pain and pray it doesn't last too long. This morning, the memory of my *mamm* dances in the forefront of my mind, and for the first time in a long time, I miss her.

I'm in my sister's upstairs bedroom, standing on an old wooden alteration platform. My police uniform is draped across the foot of the bed, my boots on the floor next to it. My utility belt and service revolver look obscenely out of place against the gray-and-white wedding-ring quilt.

"Katie, my goodness, you're fidgeting again," Sarah tells me. "Hold still so I can finish pinning without sticking you."

"Sorry," I mutter.

I can't recall the last time I wore a dress. This particular dress has a history. My sister wore it eleven years ago for her wedding. Our *mamm* wore it, too.

Our grandmother made it. And so when my sister asked me to come over to look at it with my own wedding in mind, I had no qualms about trying it on. Now that I'm here, I realize it wasn't a very good idea.

I haven't been Amish for eighteen years. To wear a plain dress with the traditional *halsduch,* its closures fastened with straight pins instead of buttons or snaps, feels hypocritical. As if I'm trying to be something I'm not in order to please a community that will not be pleased.

Of course, my sister doesn't see it that way. She's a traditionalist, a peacekeeper, and an optimist rolled into one. Worse, she knows her way around a needle and thread and has no doubt she can make this dress work despite my reluctance and somehow please everyone in the process.

"This dress is a piece of our family history, Katie," she tells me. "Mamm would have loved for you to wear it, even if you're not Amish."

"At this point in my life, I think she would have been happy just to get me married off."

Her mouth twitches. "That, too."

I look down at the front of the dress, smooth my hands over the slightly wrinkled fabric, and I try not to sigh. It's sky blue in color with a skirt that's a tad too full and falls to midcalf. "Do you think it's a little too long?" I ask.

"I can shorten the hem," she says. "That's an easy fix."

"Bodice isn't quite right."

Always the diplomat, Sarah slides a straight pin between her lips, lifts the hem, and pins. "I'll take in the waist a bit, too. Bring the shoulders out."

The real issue, of course, has nothing to do with the hem or bodice. For twenty minutes, we've been skirting the elephant in the room. Sarah is too kind to broach the subject.

"It's okay if you don't like the dress," she murmurs. "I can make another one if you like. Or you can just buy one."

"It's not the dress . . . exactly," I tell her.

Cocking her head, she meets my gaze. "What then?"

Inhaling a deep breath, I take the plunge. "The problem is the dress is Amish. I'm not. There's no getting around that."

My sister lowers her hands, looks at me over the tops of her reading glasses, and sighs. She's looked at me that way a hundred times in the years since I returned to Painters Mill. Times when I've exasperated or disappointed her, both of which happen too often.

"You're Anabaptist. That matters." She gives a decisive nod, turns her attention back to the dress. "We can do away with the *halsduch*."

She's referring to the triangularly shaped "cape" or "breast cloth" that goes over the head, the point side at the back, the front gathered and secured with pins. My wearing one of the most symbolic of female Amish garments would be perceived as insincere.

"That'll help." Trying to be diplomatic, I look down at the front of the dress. "Maybe add a sash or belt?"

"Hmmm." She makes a noncommittal sound, then

plucks a pin from her mouth and puts it to use. "I've seen rosettes on belts, for the English wedding dresses. Mennonite, too."

For the first time since I arrived, I feel a quiver of enthusiasm in my chest. Like the dress might just work after all. "I like the idea of a rosette belt."

She nods, not quite smiling, but I can tell she's warming to the idea. "Have you decided about a head covering?" she asks.

"I thought I might go with a simple veil," I tell her.

She makes eye contact with me and raises her brows. Amish women do not wear a veil. Just a head covering or *kapp*.

"Like the Mennonites," I clarify, which means the veil will be small and round, just ten or twelve inches wide, made of lace, and worn at the back of my head.

"I think that's a good compromise," she says after a moment. "Not Amish, but . . ."

"Anabaptist," I finish.

We grin at each other, a rare moment of sisterly solidarity, and something warm shifts just behind my ribs. Progress, I think.

Sarah and I were close as kids. We worked and played together; we weathered the storms of growing up. She was there for me when I was fourteen and an act of violence altered the course of my life. The summer when a neighbor boy caught me alone in the house and turned everyone's lives upside down. Our relationship wasn't the same after that. Not because of her, but because of me. Because of what happened—and what I did about it. We grew apart, and the chasm between us only widened when I left the fold four years later. I ran as far away from my family and my Amish roots as I could—to Columbus and an unlikely career in law enforcement. Despite my best efforts to sabotage everything I'd once held dear, I couldn't eradicate those ties—or continue to deny my love for my family. Some twelve years later, when my *mamm* passed away, I returned to Painters Mill, not as the rebellious and awkward Amish girl I'd been, but as a grown woman who was offered the position of police chief. I reached out to both of my siblings, and after an uncertain start—and a few bumps along the way—we set to work rekindling our relationships.

We're still a work in progress, but we've come a long way. We've gotten reacquainted, shared a few laughs, a lot of disagreements, and a few tears. This morning's fitting is a big step in a different direction and a new closeness that's not quite comfortable, but hopeful and good.

Sarah slides a straight pin into the fabric gathered at my waist. "If it's any consolation, Katie, I like your man. William likes him, too," she says, referring to her husband. "That's no small thing."

"His name's Tomasetti, by the way." I smile at her. "And I like him, too."

A giggle escapes her and she shakes her head.

The chirp of my cell phone interrupts. Sarah raises a finger. "Wait. One more." She stabs the final pin into the fabric at the hem. "Got it. Go."

I smooth the dress, then step down off the platform and reach for the phone, answering with "Burkholder."

"Chief." It's Lois, my first-shift dispatcher. "I just

took a call from a motorist out on Hansbarger Road. Says there's a DB in the middle of the road." DB is copspeak for "dead body"; we use it in case someone is listening to their police scanner.

"Who's the RP?" I ask, using the term for "reporting party."

"Julie Falknor. Local. I got her on the other line. Chief, she's still at the scene and screaming her head off. Says there's a lot of blood and she has her kids with her."

Lois has been with the department since before I became chief. She's experienced and cool under fire. This morning, she's speaking a little too fast, her words running together.

"Get an ambulance out there." I ease the dress off my shoulders, let it drop to the floor, yank my uniform shirt off the bed. "Who's on duty?"

"Glock's en route," she tells me, referring to Rupert "Glock" Maddox. He's one of my most experienced officers. If anyone can keep the situation in hand, it's him.

"Get County out there, too." Hansbarger Road is a quiet stretch a couple of miles outside of Painters Mill proper; it's my patrol beat. Even so, depending on the situation and manpower, my jurisdiction sometimes overlaps the sheriff's department's.

"Tell the RP to stay put," I tell her. "I'm on my way."

I grab my trousers off the bed, step into them, reach for my equipment belt, buckle it. I face my sister as I snatch up my boots. "I'm going to have to take a rain check on coffee."

"Of course." She cocks her head. "Something's wrong?"

"Traffic accident, probably." I don't know if that's the case, but since I have no idea what I'll be walking into, I keep it vague. "Thanks for putting up with all my squirming."

"You're entitled." She grins. "I bet your man is sweating, too."

"Literally and figuratively." Smiling, I lean into her for a quick hug, grab my service weapon off the bed, and head for the door.

Hansbarger Road is a lesser-used back road that runs between a pasture and a cornfield before meandering north toward Millersburg. I make the turn, the Explorer's tires bumping over rippled asphalt and potholes, loose gravel pinging against the undercarriage. Ahead, I see the flashing lights of Glock's cruiser. A silver SUV is parked at a haphazard angle, nose down in the shallow roadside ditch with the driver's-side door standing open. The ambulance isn't yet on scene. There's no sign of the sheriff's department.

Flipping on my overheads, I park behind Glock's vehicle and hit my shoulder mike as I get out. "Ten-twenty-three," I say, letting Dispatch know I've arrived on scene.

I notice several things at once as I approach. Glock is standing between the SUV and his cruiser, making a notation in his notebook. There's a person lying on the ground a few feet away from him—likely the victim. A bicycle with the handlebars twisted lies on its side a couple of yards away. A woman I don't recognize is standing in the grass off the shoulder, her hands on her knees. Through the window of the SUV, I see the silhouettes of children in the back seat.

"What happened?" I ask Glock as I stride toward him.

He motions toward the victim. "He's DOA." He jabs a thumb at the woman. "She says she found him like that. Maybe a hit-skip. Not sure."

Something in his voice gives me pause. Glock may be a small-town cop, but he possesses the sagacity of a veteran homicide detective.

"You check the victim?" I ask.

"Just enough to know he's gone."

I make eye contact with him and nod, keep moving, my eyes on the victim. It's an adult male, lying supine, his head twisted to one side. The victim's mouth is open. A copious amount of blood is puddled on the asphalt beneath it. *Internal injuries,* I think. He's wearing dark trousers with suspenders. More blood on the front of a blue work shirt. The brim of a summer straw hat sticks out from beneath him. Amish, I realize.

"She see anything?" I ask, referring to the woman.

"No."

I reach the victim. Something unpleasant unfurls in my gut when I get my first up-close look. The face is suffused with the telltale white-blue hue of death. One eye open and unseeing. Not yet cloudy. The other eye is half closed. Tongue is blood-covered and protruding.

For the span of several seconds, I stand there, taking in details, trying to figure out what might've happened. An old-fashioned metal lunch box lies on the ground twenty feet away, open, a sandwich wrapped in wax paper next to it. From all appearances, it looks as if he was struck by a vehicle. Evidently, the driver fled the scene without rendering aid or calling police.

I force my gaze back to the victim. The platter-size pool of blood near the mouth. The bloodstain on the front of his shirt isn't quite high enough to be from a bloody nose or mouth. Something not quite right.

I look at Glock. "Is there some kind of injury on the abdomen?"

He moves closer, his brows furrowing. "Hole in the fabric there," he says in a low voice.

The hairs at my nape prickle, and I find my eyes scanning the woods a hundred yards away. Glock is a former marine with two tours in Afghanistan under his belt. Both of us are EMTs. Judging from the look on his face, he has the same prickly feeling as me.

I motion with my eyes to the SUV driver. She's still bent at the hip, a spill of vomit on the gravel in front of her. I've seen her around town. Grocery or coffee shop or gas station.

I look at Glock. "You talk to her?"

"Just preliminaries. Name's Julie Falknor. Says she was taking her kids to school. Running late. Victim was already on the ground. Says she almost ran over him. She's pretty shaken up, so I didn't get much out of her."

It's never wise to make assumptions when you're a cop, especially when you've just arrived at a potential crime scene in which a dozen scenarios could have played out. Situations aren't always as they appear. Freak accidents happen more often than we think.

I hit my shoulder mike and hail Dispatch. "Ten-seven-nine," I say, requesting the coroner.

I scan the field, the woods, and I feel that creeping sensation on the back of my neck. I look at Glock. "That hole in the fabric," I say. "Gunshot wound?"

"I was thinking the same thing," he says. "Sure doesn't look like the kind of injury caused by being struck by a vehicle."

The last thing I want to do is risk contaminating evidence. That said, if there's been a shooting or if there's an active shooter at large, I can't wait for the coroner or crime scene unit to arrive.

"Let's check him." I dig into a compartment on my utility belt and tug out latex gloves. Glock does the same.

"Stay cognizant of evidence." I don't have to tell him that, but I do, anyway.

Side by side, we walk to the victim. Despite the breeze, I smell the blood. The other stenches of death add a uniquely unpleasant pall. The victim is lying on his back, head twisted severely. Right leg slung out and bent at the knee. Both arms above his head.

I kneel, feel that familiar rise of revulsion that comes with the sight of violent death. This man was young, late teens or early twenties. I see the red-black blood pooled in his mouth and, again, I wonder about internal injuries.

"Broken front tooth." Squinting, Glock motions. "Split lip."

"You think this was the result of some kind of altercation?" I ask.

"Mouth injuries could have happened in the fall off the bike," he says. "Not so sure about the hole in the shirt."

The victim doesn't have a beard, which tells me he was unmarried. In the back of my mind, I think of his family, his parents, and the knot in my stomach tightens a little more.

With a gloved hand, I tug the victim's shirt out of the waistband of his trousers and pull it up so the abdomen is visible. I see white flesh interspersed with dark hair coated with a thin layer of blood where the fabric had lain against the skin. An oddly shaped wound a few inches above the navel snags my attention.

"Wound there," I hear myself say. "Strange shape."

"Knife?" Glock wonders aloud.

"Maybe." But even that's a stretch. The only thing I know for certain at this point is that this is no simple hit-and-run. I let go of the shirt, let it fall back into place.

One of the most pressing tasks for law enforcement in the aftermath of any fatal accident or crime is the identification of the victim so next of kin can be notified. Normally, I'd wait for the coroner, but since I'm already here, I make the decision to check now.

"Let's check for ID." Shifting position, I reach into the front pocket of his trousers. I find a folding pocketknife. A few coins. I check the other front pocket, find a handkerchief.

I make eye contact with Glock. "Help me roll him so I can check the back pockets."

"Yep."

As gently as possible, we roll the victim just enough for me to dig into the back pocket of his trousers. I tug out a beat-up leather wallet, spot the ID behind the plastic window. It's a nonphoto ID issued by the Ohio

Bureau of Motor Vehicles. This type of ID is used by many Amish who have a religious objection to having their photo taken.

"Aden Karn." I say the name slowly, the familiarity of it reverberating in my head. "Twenty-one years old."

"Damn. He's young." Glock shakes his head, slants me a look. "You know him? The family?"

"I know his parents." I get to my feet, unexpectedly shaken, hoping it doesn't show. "Not well, but I worked for them when I was a teenager."

"This kid live at home?" he asks.

I look down at the ID and shake my head. "The Karns live in town a few blocks from their shop. According to his ID, this young man lived a couple of miles from here."

I take a moment to collect myself, scan the field, the flock of crows cawing in the trees. I feel Glock's eyes on me. We've worked together nearly every day since I became chief. We're not friends in the conventional sense, but we're close in a way that goes deeper than friendship. We share a kinship, the bond of a brotherhood to which both of us are bound. We don't talk about it, but it's there nonetheless, and in this moment I'm thankful because his very presence has lessened some of the burden I feel pressing down on my shoulders.

Cautiously, we back away from the victim, doing our best to retrace our steps.

"Call County and get some deputies out here," I tell him as I snap off the gloves. "We're going to need to tape off the area. Get the road blocked."

"You got it."

Sirens wail in the distance. I glance at the SUV, see the children moving around inside. They look young. Growing restless, probably. The body is visible to them, but I can't cover it without the risk of contaminating the scene.

"I'm going to talk to the witness," I tell him.

Touching the brim of his hat, Glock starts toward his cruiser.

I approach the woman. She's straightened to her full height, but her face is the color of paste.

"Ma'am?" I say to her. "You all right?"

"Oh my God," she says in a quavering voice. "Sorry I'm such a basket case. That poor guy. Is he dead?"

"I'm afraid so," I tell her.

I guess her to be in her mid-thirties. Judging by the bulge of her belly, she's pregnant. Brown hair pulled into a ponytail. No makeup. She's wearing a pink sweatshirt, yoga pants, and flip-flops.

"Can you tell me what happened?" I ask.

Her eyes flick to the dead man, then back to me. A fresh round of tears spill over her lashes. "I was taking the kids to school, like always. Been taking this route because it's so pretty. Kids like the ducks in the pond over there. Named all of them." She uses the tissue in her hand to wipe tears from her cheeks. "We're driving along and my seven-year-old spots him. She's like: 'Look, Mommy, that man had a bike wreck!'

"For God's sake, I almost ran over him." A breath shudders out of her. "I stopped just in time, pulled over, and . . . there he was. All that blood."

She's getting herself worked up, so I press forward. "Did you see anyone else in the area? Any other vehicles? Or buggies?"

"No." She shakes her head. "There's hardly ever anyone on this road. That's why I take it. No traffic."

I look past her to see the ambulance pull up behind my Explorer along with a cruiser from the Holmes County Sheriff's Department. I spend another ten minutes with her, asking the same questions in different ways, giving her a chance to tell me more, but her account remains the same and she's unable to give any new details.

I pluck a card from a compartment on my belt, add my personal cell phone number to the back, and hand it to her. "If you remember anything else, even if it doesn't seem important, give me a call."

"I will," she assures me.

Two paramedics and a sheriff's deputy are standing a couple of yards from the body when I approach. I've met the deputy several times over the years. He's a rookie with a cocky personality, but generally a pretty solid cop. We volunteered for a fundraiser last summer to raise money for the local library, spent an afternoon flipping bratwursts and burgers for kids.

"Chief Burkholder."

"Hi, Matt." We exchange a handshake. Behind me, I'm aware of the woman pulling away and Glock approaching.

"That guy's deader than a doornail," the deputy says. "What the hell happened? Hit-skip? Where'd all that blood come from?"

"Not confirmed, but I think he may have been shot," I tell him. "Or stabbed."

"Holy shit." He sends a look in Glock's direction, as if my assessment isn't quite trustworthy.

Glock stares back at him, his expression deadpan.

I address the deputy. "Would you mind blocking off the intersections for me? No one comes in or out except the coroner and law enforcement."

"Uh . . . sure." Looking put out that he's been relegated to a rookie task, he strides toward his cruiser.

Glock hands me a nicely-done smile.

"There aren't many houses out this way, but I think we need to canvass. Give Pickles a call to help you," I say, referring to my only part-time officer, Roland "Pickles" Shumaker. "Hit every farm. Stop all vehicles. Pedestrians. Anyone working out in the field. See if they heard or saw anything. Get names and contact info."

"I'm on it." Glock starts for his cruiser.

I pull out my cell phone and, without getting too close to the victim, snap a dozen photos of the body from different angles. I zoom in to get a close-up of the bloodstain on the front of the shirt, especially the hole in the fabric, and I work my way around the body. I notice a few details I missed earlier. Leather work gloves peek out from the back pocket of typical Amish trousers, telling me he may have been on his way to work. A straw hat is crumpled beneath him, as if he fell on top of it.

As I take in the particulars of the scene, questions begin to boil. Was this random? Or was he targeted? Was he riding his bike to work and someone drove by and shot him? Did a vehicle stop and an altercation ensued? Or was this some kind of freak accident? The only things I know for certain at this point is that the person responsible is a danger to the community and it's my job to find him before he hurts anyone else.